Rodeo Christmas at Evergreen Ranch

MAISEY YATES

Rodeo Christmas at Evergreen Ranch

HQN

ISBN-13: 978-1-335-52907-7

Rodeo Christmas at Evergreen Ranch

HQN
22 Adelaide St. West, 40th Floor
Toronto, Ontario M5H 4E3, Canada
www.Harlequin.com

Printed in U.S.A.

Haven, it's another one for you. Thanks for being my partner, my best friend and the love of my life for all these years. You're my favorite.

Rodeo Christmas at Evergreen Ranch

CHAPTER ONE

Jake Daniels had grown up knowing that life was short. When he was in high school, he'd lost his parents, and along with them, the sense that anything in this world was guaranteed.

That kind of thing changed a man.

It could make him afraid of his own shadow, worried about taking risks and filled with a sense of self-preservation.

It was either that, or he realized since there were no guarantees, he might as well go all in. Push those chips out to the center of the table and see if the gamble paid off.

He'd done some admittedly dumb stuff as a kid. Not gambling so much as acting out. But the rodeo had changed him. It had saved him.

He'd spent the last eighteen years gambling and doing pretty damn well for himself, it had to be said. Years spent in the rodeo, flinging himself around on the back of enraged bulls, had netted him a decent amount of money, and now that he was more or less ready to get out of the game, those winnings, and the amount of money his parents' life insurance had left behind, had gotten him a big spread in Gold Valley.

He was going to be a rancher.

Not cattle, like his cousin Ryder. No. He was getting into horses. High-value breeds. Another gamble. It would either pay off, or ruin him.

That was the kind of life he liked. That was the kind of thing that made him feel alive.

And if this was retirement, hell, he was pretty damn into it. Thirty-two years old, and wealthy enough to figure out a way to live his dream. Not bad at all.

Of course, there were things he would miss about the rodeo. The people on the circuit were practically family now. So many years traveling around the same venues, getting busted up together, competing fiercely and going out for a beer after.

But it had been time to leave, and all it had taken was one fierce accident to teach him that.

And Gold Valley was his home, so this had been the place to go to when his time in the rodeo was done.

The day his parents had died, his aunt and uncle had also died, along with the mother of one of his closest friends. That had left a passel of orphaned children, a big old ranch that had once been run by their parents and a whole lot of chaos.

But it had been a good life. Other than all the crushingly sad parts.

His cousin Ryder had taken care of all of them, since he was the only one who'd been eighteen when the tragedy had happened.

He often wondered how they'd made it through without Ryder punching them all in the damn face.

He was sure that Ryder had wanted to from time to time.

Hell. Jake and Colt had been absolute assholes. Neither of them had handled losing their parents well. Well, was there a good way to handle that? He didn't know. But at seventeen and fifteen, he and his brother had been mad at the world, and kicking against the one person who had been doing his best to help them.

They'd both left home and joined the rodeo, the Western take on running away and joining the circus.

It had taken some years and some maturity for him to fully appreciate what he'd had.

Because what Ryder had given to them had been bound up in his loss, and until he'd been in his midtwenties probably, he hadn't fully been able to separate those two things and think of home, and his cousin, without a measure of pain and anger.

Even now, when he pulled into Hope Springs Ranch, a strange sensation took hold of him.

Nostalgia, grief and home, all rolled into one.

He'd been contending with it a lot lately, because his—for lack of a better word—*retirement* was still fairly new, and being in one place and not on the road was unusual for him.

But that was a choice he'd made, and one that was taking a bit of time for him to settle into. It had been just over three months, and it still felt...wrong in some ways.

It was easier to pretend that all your demons were dealt with when you just spent a good portion of the time running from them. Made things simple. At least as simple as they could be.

The problem was his demons had done a decent job of catching up to him on the circuit, and that was when he'd decided it was time to move on.

When Cal had fallen...

How could he live with something happening to his mentee? Cal was his best friend and with his guidance had gotten hurt.

No, that had brought him back to a dark, raw place. One he didn't want to visit again.

That calm before the storm. That bright ray of sunshine revealed to be the headlights of a Mack truck bearing down on him.

He'd read that poem that said nothing gold could stay.

In his experience, it turned out gold was fleeting. And revealed to be fool's gold on top of it.

Good never lasted.

And it was rarely real, anyway.

He'd been… Well, he hadn't been thrilled about Cal wanting to come for Thanksgiving, but he felt responsible for the accident so in the end he hadn't been able to say no.

He pulled his truck up to the front of the farmhouse, and the door opened, three dogs spilling out the front and down the front steps.

"Back, mutts," he muttered when he got out of the truck, smiling affectionately at the creatures as he bent down and scratched them behind the ears.

He looked up and saw Sammy standing on the top step of the porch, her baby on her hip. Sammy was married to his cousin Ryder now, but she was another member of their ragtag family. She hadn't lost her parents, but her situation at home, as he understood it, had been unacceptable, and when she was sixteen she'd come to live with them. She'd never left, and she and Ryder had gotten married a year earlier.

Finally, in his opinion.

The two of them had spent way too long dancing around the truth. Not that he could blame them. Nothing in his life had ever made marriage look particularly appealing. His parents…

His parents had been unhappy, slaves to a ranch and their children, to marriage vows they'd said to each other and had always seemed like they might regret.

For just a moment it had seemed like it might all be fixed. For just a moment it had seemed like they'd be okay.

Then it had all been destroyed.

That bright spot of hope swallowed by reality.

After years of unhappiness, his parents had just died.

Jake couldn't imagine that kind of life.

"How you doing?" he asked.

Sammy shifted the baby from one hip to the other, the little girl reaching out and grabbing her mom's blond hair. Sammy laughed and unwrapped the chubby fist from her curls. She looked happier than he'd ever seen her before.

He supposed for some people there was something to be said for this life.

God knew Ryder seemed happier.

But then, it was impossible for Ryder to seem more grim. Jake felt pretty guilty about that with the benefit of age and wisdom.

"Great," Sammy said. "We've been seeing so much of you lately. I feel spoiled."

"Well, that's good, because it won't take long for you to just feel sick me."

"Never," Sammy said, coming down the steps and offering him a hug.

Sammy was like that. Effortless, easy affection with people around her.

He admired it, but he'd never much understood it. There was only one kind of touch he was free with. Sex was simple. And being a champion in the world of rodeo meant there was no shortage of buckle bunnies lining up to see if the rumors were true. His bull rides lasted eight seconds, and a ride in his bed lasted the whole night.

He took a lot of pride in the fact that he had staying power. That he gave a damn for the pleasure of the women who passed through his hotel rooms.

But that was as deep as he got.

"Come on in," Sammy said. "Logan and Rose are already here. Iris and Griffin are on their way."

It was strange to him that everybody had paired off now. Everybody except for himself, and his brother, Colt, who would rather take a stick between the eyes than settle down.

Jake was confident that would be his brother's stance.

His brother was still going out hard in the rodeo. As far as Jake knew he wasn't even interested in coming back to town and settling down the way Jake was, let alone getting married.

He walked into the living room, and noticed all the little changes.

Since Ryder and Sammy had gotten married, the place, which had actually been basically the same in all the years since their parents had died, had gotten a bit of a facelift.

Sammy had added a whole lot of real grown-up touches to it. Pretty things.

It was weird. Weirder that he cared.

Ryder came through from the kitchen and offered a greeting. "Good to see you."

"You, too. Hey, Sammy," Jake said. "Would it be all right if my buddy Cal came for Thanksgiving?"

"Sure," Sammy said. "The more, the merrier."

He was glad Sammy was thrilled. He was less thrilled. But there were a spare few things on God's earth he saw as sacred. His friendship with Cal was one of them.

The accident might have been a catalyst for Jake deciding to leave the rodeo, but it was just damned cowardly to then deny his friend's request to come visit. Why? Because he felt guilty about the fall?

Hell, yeah, he did.

But that didn't mean he had to be happy about the visit. Though even just being away and out of the game, knowing he was just out of it now for good… There were things he missed. He was looking forward to having a few beers and talking about old times.

"Good," Jake said.

Eventually, Iris and her new husband arrived, followed by Pansy and her husband, West, and West's teenage brother, Emmett. West and Pansy had taken over the raising of the kid, since West's mother wasn't hugely into the maternal thing. Putting it mildly.

And while everything with his family was good—it always was—there was an indefinable feeling of…change.

Right. Well, you haven't been here very much, so you don't have the right to have an opinion about how things have changed.

That thought galled him a little bit.

And it was true enough. He'd been gone, seen to his own affairs all this time, and something that had given him a small measure of comfort was the fact that he could come home at any time and things would be roughly the way that he left them. But not so much anymore.

There were new people. New plates. The house was fuller than it had ever been, but that made it a little bit unrecognizable, too.

It was a whole damn thing.

He finished eating, and hung out for a while.

Then he bid everybody farewell, got in his truck and started on the road back to his ranch.

Settling in Gold Valley.

There was a time when he'd been sure he'd never do that. And as he drove down the familiar highway he had a strange sense of…dread.

He hated that.

He chased dread. The kind of fear that held other people down, he pursued it. He'd spent years riding bulls because he'd figured why not give fate the biggest middle finger of all.

It was the quiet moments that seemed to bring the fear. The still moments. The golden hour, when the sun lit up the world around him and everything looked new. And there would be a moment. A breath. Where peace rested in his soul.

And right on its heels came the hounds of hell.

The arena had stopped it. The pounding of hooves, the danger.

It was just that it had followed him to the arena now so he'd figured he'd take his chances here.

Maybe that had been a mistake.

Too late now.

He drove through town, trying to get a look at how it might seem if he were an outsider. If he was someone who hadn't grown up here. The brick facades were the kind of thing tourists lost their shit over. But he lost the ability to see them a long time ago.

For him… For him, Gold Valley had just represented everything he lost.

He'd been running when he'd left.

He'd run for a long time. And he'd achieved a hell of a lot.

But whatever he thought he'd feel when he got here… He didn't.

And so he was trying to see everything with new eyes, like he was a new man, because he felt just so damned much like the old one. And he wasn't the biggest fan.

Hope Springs always put him in this kind of mood.

So he shrugged it off and started mentally going over the timeline that he had in place for getting his ranch going. His first five horses were coming at the new year.

It was a new challenge. And it reinvigorated him. That was the problem. The rodeo had gotten stale. He'd want everything twice. You didn't get better than that. He'd done it twice in a row, and he didn't want to get to the point where he wasn't winning anymore.

He'd peaked. Basically.

So now he had to go find somewhere else to do that.

That was something, anyway.

It was one reason he'd backed his cousin Iris when she had decided to open her bakery.

He knew all about needing a change.

Maybe that meant he actually was still running.

None of it mattered now, though.

He hadn't had enough to drink tonight because he'd needed to get his ass home, but he was going to open some whiskey the minute he got in the door.

The place was out about ten miles from town, a nice flat parcel of property with the mountains behind it. The house itself was a big, white farmhouse with a green metal roof. Different to the rustic place at Hope Springs, but he liked it. The driveway was gravel, long and winding, with tall, dense trees on either side of the road.

But when he came through the trees into the clearing where the house was, there was a surprise waiting for him in front of the house.

An old, beat-up pickup was parked there, and he could see a lone figure leaning up against the hood. He parked the truck and got out, making his way over to the figure.

In the darkness, he couldn't quite make it out, but he had a feeling he knew who it was. Early and unannounced.

Entirely in keeping with what he knew of his friend.

"Cal?"

And two wide, brown eyes looked up at him from beneath the brim of a white cowboy hat, long, glossy brown hair shifting with the motion. "Jake. I'm really glad to see you. Because... I don't just need a job. I need a husband."

CHAPTER TWO

Callie Carson wasn't known for her shy and retiring demeanor.

But she was a woman of her word, and always had been.

She'd been raised to follow the Code of the West, and she took it seriously. Applying it equally and fairly across all situations and circumstances. She believed in truth and justice, and that made this entire situation a whole big mess.

Because it required her to lie.

Required that she take something as sacred and important as marriage—not that it was anything she'd ever wanted for herself, but still, she respected the institution—and turn it into a tool that she could use to get what she wanted.

She wasn't thrilled about subterfuge. Not remotely. But there wasn't a whole hell of a lot she could do. Her father hadn't left her with any good choices.

Her father, who she'd always felt was on her side. He'd raised her as one of his sons, had begged her mother to let him do that after her sister had died. Pale and weak from an illness that had ravaged her from birth.

Let me have her. Let me make her strong.

And he had.

But then… Then this had happened and he'd apparently hit his limit with his belief in her, and Callie wasn't sure she could ever get over that.

Her dad was her best friend. Her ally.

But when she'd fallen off that horse fourteen weeks ago, more had shattered than just her arm. Jake had left, and even if it wasn't related, she'd been broken and he'd been gone.

And then there was her dad.

Her dad, who'd been her constant support, her biggest champion through all of her endeavors in the rodeo, calming all of her mother's fears, had turned into a near stranger.

He'd put his foot down, said that there would be no discussion of her going out for saddle bronc. And the fight had been…epic. But he'd raised her to be who she was. She stood her ground, and fought for what she believed in.

And in the end it came down to the insurance. To money.

She'd wanted to do it aboveboard. She'd wanted to do the right things, but he'd made it impossible.

And now she was going to lie to him.

"Say again?" Jake asked.

It would be funny if she didn't feel so serious. She had stunned Jake Daniels into silence. Jake was the kind of man who wore *in charge* with all the ease of worn work boots. And she had effectively silenced him. Put him on the back foot.

In fact, right at the moment, her friend's ridiculously handsome face was incredulous, even in the dim outdoor light.

That face had felled a thousand buckle bunnies, girly women who had the secrets to femininity stitched into the sequins on their jeans. But she doubted any of them had ever gotten him to make *that* face.

Her lips twitched. "Did you need me to get down on one knee, Daniels?"

"No," he said slowly. "You can skip that. But you might want to give an explanation of some kind, Cal."

Only *he* called her Cal.

Jake Daniels had been her best friend since she was sixteen years old, and she knew that most people wouldn't get it. But that nickname was a piece of it. Cal. Like she was part of the rodeo, really and truly. A friend to *her*. Not just Callie Carson, daughter of the rodeo commissioner, Abraham Carson, but someone who mattered to him specifically. Someone with her own relationship to him. He'd been a mentor in many ways from the first moment they'd met, and there was something about his renegade recklessness that called to her. That reached down into something inside of her that she never accessed before and woke it up.

He made her feel brave.

He was a daredevil of the highest order. A bad boy who cut a swath through the buckle bunnies of the rodeo circuit, and even if she didn't approve of that sort of behavior, what she appreciated about him was the commitment. To every single thing he did.

The complete and total lack of fear in his every action.

The way he didn't care about what people thought.

She had tried her best to take on some of his attributes. Oh, not going after the buckle bunnies. That wasn't really her thing.

No, as far as Callie was concerned the rodeo was all there was.

Ever since she'd first witnessed the spectacle of the rodeo when she was too little to walk, and had known her future was on the back of a horse. To when she'd learned to barrel race and had started competing in her teens. All the way to discovering that what she really wanted was to break new ground in saddle bronc, and become the first woman to compete in the event in this particular Pro Rodeo Association.

She'd been working toward it, and her dad hadn't been thrilled with it, even in the beginning. But he'd fostered that tenacious spirit in her so he hadn't stopped her, either.

Until the accident.

"Let's go inside," she said. "And I'll explain."

"I think you can explain just as well from out here."

"I can't," she said. "Because I can't see your face well enough."

He paused. "And that has to do with…?"

"I need to know. What you think about all this."

He shook his head. Then he walked over to her truck and opened the driver's side door. He took out her duffel bag and retrieved her hat from the dashboard, then plunked it onto her head. Then he slung the bag over his shoulder. "Come on. Explain yourself."

They made their way up the front steps of the surprisingly nice ranch house.

"Well, I didn't expect this," she said, looking around.

"What?"

"This place is clean, Jake." She turned a half circle, looking around the place.

"I'm not an eighteen-year-old bachelor out on his own for the first time, Cal. I know how to keep my place clean."

"And how is that?"

"I hired a maid."

She laughed in spite of herself. "I should've figured."

The whole inside of the house was immaculate, too. Nice. Her family ranch in the small Eastern Oregon town of Lone Rock was damn near palatial. So it wasn't that she wasn't used to nice. It was just that accommodations on the circuit were different. She had opted not to stay in the elaborate trailer that her father brought when they were traveling around to different locations, and she tended to camp, or crash in the horse trailer, or crash in a motel, whatever worked for the situation.

She'd heard her dad make comments over the years. About her mama needing a fancy-ass RV or a nice hotel if they were going to travel. Remarks about how the other cowgirls needed softer beds, nicer places to sleep.

He'd said it was why there were fewer women in the rodeo.

Her dad didn't openly see women as less, or anything like that. Rather he was... Well, he acted like they were more breakable.

And Callie had determined she'd never show her weakness like that. She could handle uncomfortable beds, cramped conditions, whatever. If it was good enough for the boys, it was good enough for her.

Her anger bristled anew. She'd earned this. Every time she'd bunked in a horse trailer. Every time she'd gone camping and complained less than her brothers while it poured down rain on them. Every time she'd cut herself or bruised herself or fallen and gotten back up without so much as a whimper.

The trouble with breaking your arm was you didn't get to stop and make a choice about whether or not you howled in pain and cried like a baby.

One moment of vulnerability. Just one.

And it was like her dad had suddenly noticed she was a girl and therefore potentially breakable.

Jake straightened, hefting her duffel bag down to the floor and pushing his black cowboy hat up on his forehead with his knuckle. "Okay. Explanation time."

She let out a frustrated growl. "You know what I want."

He arched a dark brow. "Do I?"

"Yes. You do. I want to ride saddle bronc. I want to do it more than anything. It's in my family's blood—why wouldn't it be in mine? Just because I'm a woman?"

"Historically speaking, I guess that's the school of thought."

"But it's not *yours*, Jake. It never has been. You always treated me like I could do whatever I wanted. You have. You've been my biggest support—hell, you were the one who encouraged me to get up on the back of that horse and try it for the first time. You were the one who showed me that I couldn't live without it. The exhilaration. The... The everything. You're the reason that I know how much I want this. And now I need your help to make it happen."

"You are going to have to get creative to figure out how the hell you draw a line from saddle bronc to needing to marry me."

She shrugged. "It's not even that creative. It's that my dad... Look, he couldn't specifically bar women from the competition. But the fact of the matter is the insurance insists women are at greater risk than male saddle bronc riders. If I want to ride, the cost goes up for entry. For everyone. So he's put me in a position where I would make things harder for everyone else, and where I can't afford to pay my own entry. I don't have that kind of cash just from barrel racing and traveling around with the rodeo. I'm not like you. I'm not a bull rider—I didn't do the big events. Barrel racing... It doesn't get treated the same. There's not an expo in Vegas for everyone to watch. There aren't endorsement deals on the level that you get."

"Cal, if you need money..."

She'd known he'd do that. That he'd try to just fix it that way. By throwing money at it. Being her protector and all that, in the way he was. But that was just what she didn't need. And she was aware there was a little irony in needing his help but refusing a certain kind of help.

But this was like... The difference between giving a man a fish and teaching a man to fish.

Taking his money was a gift fish she could only use once. Marrying him and getting her trust fund was a fishing rod.

"No. I need freedom. That's all. Just the freedom that I deserve to have as a grown woman."

"And explain to me how marrying me is going to give you that freedom?"

"I have a trust fund."

"Well... Hell. I knew you guys were fancy, but I didn't know you were trust fund fancy."

"My father isn't the commissioner of the rodeo for nothing. He's from a big old oil family. Lots of money that he kicked into programs over the years. But, anyway. That's not the point.

The point is that if I really want to have freedom, I need access to that trust fund. And I'm not waiting until I turn thirty. It's too far away. The only other way that I can get my hands on it is to get married."

"So, you want me to marry you. *Marry you*. Like sign a document, link up our tax filing status, marry you."

"Yeah, that about sums it up."

Something in his face changed, and she didn't like it. It made her stomach feel weird. And a slow smile slid across his insolent mouth. "Wedding night?"

She felt like she'd been doused in liquid flame. Her whole face went burning hot.

A wedding night.

A wedding night.

For a minute there, her brain sort of stalled out. He was teasing her, of course he was. He liked girly girls with big hair and big boobs. With shiny smiles and shinier sequins. And that was all fine because she wasn't that, and she didn't want to be.

Couldn't be.

Didn't care to be.

She'd made that choice a long time ago and she didn't regret it. And he was screwing with her, anyway. To get a reaction, which he had. Which was dumb.

She ground her teeth together, gritted out the heat.

"*No.* It's a temporary thing. Just until everything is set up with the trust fund. I need to get married as soon as possible so that everything can get rolling, and I'll have the money. I need to cover the excess on everyone's entry fees."

"One problem with that," Jake said, walking away from her, heading toward what she guessed was the kitchen. She scurried on after him, confirming what she thought. He opened up the fridge and took out two beers. She grabbed one from his hand and popped the cap off on the edge of the counter. "How many of those cowboys are going to like the little rich girl playing around a competition, paying their entry fees."

"*I'll* be the reason the fees went up," she said.

"Still. Men have pride, Cal."

"Men have dumbass egos and ridiculous complexes about being a white knight when nobody asked to be saved. I want what I want. I want the control of my life. If those pansy asses can't handle me paying for the costs that I created, that's on them. They don't have to take it. Fact of the matter is, I didn't ask for any of this. I just want to compete. Same as everybody else."

Except she didn't want to be just the same as everyone else. She wanted to be better. She wanted to be special.

She had this fantasy… Buried deep inside of herself. That if she could just do something big enough, decisive enough, unique enough, her mom would suddenly understand her. And why she was so driven. That her dad would bring her in for a hug and tell her she was amazing.

That she would somehow set herself apart from her brothers.

And from her sister.

No longer just a replacement daughter who didn't quite measure up.

Conviction burned in her chest and she wasn't going to let him scare her off by being a smart-ass about wedding nights and whatever.

Her arms felt prickly.

He didn't mean it, anyway.

"Marriage is important," she said. "And I don't like this. I'm sorry to have to ask you…"

"Marriage doesn't mean a damn thing," he said. "It's a legal institution. Who the hell cares?"

"It's *sacred*. You make vows. Before God."

"Yeah, but I've always believed that if God is paying attention he's well aware of who's full of bullshit. So, he's not going to take them too seriously."

"That's a terrible thing to say," she said, taking a step to the side, like she might need to dodge a lightning bolt that would come through his ceiling at any moment.

He shrugged. "I say terrible things all the time. It's kind of my thing. I say honest things. There's no point in anything else. Life is short."

"Yeah. Well. Too short to not do what I want. So… Will you marry me, then?"

"Sure," he said, lifting his shoulder. "But you need to make it real clear exactly what's happening here. Name your terms and conditions."

"Just that…" She crossed her arms and stared him down. "I don't need to be married for longer than sixty days. Not per the terms of the will. We should be able to get married December 1 and be divorced before spring. As soon as I have access to the trust fund. But it has to *look* real."

She was shaking. Vibrating with an intense need for him to say yes coupled with the guilt that she felt over this whole thing and with her nerves over being dishonest. She wasn't dishonest. That was the thing. But she had to be. For this. If her dad knew that she was marrying Jake just to get her hands on the trust fund, then he would… He would change things. He would make it so she couldn't get it. He would do something to block her. He had to think it was real. He had to think it was real until the minute she got her hands on that money. That money that represented freedom. She didn't give a damn about fancy… Anything. She didn't care about any of that. It was about what it represented. About what…

He looked like he was considering it. "How do you see this going?"

"What?"

"I mean, what's your strategy for after? Marriage isn't any skin off my nose," he said. "But I've to get this place in shape for when my horses arrive after the first of the year. And let's get one thing real clear. You wouldn't be able to pull this off around your family."

She frowned. "What?"

Suddenly his expression changed. His face went intense and he took a step toward her. Then another and another until she was fair certain he was going to run smack into her. And she sidestepped him like he was a bull and she was the fighter, a small squeak escaping her lips. "What in blazes?" She blinked and looked at him like he was insane. "You were going to run into me."

"I was leaning in for a kiss, Callie. And as your fiancé that's something you should be real happy about. You shouldn't be… skittish."

Heat rash—from rage—broke out over her skin. "I am not skittish, you boneheaded periwinkle, you were random. You have to announce things like that."

"Not if I'm your fiancé."

"What's your damn point, Daniels?" She was ruffled now, and her clothes felt like they were sitting crooked on her body.

"My point is you don't know what the hell you want, or what you're doing. And if this is supposed to look real we'll have to play house here."

She hadn't considered that. The really annoying thing was she realized right then that he was right. There were things she hadn't thought through. What she had figured was that she would come for Thanksgiving, make up some story about how they'd… Fallen for each other in that time, and then somehow go back to… Her life. She had figured maybe he would come with her. But of course that wouldn't work. Of course not. When she wasn't traveling with the rodeo she mostly lived in her family's sprawling home on their Lone Rock property.

And there would be no way she'd want to live in that kind of proximity to her parents for this whole thing.

But she hadn't considered staying *here*, either. Not for an extended period of time. But of course she would have to.

And then Christmas…

Well, at Christmas they would have to deal with her family. Maybe she should tell him.

"I…"

"I just got this place going, Cal. I've got work to do. I don't really need a wife, truth be known, but I could use a ranch hand." He assessed her for a long moment, and she shifted uncomfortably, unable to read the glint in his blue eyes. "And if you're going to be doing saddle bronc, then you need more training. And no one is going to handle that except for me."

Hell. He'd been gearing up to deal with the reality of having Cal show up, but nothing could have prepared him for her declaring that she wanted to *marry him*.

Cal had somehow become his best friend. And he was a man who'd never claimed a best friend before, never in his life. It was unexpected. He hadn't figured the sixteen-year-old spitfire he'd seen doing laps in the arena could teach him anything. But she had. About resilience, and humor in the face of defeat.

He'd come into the rodeo with demons on his heels. He'd ridden hard, drank harder. Slept with a new buckle bunny every night. Losses had been unacceptable—and there were a lot of losses. He'd been at the mercy of bulls with bad attitudes happy to grind him into the dust, and part of him had taken that punishment and relished it, even while losing put him in a rage.

It had been an endless cycle.

He'd chased winning, but he didn't like anything that felt too good. Didn't trust it. So winning always came with a steeper cost, a darker night of the soul. And everything came with whiskey.

But there was something about Callie. He'd encouraged her spark, and there had been something in that—something in giving—that had mended a tear in him he wouldn't have thought possible.

Yeah, everyone figured he was close to his brother, Colt. They all thought that since the two of them had left Hope Springs and Gold Valley behind they had some sort of bond out there on the road, but that was far from the truth.

They drank in different circles and they screwed different women. At least, to the best of their ability. And at the very least they had a "don't ask, don't tell" policy about it.

It was just easier to keep home distant.

Obviously Colt agreed, because he conducted himself the same way.

He had his circle, Jake had his. Well, Jake had Callie.

But that bond had grown, and on his end it had started to change.

Though he hadn't realized how much until she'd fallen.

That was part of his reluctance over having her come for Thanksgiving.

He'd dealt with it, though. All of the reluctance. And pushed forward into just being glad to see her. She was his friend, after all, whatever had shifted inside him in the time since she had been bucked off a horse in the middle of the arena and he'd left the rodeo to come here.

The two were related, but she didn't need to know that. She never needed to know it.

It was why he agreed to have her come visit without a fuss.

But he'd been trying to get away from Cal, not spend more time with her. And now that wasn't looking like it was going to be a possibility.

No way was he letting her go off and marry someone else. Who would it even be? He thought of the men she'd know. The guys in the rodeo who were about her age...

No. Hell, no. Helping her wouldn't be the motive. It had disaster written all over it.

And he might not have a very deep sense of responsibility when it came to much of anyone…but Callie.

In some ways he felt like her connection had saved him. Pulled him back from the brink because the rate he was traveling was bound to meet with disaster at some point.

And she'd given him peaceful moments. Smiling, laughing. Not that he didn't do that with the other cowboys, and even his brother, when he had some whiskey in him.

But with her it felt like something else.

Something deep.

He owed her this.

And then after…after this he'd make his life here and she'd go off and make hers.

"I don't need more training," she said stubbornly. "That's what you said when you left. When you stopped training me, if you recall."

"I don't think I told you you didn't need more training. I think I told you to forget it all when you were wrapped up in a cast looking mean as a pinched chicken."

She didn't let the jab derail her.

"How many broken bones have you had, Jake? Don't put your overprotective alpha male bullshit onto me. I'm not fragile. Not any more than you. I'm made of flesh and blood and bone and an animal can crush you just as easily as it can me."

Everything in him went still, his anger rolling through him like a thundercloud, his muscles tensed up, and he moved to her, gripping her arm. She was soft. Well-muscled, sure. But on a feminine frame, and there was no denying it.

He and his brother, Colt, had ridden bulls for years, and the skill it took, the strength that it took on the back of those animals, was intense. It turned your body into something as hard as granite, and the best thing about that was when you did— inevitably—get stomped on by one of the giant animals, you had some defense against it. Everything in you went tight. Callie was strong, it was true. She couldn't do as well as she did in her events without being strong. But it was still not enough.

She was breakable, whether she wanted to acknowledge it or not.

She was also stubborn. And he knew that she wouldn't stop. That she was here, that she had taken it this far, was evidence of that.

So all he could do was take control of it. Make sure she was as ready as she could be.

The best she could be.

"Come on," he said. He grabbed her other hand, and pushed it firmly against his chest, ignoring the tightening in his whole body that resulted from the casual contact. "Feel the muscle on the two of us, and you tell me that there's no difference. Tell me."

She jerked her hand away, and the only spark in her eye was anger.

The spark on his skin was something else.

"I can do it," she said. "I don't have to be as strong as you to be able to do this."

"I'm just saying," he said. "Don't go acting like you have no idea why there might not be as many women competing in saddle bronc. Why your father has a concern."

For whatever reason, Callie was hell-bent on this, and he could understand it. She was from a rodeo family, and rodeo was what they did. But this seemed deeper than that. And to not get why her dad might not be thrilled with her competing in a man's sport...

She was too smart for that.

"Right. But why are you acting like an overbearing hen?"

She looked up at him, the sparks in her dark eyes shooting through him. This was the problem. He'd befriended Cal back when she was sixteen years old, scrappy and determined and bound to get injured if somebody didn't take all that energy in hand. She'd reminded him of... Well, of him. Heedless and daring, but she had a joy to her that he just didn't. Her father had been happy enough letting her compete in barrel racing events but she'd wanted to learn more.

They'd practiced tie down roping and raced each other all over the place. Most other people were scared of her dad getting the wrong idea if they hung around her too much. Jake had never cared.

Childhood was a time of hope, if all went well. But being one of the unlucky kids who'd experienced inalterable shattering of hope in an age that should have been full of innocence had broken something in him.

How well he'd learned that the promise of fresh beginnings meant nothing.

That when things looked brightest you could be on the verge of being plunged into darkness. And that there was no damn guarantee at all that it would be darkest before any sort of dawn.

Sometimes it was just dark.

No light on the horizon.

There were no such things as gut feelings, signs, wonders or miracles. The idea that you could sense whether something would be good or bad. That there was something bright out there waiting for you...

He knew better.

That life was always waiting to yank the rug right out from under you, and all the better if you thought that things were going fine.

And anyone who felt secure... Well, they were living in an illusion.

He'd been disillusioned completely at seventeen.

Other than the horrendous grief and loss, it had served him well.

"Fine. If that's what it takes. You can train me. Whatever. As long as you agree to the marriage thing."

"Yeah. Fine with me."

Cal took her white hat off, and set it on the counter. Her brown braid had grown scraggly around the edges, and he could see a slight dirt band around her head. She'd come straight here from riding or working. Which was just like her. She was the least feminine female of his acquaintance, and the least fussy about things like fixing up. Which made it all the more insane that he had such an attachment to her.

An attachment that he'd spent a hell of a long time playing off, pushing off.

She was a woman, and he wasn't blind to that, so the occasional moment when she bent over and her jeans had displayed her ass and he noticed... He hadn't thought much of it.

But when she'd been bucked off her horse a few months ago, and had lain on the ground motionless, knocked completely unconscious...

That was when he realized that all his thoughts about fate didn't apply to everything. Not to everyone. Because when he'd seen her lying on the ground like that, he'd seen his whole life flash before his eyes like he was the one who could've died. He didn't mind the occasional moment of checking out her rack while she was wearing a tight tank top.

He had minded the clutching terror in his chest when she'd been thrown from that horse. Yeah. That he'd minded a whole lot.

It was that dread. That dread that he'd only before ever experienced here. In the house at Hope Springs, in this town. Dread tied to loss. The loss of people he cared for.

It had followed him to the rodeo.

To her.

And it was why he'd left.

But she had followed him here.

And what was he going to do? Turn her down now?

He couldn't have her going into competition unprepared. In both cases, he was her safest bet. He would die to protect her.

And for a man who prided himself on holding on to nothing all that tight… It was a strange realization.

She wiped the back of her hand over her forehead, and he thought again about the fact that she'd clearly driven here without a shower.

"You want to grab a shower?" The words felt heavy on his tongue and something in his body reacted like he'd given an invitation of some kind that he absolutely hadn't.

God bless Cal, she didn't notice.

"Oh," she said, turning her head and sniffing the front of her top. "Sure. Thanks."

That ought to cool him off. It didn't.

"No problem."

He did his best not to imagine her standing underneath the spray of water. Slick and naked.

He didn't know why he was so unable to keep himself from fantasizing about her when she was around. He had all the women he could possibly want, when he wanted them. And his taste ran a lot more toward girly girls than women like Callie. But maybe that was the thing. There was something unknown about her. Untamed. She was serious and private, and he didn't really know what she did with that part of her life.

Men.

Or whatever she was into.

She was unreadable on that score. It wasn't anything she ever talked about.

She could talk about horses and rodeo from sunup to sundown. Had tons of great stories about growing up on the circuit. Laughed at a dirty joke as hard and loud as anyone. She was… one of the guys. Except that she never talked about conquests or anything of the like. And except he thought she was beautiful.

Yeah, one of the guys.

Except for *that*.

And except for the fact that when she'd fallen off her horse he'd felt like his life might be ending.

"Come on this way," he said.

He swung by the entry and grabbed hold of her duffel bag again, slinging it up over his shoulder and leading the way down the hall. He pushed open the door he'd prepared for her to use as the guest room. He hadn't lived here long enough to have ever used it for that purpose.

He stood there for a second, and marinated in the ridiculous lie that he'd just told. As if he'd ever been planning on using it for anyone else.

He hadn't really been planning on using it for her. But it wasn't like he'd moved back to Gold Valley to suddenly start throwing dinner parties and having guests stay. Hell, no.

She turned a circle in the generous space. Looked at the large bed and leaned over, pressing on the mattress with both hands. She bounced.

Well, she bounced the mattress, but it bounced her body.

Dammit.

"Well, this is great. Thank you. I mean, a hell of a lot fancier than what we usually get when were out on the road."

"But not as fancy as your house, I bet you. Given that you're trust fund people. Turns out."

"I told you. It doesn't really matter to me. It's not about money or getting nice things or anything like that. It's about the rodeo. It's in my blood. My bones. So if they break, it better be because of the rodeo. That's all. That's it. And if I'm breathing, it better be arena dirt and horse manure."

"That's real romantic."

"I don't know what else there is."

"You've got a big family," he pointed out. "Big family house."

"Oh. Yeah, sorry, I didn't mean to be insensitive about your… About…"

She knew about his parents, about how he'd grown up. The bare bones of it, anyway. Less so the nitty-gritty details of the whole situation.

But no one else knew about that.

He waved a hand. His loss wasn't anyone else's problem. It wasn't up to her to watch every word that came out of her mouth to avoid skating too close to his family stuff. "No worries. Do you have a Thanksgiving favorite?" he asked.

She wrinkled her nose. "I don't know. We never really get the same thing—my dad caters it every year. We go out on Christmas Eve."

"Well, you're in for traditional home cooking. My cousins are pretty spectacular in the kitchen, and my cousin's wife is really something."

"Sounds good."

"Wait till I tell them about the marriage."

"You *can't* do that," she said.

"And why not?"

"It's embarrassing."

"I can't tell my family that we're getting married for real. I can't do it."

"Well, tell them about it when I'm not there. And not Thanksgiving. Or at least wait until the pie so that I can split. But I need to be able to get some pie."

"Sure. Whatever you need."

He'd been saying that a lot. Whatever she needed.

What she really needed was to get the hell away from him, and he didn't have the strength to say it. Didn't have the strength to send her off on her own, and let her do this without his intervention.

Because God knew she needed his intervention.

Yet another moment when Callie was throwing all his bold proclamations about being blasé regarding fate into the wind.

"Bathroom is down the hall. Anything in the house that you need…it's yours. And we report for work bright and early."

She grinned. "The only morning I know is an early morning."

He chuckled. "Yeah, spoken like a girl who doesn't go out after buckle bunnies." He frowned. "What do they call the male equivalent?"

"I think they call them cowboys," Callie said. "But they're too busy with the buckle bunnies. And anyway, not man enough to take on a real cowgirl."

"Harsh."

She shrugged. "Call it like I see it."

And as he turned to leave Callie alone to do her thing, he figured it was best to let her have that illusion. He was more than man enough to handle her. It was just that it would only ever be a roll in the hay. And Callie wasn't someone he could ever do that with.

She was everything bright and earnest and passionate in the world.

And his soul was a dried-out dust bowl with nothing left to give.

You can give her this.

Yeah. Well. It would have to be good enough.

And he would have to keep his hands to himself.

CHAPTER THREE

"Were you trying to sneak out without me?"

It was dusky outside, the sun not yet risen over the mountains that Callie hadn't entirely gotten a glimpse of last night. It had been dark when she'd arrived, but from what she knew about this part of the state, there had to be mountains all around.

Jake snorted. "I'm not sneaking anywhere. It's my house."

"You said you needed help."

Jake was ready for a day out on the ranch. He had on a tan cowboy hat, a denim jacket and blue jeans. He was wearing work boots, rather than the cowboy boots that she was used to seeing him in during rodeo events and nights out at the honky-tonk bars they frequented after the rodeo.

"Well, I didn't figure it was polite to roust my guest from bed on the first day of her arrival. Anyway. You're here for Thanksgiving."

"A ruse," she said.

He chuckled, shook his head and opened the door for her. She didn't like any of those things. Because the chuckle felt paternal, and the opening of the door felt like he was emphasizing the fact that she was a lady and he was a man.

She didn't care for either, since she was chasing both issues at the moment. She stepped past him, and stomped across the porch and down the steps.

"Get up on the wrong side of the bed this morning?"

She turned around, huffing.

"No. But I didn't come here so you could treat me like I was fragile. I came here because I thought you were about the only person on earth who really respected me, Jake. And now you're being as weird about me riding saddle bronc as my dad."

He paused, and he looked at her, his eyes going sharp like they'd done yesterday when he'd approached her suddenly. When he'd tried to throw her off balance by pretending he'd intended to kiss her.

"I saw you fall," he said. "I saw you fall, and I can't forget that. I heard the sound of your bones breaking on the ground."

The intensity in his tone stopped her short. It made her feel strange. Like her boots had been tacked down to the dirt with a couple of horseshoe nails.

Then he did something totally unexpected. He reached out and touched her face, cupped her chin and held her steady. "If something would have happened to you, more serious than it did, I would have never forgiven myself."

Something jittered through her body, and she didn't like it. Not one bit. She pulled back, shaking off his hand.

But the impression of his touch wouldn't go away.

"You're being a drama queen. It was a fracture. And I'm fine."

"But I remember it. And I don't like it."

"Well, as much as I'm sure it pains you to hear this, I am not in existence for the sole purpose of you liking or not liking what it is I want to do, Jake Daniels. It doesn't much matter to me if you like it. But if you're my friend, you'll help me."

"I agreed to help you, Cal, so quit being prickly. I signed up to spend time with my friend, not a cactus." And then he walked past her, jerking open the passenger door of his pickup, another misplaced show of chivalry.

"You know women are more than capable of opening doors." She held her hands up and wiggled her thumbs. "Damn if we don't also have opposable thumbs."

"And as a gentleman, I opt to use my thumbs to open doors for women, regardless of the state of their ability, just because it's what I was taught to do."

"Doing what your daddy taught you like a good boy?" The words landed flat, and it took her a moment, just a moment that came abreast too late, to realize what she had said. "I'm sorry."

That was stupid. She knew about Jake's family. She hadn't meant it that way, and it had still hit that way. He'd trusted her with his ghosts.

She felt a slight bit of guilt she hadn't returned the favor.

And now she was being a jerk about it.

"Jake..."

"Okay," he said, backing away from her and making his way to his side of the truck.

When they were both inside and headed down a dirt access road on the ranch, Callie's eyes blurred, and she finally spoke again. "I wasn't thinking. I'm really sorry that I said that."

"You were just giving me a hard time—you didn't mean anything by it."

"It doesn't matter," she said. "I should have thought."

"It does matter actually. Because you didn't mean anything by it. But to answer your question, yes, my daddy did teach me that. And he wasn't around long enough to teach me as much as I would've liked. So yeah, that stuff matters to me."

"I'm just... I'm being sensitive," she said, kicking a piece of gravel and sending a cloud of dust up with it. "And I apologize. I should never be so touchy that I end up hurting my friend without thinking. You're not trying to upset me by opening doors for me. I get that. It's just sometimes it really bothers me… The difference between us."

"What's wrong with the difference between us? It's not a bad thing to be different. It just is what it is."

"Not when it holds me back."

"Do you wish you weren't a woman?"

She was taken aback by that question. Because that wasn't it at all. It was that…she wanted to matter. She wanted to be special. Singular.

And she had her reasons. Reasons she hadn't shared everything with him.

She lived with enough ghosts—she hadn't wanted them to follow her to the circuit. And it was clear her parents didn't, either, because there were no whispers about their tragedy among the other riders.

She just wanted to be herself, as much as she wanted. Why was that so hard?

"I just want to be able to be everything I want. As a woman. And it makes me angry that it's so difficult. I don't want to change who I am. But I want the other people around me to stop acting like I can't be all that I am. I mean, it's sad. That you would have to think I don't like being a woman just because I want to do these things."

"That isn't what I meant. I didn't mean it's not—"

"Ladylike? My mom does. My mom despairs of me." She tried not to let those words hurt. "Her only daughter, out of all those kids, and I was supposed to be something different. I was supposed to want to dress up like her, be a rodeo queen. Big hair and lots of sequins. I was supposed to be shiny. And probably married by now with lots of kids."

"You're too young for that," he said, frowning.

"My mom was married when she was nineteen, with her first kid by twenty. It's what she cares about. And that's fine for her, but it's not what I care about. I know that it hurts her. I know she figured I was her one great hope for a child that she could actually understand. Identify with. I know that she wanted me to be the one that painted my nails with her and all that." She looked down at her hands. At her dirty, busted-up hands with chewed-on, ragged fingernails. "You know she doesn't have any other daughters." The words felt like a lie. "I was her hope."

She did not have the hands of a lady.

Good thing she wasn't interested in a real marriage. What man would even want those hands on him?

The thought was strange, so dissonant and off-key to her usual line of thinking that she paused. And tried to imagine her hands on a man's skin.

His face.

His chest.

She looked up and her eyes collided with Jake's, and she felt... suddenly uncomfortable. Guilty.

"Ladylike's not a real thing," he said. "Bottom line, this whole conversation is regrettable. You should be able to be who you want to be. You should be able to have your dreams. But you know, the people that care about you are going to worry. Because... I do not want to say this without upsetting you, Cal, but your dreams are going to be more challenging for you because you're a woman than they would be if you were a man. And they're more dangerous."

"Well, maybe I'm twice as brave to make up for it."

He said nothing, then huffed a laugh a moment later. "Maybe twice as stubborn."

"Only twice?"

She realized that she'd been so lost in their conversation she hadn't looked at any of the scenery at all. And at this point, the sun was coming up over the mountains, a brilliant, golden glow casting a stringent yellow filter on the scenery around them. Turning evergreen trees into gilded bottlebrushes and making the meadows around them look like they'd caught fire. It was a beautiful ranch. The fields empty right now, the outbuildings they passed dilapidated.

"What exactly are you going to do with this place?"

"I'm going to breed horses. Horses are what I know. My cousin has beef, my dad did beef—I don't want to do that. I don't want to do the same thing."

"The same thing is bad?" she asked.

He didn't look at her. "I never wanted that life. This is a hell of a lot closer to it than I ever thought I'd get."

So there were things he didn't tell her, because he'd never told her this before.

"So why did you leave the rodeo?" It had hurt her when he'd left. She'd felt abandoned. And he'd done it in the weeks following her injury. It had felt personal. It had hurt worse than the bone fracture.

"You haven't spent a lot of time here, have you?" His face was carefully blank when he said that and she had a feeling she was being redirected.

She shook her head. "I mean, obviously I've been all over traveling with the rodeo, but not any more notable time here than anywhere else, no. Mostly, just Lone Rock. It's beautiful here."

"It's home," he said. But he didn't sound… He didn't sound warm or affectionate when he said it. There was something else to his tone, and she couldn't quite sort it out. But before she had a chance to linger on it, he was ready to move on. "Hope you brought your work gloves."

"Who do you think I am?" She reached into her pocket and took out the battered pair of leather gloves. "I'm ready to go."

"Good. Because we're stringing barbed wire."

"Somehow I knew it would be fences," she said. "I hate putting up fence."

"Yeah, well, a whole lot of this life is fencing."

"I'm aware. Do you think my dad doesn't put us to work on

his ranch? You know full well he does. Puts me to work the same as the boys."

Her dad had always treated her like the boys. And the better she did on the ranch, the faster she ran, the heavier things she lifted, the more attention she got. She'd learned to drive a four-wheeler at nine so she could help haul equipment around. She'd gotten good at barrel racing at ten and her dad had thought it was a revelation.

Her mom had watched distantly and she'd seemed fine with it for a while. But as Callie had gotten older, the more it became clear she'd expected Callie to stop loving ranch work, to stop loving the same things as her brothers and father and get more invested in cooking and baking and nail polish.

She had not.

Jake chuckled. "I imagine he does."

They got out of the truck, and Callie's boots sank into the muck. It was drizzly and gray so she hadn't expected the ground to be so soft.

"Rained a hell of a lot yesterday," he said. "I expect the clouds are going to roll in a little bit later. But I'm always thankful for a clear fall morning. A chance to see the sun. By the time we get through to December we're not going to see it at all."

"Well, it's already colder than a witch's teat in Lone Rock, so I don't mind."

His expression turned serious. "I always wondered how cold exactly that was."

"*Cold,*" she answered. "This is downright balmy." She let out a long, slow breath. "It gets really cold in Lone Rock around Christmastime. Dumps a whole bunch of snow. The ranch looks beautiful, though. And there's a whole bunch of cabins on the property. Basically, every time the family decides to upgrade houses they just keep the last one. It's hundreds of acres, so there's cabins enough for every member of my family when they decide to come to stay. Lots of space. In the main house... My mom gets a huge Christmas tree. Puts it in the living room. The ceilings are twenty feet high, so she's got a tree that complements it. That's another thing she loves that I've never been that into. But I'll tell you, I might not like doing the decorating, but I love the way it looks."

"Okay," he said, his tone letting her know he was good and suspicious.

"You *really* ought to see it sometime," she said.

"Yeah, I'm not really into that sort of thing."

"What? Christmas?"

"Yeah. I mean, I go to my family's place for Christmas. It's our tradition. And if it wasn't, I probably wouldn't go. But I always show up. I always do the thing."

"Right."

He had a family Christmas tradition. Well, what was she going to do with that?

"But you like Thanksgiving."

"It's a giant meal. And frankly, that's how I see Christmas, too."

"What was Christmas like when you were a kid?"

Another thing they'd never talked about before and now it seemed important because she wanted him to come with her to her parents' house and…

What if Christmas was awful for him?

She'd been so focused on what she wanted, on what she needed, that she hadn't really considered him as a person. She'd thought of him as a solution.

"I mean, you don't have to tell me. I just…"

He laughed. "Same as it is for anybody. I… I, well, I wanted presents. That was about all it meant to me. Then I lost my parents and I realized how much more it was about my family all being together, going to Mass and all that."

"Mass?"

"Oh, my dad was very Catholic. *Very*. It was a big part of our lives growing up."

She hadn't known about that, either. "And now?"

"Didn't work for him, did it?" he asked.

"I see."

"There's not much to see. It just is what it is. They were here, they're gone now. Christmas changed for me. I mean, I always liked it with the cousins. But then, we spent Christmas together before, too."

"Have you spent every Christmas with them? That is, every year even since they left?"

"No," he said.

That made her feel a little bit better.

"I have spent a few Christmases lost in whiskey instead of family. Now I try to make it back to avoid that."

She had never really been all that conscious of the age gap between them, but something about the way he said that made her feel every bit of the seven years that separated them. She had certainly never lost a Christmas to alcohol.

Though maybe that was more life experience than it was age.

She still felt guilty about telling him what she needed from him. In light of everything. So she figured she would wait until she had put in a little bit of labor.

They got to work, getting out big rolls of fencing and stretching it across the posts that were already put into the ground. It was sweaty work, even though it wasn't all that warm in spite of the sun. She began to get clammy beneath her jacket, and a couple of times she lost hold of the barbed wire, and got what would've been a big old gouge in her hands if not for her gloves.

And finally, when they sat down with lunch—which consisted of half a sandwich that he gave her out of his own box since she hadn't brought anything—she looked up at him. The moisture from the ground soaked through her jeans, but she didn't much care. And he didn't seem to mind, either. He was sitting there with his knees up, his forearms propped on the top of them. His cowboy hat shaded his eyes, and the glare from the sun highlighted whiskers on his chin, showing that he hadn't shaved that morning. His face was familiar. Not only that, the shape of him was familiar. Her whole life was cowboys. And Jake was one of the most important cowboys in it. But for some reason, that moment felt like a piece of time that had been pushed slightly sideways, and as a result, the way he looked felt slightly sideways, too.

His familiarity.

It just seemed... It seemed different. And something about the shape of him seemed new. Like she was noticing the squareness of his jaw for the first time. The way his upper lip curved, and the strength and straightness in his... His nose of all things. It was a strange way to think about a nose. He was a well-formed man. Like a big hunk of clay that had been shaped by a master sculptor. It was no mystery why he had endorsement deals coming out of his ears. Why he was used in advertisements for Wrangler jeans and work boots. For whiskey and barbecue grills. A strange sort of longing filled her, and she could only attach envy to it. Envy that he was... Everything that a man with his set of dreams needed to be. That he was so strong, so broad. So striking. And that all of those things worked for him, and not against him the way her particular makeup seemed to do.

She'd never felt envy that was quite like this, though. Big and expanding and threatening to crack her chest. No. She never felt anything quite like that.

"I need you to come for Christmas."

CHAPTER FOUR

Jake looked over at Cal. "Excuse me?"

He'd been having a hell of a time keeping a handle on things all day. He had, in fact, been trying to sneak out without her noticing.

And the little sprite had caught him. And then he had to play like there was nothing going on. Like having her sleeping down the hall in his house hadn't played some kind of havoc on his body.

It was irritating as hell.

And frankly, his ability to hide it from her was suffering. Or maybe his drive to hide it. She was asking a lot of him, and she was as wide-eyed as a cartoon deer when it came to this kind of thing.

He could easily recall how she'd nearly fallen to the ground trying to back away from him when he'd made a move toward her a couple of days ago.

She hadn't even realized what he was doing.

Yet another reason to never, ever touch her.

He was a man with ample experience with sex and women, and there was no way that Cal should cause the amount of issues inside of him that she did. But the problem was, the distance he had put between them hadn't solved the damn thing. If anything, it had only made matters worse. He hadn't truly been prepared for what it was like for her to be here. For her to stay with him.

And now she was throwing all these curveballs into the situation, and it was only making matters worse.

He might not touch her, but he didn't need to protect her from all signs of his attraction, either. That appealed to his sense of dark humor.

She was telling him that he had to come for Christmas, after all. Suddenly it was bigger than just a marriage license.

It was a family holiday.

"Say that again?"

"It's only that it's really important that I have Christmas with my family. And there's just no way, there is no way in hell, that my father will believe I married a man who didn't come home for Christmas."

"And all this... This believability business is a really important part of all this?"

"Yes. It's really important. Because otherwise he's going to change the stipulations of the trust fund."

"Why can't you just have a chat with your daddy," he said.

"Have you *met* my daddy?"

Rhetorical, since she knew full well he had. And had shared a couple of drinks with him at that.

"Cal, he loves you."

"Yes," she said, sounding angry. "He does. I know he does. But he lost his mind after I broke my arm. It was just an arm! And all this stuff...he thinks he's doing it for my own good. And I get that. I do. I really, really do. But the fact of the matter is, it's bullshit. I am... I'm my own person. And if I have to take control like this for him to understand that, then I have to take control. But I can't have him knowing that's what I'm doing.

We can… We can figure out how to wash all this out later. I can figure out how to fix it later. But I just have to do this bit first."

"He's going to be real pissed off at you."

"I know," she said. "I do know that. I do know that I'm going to hurt some things. Damage some pieces of our relationship. I get that. But that's how worth it it is to me."

"Callie…"

"Please do this for me. Please. I know it's not perfect, or good, or… I mean, I know it's going to hurt people… But I just…"

And he couldn't tell her no. He really couldn't. Because life was an absolute asshole. And he knew that better than a lot of people did. And if she saw a way to make hers better, who was he to stand in her way? If he had a way of helping her, why wouldn't he do it?

"But part of this deal is that I'm training you," he said. "That doesn't change. Here, in Eastern Oregon, doesn't matter. I'm training you, and if I tell you that you're not ready you'll listen."

"You'll come for Christmas?"

"You agree to my terms?" He took a step closer, some devil inside him pushing him. What would she do if he outright kissed her?

He turned his head and let out a breath.

She fidgeted. "Yes."

"If I have to come for Christmas to look like a real husband, then I'll do it. But we better have our own accommodation. We're not playing some ridiculous sitcom game where we're running in and out of rooms and hopping into bed to put on a show or whatever the hell."

He was not going to be playing roommate to Callie Carson. It just wasn't going to happen. He was only a man, after all. And Callie didn't even have any idea of the way she made him feel. Of the kind of pressure she put them under physically.

"We will. I told you. There are cabins everywhere. We'll have one to stay in. Everything will be fine. In my family... They already know you. And they like you."

"Somehow, I have a feeling your dad is going to like me a hell of a lot less when he finds out that I eloped with his daughter. And then he's going to hate me once he discovers that it was entirely made up so that you could get your money."

"We'll cross that bridge when we come to it. And anyway, in the meantime... Maybe if you're training me he'll see things different. I mean, if you're my husband I'll be under your protection, after all." She made an extraordinary gagging sound.

"You really think he's going to see it that way?"

"He's old school, it turns out. And none of the things that he taught me all my life seemed to matter when it actually came down to it. I know he's going to see it that way. He may not like it, but he's going to respect the fact that you're the man in my life." She suddenly looked morose. "I just wish that I could be enough. That what I wanted for myself was enough."

"It's enough for me," he said.

He couldn't fix her situation, but he could help her along.

And he was pretty well determined to do just that.

"All right. But we *are* telling my family."

"Oh..."

"I have to explain the situation to them. And I'm not lying to them."

"But..."

"Anyway, my cousin's wife would sniff it out."

"She would?"

"She's like a mystical elf. She can always tell what's going on with people." He did not add that the real truth was that Sammy was going to be able to tell if two people were sleeping together, or if they weren't. Because he did not want to introduce that topic of conversation. Not between them. Not right now.

There was flirting with the line, and there was crossing it.

She sighed, heavily. He'd find it funny if this whole situation weren't so messed up. "I guess this is my payment, then. I owe you. And so, I'll be honest with your family."

"I like how you're acting as if you have any sort of bargaining power here, Cal."

"Bite me."

He didn't respond to that provocation. Because part of him would like very much to bite her. Then she would know what the hell that meant.

So he just elbowed her. "Get back to work."

"Fine, fine. When do we start training?"

"After Thanksgiving. After the wedding."

The words felt weird on his tongue. Marriage didn't matter to him. Not one bit. But he'd still never thought he would be doing it.

"Well, all right, then. I guess we get back to stringing fence."

"I guess so."

Jake had always liked Thanksgiving. It was one of the easier holidays to get through, even after his parents had passed. Because it was just… Loud and filled with food and people. And he and all his cousins, and his brother, had always done their best to make it the most chaotic, crazy event possible. There was always football, on TV and played out in the yard in the freezing cold, sometimes thrown around the living room. There was dinner, and then there was a second dinner, which they always ate on TV trays in the living room, and there was every kind of pie imaginable. The season itself didn't come with the melancholy of Christmas, of the pressure of family memories, of his parents waking him up early in the morning so that he could open presents, of dressing up for church.

He primarily remembered everyone at Thanksgiving, not just his own family unit.

It was just the right amount of celebrating, without digging too deep into childhood scars, that he appreciated.

And today would be no exception. As they drove beneath the big sign that proclaimed the place Hope Springs Ranch, he smiled.

"This is it," he said to Cal.

"Wow," she said, looking around. "It's... Well, it's bigger than I expected it to be."

"My dad had a pretty good spread here, but Ryder has made it something else. Our fathers worked together, though his dad was chief of police, and that was his primary work."

"How come Ryder ended up running the ranch if it was your dad who ran it while your parents were alive?"

"Because Ryder was the only one that was eighteen. He was the one who had to take care of everybody. For years. He and the kids needed the house. And in the end, he was the one who really saved us all. Who established our roots here. Who grew this operation so that it supported us, and supported him, as well. Besides, I had itchy feet. I wasn't ready to stay here. Not yet."

His relationship to home was complicated and always had been.

It was the circumstances of everything, he was sure. Because Ryder had to be the father figure. There had been no other option. And he'd done it. He'd done it well. And he'd made sure that everybody was well taken care of.

He'd been a teenage boy, not a kid, not a man, not yet. Ryder had to become a man, and Jake had been... Lost somewhere in between.

He knew he'd been a pain in the ass. Sneaking out, getting drunk, in general being a dick to the one person that he was counting on to see him through everything, to keep the family together, and he just hadn't seen it that way. Not at the time. He regretted that. Being so difficult for his cousin. And it was one reason that he'd always used pieces of the earnings he'd gotten on the road to help support the ranch at Hope Springs. Because it mattered. Because he'd had some atoning to do.

But yeah, for him the place would always be a haunted ground of what could have been. Because maybe this would've been his. In another life. Or maybe Colt's, but they wouldn't know. It was Ryder's, and rightfully so. Nobody contested or questioned it. Things were just too different. You could never go back and pretend...

They could never pretend they hadn't lost their parents. And that had reshaped the entire fabric of what this place was and what it could be. They couldn't pretend that it hadn't altered the fabric of who they were completely.

"If I open the door for you are you going to get mad at me?"

She narrowed her eyes and pushed the door open, letting herself out. And he chuckled, getting out and leading the way up the front porch. As soon as his boot hit the bottom step, the door flung open, and his little second cousin came charging out, all pudgy legs and a four-toothed grin, her wild blond hair sticking up at all angles. And her mother followed behind her—Sammy, in a flowing white dress, her blond hair not any more tamed than her daughter's.

"You're here," she said, folding him into a lavender-scented hug.

"And you must be Cal," she said, looking from him back to Callie.

He frowned at Sammy's speculative look. "Yeah."

Then his cousin Ryder filled up the doorway, standing behind his wife. "Hey, Jake," he said. "Who's this?"

"Cal," Jake said.

Ryder laughed. "Hell. We thought your friend was a man."

He saw Callie turn a shade of beetroot, all the way up into her hair. *"Oh,"* she said.

"Oh, well, then you're going to think the rest of the story is even funnier," Jake said, planting his hand in the center of Cal's back and propelling her forward toward the house. They all collected inside, where his cousins Pansy, Rose and Iris already were, with their respective partners, as was his brother, Colt, who was sitting in the corner fiddling with the tuning pegs on his guitar.

Logan was next to him. Logan, who had been part of their ragtag band of misfit toys here in Hope Springs, as he had lost his mother in the same accident that had claimed their parents. Him getting together with Rose last Christmas had come as a source of shock to the family, since they'd all felt the family kind of way about Logan, and clearly Rose had not.

But they were happy, and that was what mattered.

"Everybody," he said. "This is Callie Carson. Callie, everybody."

They greeted her with an uneven roar, and he leaned in. "You'll figure them out as we go. I figure if I tell you all their names now, you're not going to remember, anyway. But you know Colt."

Colt treated them to a half wave.

"I thought your friend was a man," Rose said.

"What did you *tell them* about me?" Callie asked.

"I just said that my buddy Cal was coming up for Thanksgiving."

"Oh. Well," Callie said, sounding exasperated.

"Callie is my fiancée now," he said.

The entire room went silent. Of all the things he'd expected from this pack of assholes, silence wasn't it.

"It's a funny story actually," he said.

He had expected some kind of eruption. But none occurred. Instead, his entire family was staring at him openmouthed.

"You're a bad person," Callie muttered. "He's helping me out."

"You make it sound like you're pregnant," he said.

"Good God, Jake," she said, going right at him again. "I told you this was going to embarrass me, and not only are you not trying to not embarrass me, you're making it worse."

"How am I making it worse? I'm just saying. I'm helping you out. And it's true. It's a trust fund thing. Callie is a saddle bronc rider. At least, she wants to be. Her dad is the rodeo commissioner, and long story short, in order to get her freedom so that she can compete in the event she wants to compete in, she needs to get married for a minute."

"That *is* a good story," Sammy said, looking keen. "You weren't joking."

"I said I wasn't."

He was grateful for the ribbing of his family, and for the general mayhem around him. Because it took away some of the uneasiness that he felt over the whole situation. The uneasiness that he was feeling because of her.

The dining room had two tables, set up end to end, and all the plates matched, which he thought was kind of weird, but the chairs didn't. There was a high chair for Ryder and Sammy's little one, Astrid, and a whole lot more people than they used to have, since everyone was now paired off. And in the case of Pansy and West, there was an extra associated with them because West's half brother lived with them.

They were going to be very unhappy that Jake was going to have to miss Christmas.

"I'm glad everyone's here," Sammy said. "Because before we cut the turkey I have some family business to go over."

"Who elected you supreme leader?" Logan asked, taking a scoop of sweet potatoes with marshmallows—both varieties were present—and putting them onto his plate.

"If you would like to run the proceedings, Logan, you're welcome to. But you don't know what I have to say."

"Agreed," Colt said. "I don't want to hear what Logan has to say."

Jake shared a grin with his brother.

"Anyway," Sammy said. "I'm proposing that we celebrate Christmas a week early."

"What?"

"We got everyone for Thanksgiving, which I'm very grateful for, and it required other families to make various arrangements. But Iris and Griffin want to travel to California for Christmas to spend the holiday with his family, West and Pansy have the Daltons, and so do you, Logan," she said.

Logan shifted uncomfortably. As far as Jake knew, Logan was still in the process of making peace with his father's family. He'd spent his whole life disenfranchised from him, but when West, another of Hank Dalton's secret sons, had married into their family, it had created a bridge between the two worlds that Logan could no longer ignore. As far as Jake was concerned, it wasn't any of his business what Logan wanted to do one way or the other.

"My family is trash, regrettably," Sammy said, spreading her hands, "but we understand that many of you have other family to see, and we don't want to not have a big Christmas celebration, so we'll make it earlier."

"Well," Jake said, feeling deflated, because it solved the entire problem, and all of his objections about going to Eastern Oregon with Cal over Christmas.

And just like that, somehow, he seemed to be facing down two Christmases, and he wasn't sure how in hell that had happened.

But by then dinner was served, and there was such a fantastic array of every good thing he could've hoped for that he quit thinking about Christmases of any kind. He knew well that Callie was used to big noisy families, and his didn't seem to bother her at all. In fact, she appeared to blend in pretty effortlessly, something that he appreciated. He was glad that his family liked her. Because she was important to him. And that mattered.

After the turkey was demolished, but before Sammy had brought in the pie, Ryder brought out his football, and they started trying to urge people to go outside and play. His cousin was the current football coach at Gold Valley High School, and had always been a major enthusiast. Which Jake thought was sort of unfair, since Colt liked to play his guitar, but only sat in the corner with it and didn't force his hobbies on others. Though, he had to admit, finding an excuse to crash into his family members was always a good time.

"Before we disperse," Sammy said, "we have to see who gets the wishbone."

Sammy was big on all things mystical, and if there wasn't an inbuilt mysticism to something, then she would create it. And she had begun spinning forks and handing out wishbones fifteen years ago, and there was really nothing anyone could do to stop her.

She gravely set the fork at the center of the table and spun it—whoever the tines faced would become the recipient of the wishbone.

The tines faced Cal.

She looked at him, her eyes round. "What does that mean?"

"You get to pull the wishbone in half with someone. Whoever gets the bigger half—"

"I mean, I know how a wishbone works," she said, looking grumpy. "I just didn't know about the spinning forks."

"That's because I made it up," Sammy said proudly.

"Well, who do I… Who do I pull it with?"

"Jake can do it," Sammy crowed.

"Sure," Jake said, casting her a sideways glance.

Sammy passed the bone down to him and Cal. He gripped one side, and held it out in front of Callie. "Are you ready?"

Half of her lips lifted into a rueful smile. "Sure." She stuck her hand out and grabbed the other end, and their eyes met.

She pressed her lips together, and he couldn't help but…

Dammit.

He didn't have a wish. All he had was a brief flash of what it might feel like if his mouth touched hers. And then she broke the bone.

And he was left with the big half.

"I guess you win. Doesn't that mean your wish will come true?" she asked.

His gut went tight. Hell.

"Football," Ryder said.

Saved by his cousin and his unfailing commitment to tradition.

"Don't I get to know what you wished?" Cal asked.

"That's not how it works," Sammy said gravely. "He can't tell you what he wished or it won't come true."

That was a catch-22 if Jake had ever heard one, but it didn't much matter, because he was already being ushered outside with a football, and his family. He could only hope that the women-folk didn't consume Cal. And that she wasn't angry that she'd been left behind with the women—maybe she wanted to play football? He didn't know. He hadn't asked.

"Getting married?" Ryder asked as soon as the door closed behind them.

"Shut up and play, Daniels," Jake said.

"Seriously," Colt said. "You're going to marry Callie Carson, and you think that Abe Carson isn't going to wring your neck?"

Yeah, well. His brother had a point. "Not my problem, since I'm not in the rodeo anymore."

"But he might kill *me*," Colt said. "And that's relevant to my interests. Or dis-interests, as the case may be."

"What you do has nothing to do with what I do, and he knows that. Everyone knows it. We're not the same person."

"It's not like family and the rodeo is rare," he said.

It was true. Brothers often found themselves competing, and they were often carrying on a legacy left behind by their fathers. It just wasn't unusual for families to be part of the business. And sure, families did tend to get lumped in together, but it was also just usual enough that it wasn't like people assumed you were the same just because you were related. And Jake and Colt were not the same.

They never had been.

They loved each other, sure as hell, but they'd always been of two minds. And for all that they spent years out on the circuit together, they tended to gravitate to different groups. He had a feeling that it was related to the way their lives had been, the way that everything had gone when they were kids.

And there were certain things that Jake knew…things that he didn't want his brother to know. And pulling away from Colt had been a natural way to do that.

"I don't need any drama," Colt said.

"I'm not giving you drama. Callie wants to ride. It's not up to Abe to stop her."

"I guess I agree with that," he said. "Reluctantly."

"No need to be reluctant about it. It just is what it is. Callie is a grown-ass woman, and she can make her own choices. She needs access to her trust fund. And to do that she has to get married."

"What year is it?" Logan asked. "That's some weird shit."

"Rich people, man," Jake said, shrugging. "Hell if I know."

"And you're *not* sleeping with her," West asked, looking deeply skeptical.

"No," Jake said. "I'm not." He gritted his teeth against the images that statement conjured up. "She's a friend. She has been for a hell of a long time. She's a good kid. But that's the thing, she's a kid." And he wished like hell that he believed his own damn lies.

"Doesn't look like a kid to me," West said, a half smile curving his lips.

That earned West a glare from Ryder.

West lifted his hands up. "I am wholly and completely committed to your sister."

"See that it stays that way, dickhead," Ryder said, pointing at West while holding the football.

And Jake had a feeling that West was cruising to get his ass handed to him during the game.

"I have to spend Christmas with her family," Jake said.

"*Damn,*" Colt said. "I would not want to be you."

Jake shrugged, feigning a nonchalance he didn't feel. "They're nice enough."

"Sure. All of them. *Before* you were banging Callie."

"I'm *not* banging Callie," he said, making sure to enunciate very clearly.

"But her family doesn't know that. And they won't know that. Because all they are going to know is that you married her. And quickly. And I'm just saying..."

"Yeah, I get you. This is what I get for being a good friend. And frankly, for being a good family member, being here in the first place."

"We all think you're very good," Ryder said. "Is that what you're looking for? A cookie?"

"I don't want your damn cookie," he said. "A little respect, though, that would go a long way."

"You have it," Ryder said. "And I think you know it. Anyway, let's quit talking and play some football. And make sure not to damage Jake too much. He has to look pretty for his wedding."

CHAPTER FIVE

Jake's family was so nice. Really, they had been exceptionally wonderful to her during Thanksgiving, and they had made fun of Jake for agreeing to a fake marriage, but they had been supportive in a way she had not imagined anyone's family could be. But then, they were unconventional, the lot of them. While Jake been outside playing football, she'd spent time listening to the women chatting. They were all different from each other, though they were all married. Rose was a spirited tomboy around her own age. Pansy was the chief of police, tough as nails and filled with spirit. Iris was softer, sweet in a more traditional way, with Sammy as earth mother, bringing a different kind of airiness to the group. It was sort of fascinating to her, to be surrounded by all these different kinds of femininity.

Sure, there was a bit of that in the rodeo. It was inescapable. But mostly, the women affiliated with the rodeo were easily categorized into three different buckets.

You had your tough cowgirls, which she considered herself among. Then you had your sparkly cowgirls. Your rodeo queens, and your barrel racers who liked to spend time gluing jewels to their horses' butts. She was not that. And there was a little bit of friendly ribbing that happened between those two types of cowgirls.

Then there were the buckle bunnies, of which none of the cowgirls were fans. It was cowboys that liked those ladies. Who were there for only one reason. To dress the part for a few minutes so they could get down and dirty with one of the men riding the animals. And she heard it expressed more than once by the girls on the circuit how unfair it was that the boys messed around with those fake cowgirls.

"Because they can't handle a real one," she remembered Lara Pritchett saying once. One of the more gussied-up types of barrel racer, she always had nice, fancy braids and pretty makeup done.

"I guess you're welcome to put out the same as they do," one of the other cowgirls had said.

"None of those boys are worth that kind of carry-on," she'd said. *"If they want to man-up and get serious, then they're welcome to it, but until such a time as that, I will not be competing with some trumped-up skank in a plastic belt buckle."*

And Callie hadn't really seen the issue.

They all wanted to compete in their events the way they wanted to, as she saw it. The buckle bunnies were just looking to complete a different ride, so to speak.

And it didn't interest Callie. It just wasn't what she was going to pour her energy into. Trying to get into the sack with some cowboy who would never remember her name, and who would make things uncomfortable for her around the circuit, yeah, that didn't appeal to her at all. But she wasn't going to sit around stewing like the other women, either. If she wanted to do it she could.

She just didn't. That was it.

Nothing to be pissed off about.

But anyway, that was her experience with different kinds of women, and the ways they sometimes competed rather than getting along. But the Daniels house was an interesting mix of a great many things that seemed to simply coexist and not compete at all. Different types of people who let each other be.

It was an interesting contrast to her own household, which was... Homogenous.

It was Western, unambiguously.

Her brothers were rodeo cowboys, her father was a former rodeo cowboy and her mother was a former rodeo queen.

And there was no kind of model for her to emulate other than the boys, because she sure as hell didn't want to be a rodeo queen. It just didn't suit her.

She wasn't like the other cowgirls in the rodeo, either, not exactly. And it just felt easier to emulate her brothers. She had five of them around all the time, after all. Though her oldest brother hadn't been home in years, six brothers was a little excessive anyway, and Kit, Jace, Boone, Flint and Chance were more than enough of an influence without Buck around.

And the tougher she acted, the less her dad hovered and the more he supported her in what she wanted.

But anyway, her like of his family aside, her palms were sweaty because they were having to get themselves a marriage license today. And she just felt guilty. Because she wasn't going to tell her parents until the wedding happened. Because she didn't want it to turn into some kind of a circus. And she really didn't want them all there. It was bad enough doing it at all without having an actual ceremony, and her mom wanting her to be a bride and... No. That just wasn't happening. So it had to happen without their knowledge. And it needed to happen quick.

"I guess we need to get our paperwork," she said at the breakfast table that morning.

"Right. What all does that entail?"

"I don't know. Birth certificates and things. You have to get a blood test in some places to prove you're not related."

"I don't think you need to do that here," he said.

"Well, we just need to make sure. And then, I guess we make

our appointment with the justice of the peace. No point having anything other than a civil ceremony."

"Sure. I mean, what exactly do you have to do legally to make it... Real?"

She was starting to feel twitchy. "I don't know. You need a witness, I know that. And I don't actually think someone can stop the wedding by objecting. That much I kinda know."

"Sure," he said.

"So, I guess we better go get ourselves a marriage license."

"Yeah, all right, we can go do that today. But we have to wait for things to open up."

"The courthouse is open at eight. I checked."

"Aren't you industrious?"

"I am," she said, feeling pleased with herself.

"Chores first," he said. "Then we can get on to the marriage license."

"Well, it's a good thing it's not a real marriage, because that's not a very romantic sentiment."

"Callie, nothing about this is overly romantic. But I figure that's by design."

"It would have to be by design for it to be romantic," she said, snorting. And then she realized that maybe she didn't want to be snorting like that. It was a little bit embarrassing.

She tramped out to the fields with him, and they spent the morning working on barbed wire, and then they decided to go sweaty into town with all their documentation. It was a painless process at the courthouse. They filled some things out, finishing them off with their signatures.

"I didn't know your birth date," she said as they were walking out of the small, redbrick building.

"Is it a deterrent?" he asked, lifting a brow. "Does it make me ineligible?"

"No," she said. "I just didn't know it. It's more a point of interest. An observation."

He huffed a laugh. "Kinda makes it seem silly that we're doing this."

"I thought you didn't care about marriage."

"I don't. But you do. You said something about it being sacred. A promise in front of God and all that."

"Well, yeah, my parents have been married for forty years. It's a relationship that means everything to them, and living a life like my father did... Well, he could've been unfaithful. That's the thing. A lot of them are."

"Hank Dalton as exhibit A."

She nodded. "I know Hank. He and my father used to ride together, and they were good friends, but he could never condone the way that Hank treated his marriage. He never wanted to be like Hank. My dad talked about him as an example of what not to be. It's just... Yeah, my dad never wanted to be like that. And I respect that. I do. I know that it means a lot to them, to my parents. That their kids respect marriage and relationships in the same way that they do."

"This isn't real. Don't worry about it."

"Why don't you care about marriage? I mean, I know you didn't have your parents in your life forever, but... Were they unhappy?"

"They built up our house like this sacred thing, treated our family—me and Colt—like we were something special. Like the home was the most important thing, our family, no matter what. No matter what else was happening. You know how it is. And it felt that way for a while. Like the Daniels family was the most important family that there could ever be. When you lose something like that you realize it's not magic. The *world's* not magic. It's just dirt. Dirt and sweat and death. And that's about all you're guaranteed in life. You know where you're headed, right?"

"That's grim," she said, shivering slightly. But she could understand how he felt, because his words broke something open in her head. Her family felt magic. With their beautiful ranch out there in the middle of nowhere, her brothers… She knew they weren't, though. They'd been touched by a grief that she'd never had to experience. But she had always known that bad things can happen. Just because she hadn't been around to see it didn't mean she didn't understand it.

The secret she hadn't told him.

But how could she keep it from him?

She knew his birth date now. She supposed he should know this.

"You know, before I was born, there were seven kids in the family." She didn't know why it felt like trying to shove a brick off her chest. Why it felt so heavy.

He frowned. "I don't follow."

She felt… She didn't want to talk about Sophie. Because then he would know about Sophie. And part of her felt like by just knowing about her would make him wonder…what she'd been like. What another girl in her family would have been like.

Maybe he would find her lacking, too.

She cleared her throat. That was silly and it wasn't important now. "They had a little girl before me. Sophie. She was just a couple years younger than Kit. She was sick. From the time she was born." She swallowed hard. "They tried to keep her safe but she was very fragile. She died when she was five."

"Shit."

"I know. I just… I know. My dad thought the answer was to take me and make me tough. I mean, I wasn't born with a genetic disorder. But he begged my mom, begged her to let me be his. To let him make me tough. And she agreed because she was so broken up about Sophie, too." She swallowed hard. "But I don't know what my family was like before… I don't know how things were between my parents. It all happened before I was born, or even a thought. But I know it changed things. I know the boys remember it. And I know they were affected by it. It was one thing and now it's not. It hasn't been since before I was born."

"How is it that no one knows about this in the rodeo?"

"It just happened too long ago. Twenty-five years ago. It's not something that comes up and I think…after she died was when my dad took the position as commissioner. It's when the family got more involved. He was a rider first and my mom was the rodeo queen for a season and…they retired for a while and had kids but it was losing Sophie that brought them back. And I think they wanted it to be free of sadness even though their lives really couldn't be."

"That's a whole lot, Cal. I'm sorry."

She nodded. "It is. It's just…there. And there's no way to fix it."

"Things always change, that's the problem. I just had to deal with it a little sooner than other people do. Losing your parents is nothing special. Most everybody goes through it at one time or another."

"Sure. But most people aren't as young as you."

"Doesn't matter. It's just part of life, like I said. Nothing to get precious about. But I don't feel that kind of reverence toward marriage or anything like that. I'm sure it's a direct result of my experience. Even when things look like they might be going well…everything can fall apart. The plane can go down. You can't control it. Everything's just twists of fate here and there. You can't make yourself safer."

"And you ride bulls."

"Yeah," he said, grinning. "I ride bulls."

She couldn't quite put all those pieces together, but it was a strange thing, to have been friends with this man for as long as she was, and feel like she had just learned something singular about him. To feel like she had just made a discovery about what put him together, what made him click.

But they were here, sharing old grief together, and it made her ache. Hers and his. But it felt good, too. To say it out loud.

"Let's get some lunch," he said.

She walked behind him, and into a diner called the Mustard Seed. It had glimmering, coppery pennies glued down for a floor, and whimsical little animals made from forks and beads set up on the tables and windowsills. There were red diner seats, and clear Christmas lights strung around the perimeter.

"I guess Thanksgiving is over," she said.

"Sure is."

"Thanks for agreeing to marry me."

He smiled. "Sure. No problem."

They took a seat at the bar, and the owner of the diner, who introduced herself cheerfully, came and took their order a few moments later. They both got cheeseburgers and fries. Callie got a milkshake. She dipped one of her French fries down in the chocolate shake when it came, and took a bite off the end, chewing thoughtfully.

"We need to start the training as soon as possible. I really want to get in this season."

He stared at her, his blue eyes unreadable.

She felt pinned to the spot. And for some reason, the breath was coming a little bit faster into her lungs. "What? It's really important to me. It's why I'm doing this in the first place, so I need to get ready. And you seem to think I'm not ready, so you better have something interesting to show me."

"Yeah, there's some things that I'm going to show you. Fundamentally, you've been around it your whole life. It's not like you don't understand, but you need to make sure that you're not overconfident. You need to make sure that you're safe, and I would feel better if we ran through the routines as often as possible."

"Every ride is different, and you know it. You can't practice for it. Animals don't do any one thing. They do what they're going to do. And the horses are going to do what they're going to do, regardless if I practice or not."

"You know what you're gonna do? You're going to practice being strong. You're going to build up your leg muscles. You're not going to be caught off guard. You're not going to panic when you fall, you're going to relax. And you're going to let them fling you around like a ragdoll, and if you fall, you're going to figure out how to hit the ground and move your body as quickly as possible. Do you understand me?"

He stole one of her French fries, which was just patently unnecessary, because he had his own.

"I understand."

He reached his hand back into her fries at the same time she did, and their fingertips brushed. And for some reason, it made her heart jump up and hit the bottom of her throat.

Maybe it was just because this whole situation was weird, and it was taking her friend and shoving him into a role that she wasn't entirely familiar with.

But this, she was familiar with. His instruction, his guidance. He was good at that. He had been coaching her for a long time in other skills, and this was nothing new.

Yeah, the marriage thing was new, but that was it. And it wasn't real.

She needed to practice thinking of it the way that he did. She needed to practice thinking of it as something that didn't matter at all. It was just a function. A function to get her money.

To get her freedom.

Ultimately, the trust fund itself, and the amount of what it had in it, didn't matter. She didn't care about riches. She didn't care about fancy things. And she loved her family more than anything in the world, so tricking them wasn't something she relished. But she really, really needed this freedom, and that was what she required. Beginning and end of story. This was all in aid of that. It was all helping her get there. And that was what mattered. That was really the only thing that mattered.

That she could make her own history. That Callie Carson could feel like she had a place in the world on her own merit.

"All right. We'll start training as soon as possible. Three days until the wedding, so tomorrow we saddle up."

"Sounds good to me."

"Sounds good."

The next morning, Callie was up bright and early, and she was excited. Because if he was going to teach her how to ride, then she was ready.

Not that she didn't know. She was confident enough that she could step into the ring and compete against the men, but she understood that he was doing his best to fortify her against anything that might happen. If he needed to do that, that was fine. The bottom line was, he was a great rider. He was a great cowboy, and she didn't resent having to take lessons from him at all. Any tips that he might give her would be helpful. He had won it all before in the bull riding stakes, and while broncos and bulls were quite literally two different beasts, the function of riding the two of them wasn't entirely different. The mechanics of it all.

Anyway, the mindset of a champion…that was what mattered.

The more she thought about it, the more she realized she didn't just want to compete—she wanted to win. She wanted to prove that she belonged there. That it wasn't just that she could buy entry, but that she could really and truly compete. She had a feeling that as much as Jake supported her, not even he fully believed that.

But he would see. He would. She would make him see, and then he would be… He would be proud of her, and so would her parents. They would understand. In the end, they would understand.

"You actually have bucking broncos out here?"

"I do, in fact, have some horses that are retired from the rodeo, but it doesn't mean they can't still buck."

"This is fantastic. I haven't ridden since the accident."

"Are you strong enough?"

She laughed. "Yes. I did physical therapy, religiously. Everything is great. It's the fact that my dad won't let me near the horses."

"Your dad?"

She blew out a breath. "He lost it when I broke my arm. He said...he said he'd been an idiot thinking I could handle it and that I obviously couldn't. It's not fair, Jake. Kit, Boone... They've all had their injuries. But the minute I couldn't walk it off, I have to quit? He doesn't want me to be equal, he wants me to be better. And I can... I can."

"He's afraid, Cal," Jake said, his voice suddenly rough, and it caught Callie off guard. "You know, it's not insane that your dad lost a child and he's worried about you. Losing people messes you up. I know. It's not like I took care of my parents or anything like that. It's not the same. But still, it... It did something to me to lose them. It wasn't nothing."

"He told me I could do whatever I wanted. Be whoever I wanted. I feel like it was a lie. All of it."

"I get it. I'm just saying... Look, I get it. I get why they're scared. I don't know how anyone does it. Has kids like that. And... Just has them, knowing how things are."

"Oh. So... That idea scares you?" The idea of anything scaring him was... So foreign. So strange.

"I don't know that I'd say *scares*, because I'm not going to do it. I'm not going to have kids. Like I said, none of that stuff means anything to me. I'm not a family man. Not cut out for it."

"Me, either. I mean, I don't want to actually get married. It just doesn't fit in with my plans."

They wandered over to the barn, and her heart leapt when she saw the horses out in the field. "I get to ride one of them?"

"Yes. And you have to wear a helmet."

"I hate that," she said. "I hate it when the cowboys put on those helmets with face masks."

"It's not wimping out to protect your brains," Jake said, his tone dry.

She still groused.

"You can't ride forever," he said. "Even I quit. You have to have a body to use when you're done."

"Well, all right. Maybe I'll think about that other stuff when it comes time. But… It's not time. Not now. This is what I want. Besides, you know you never wanted it—why can't I know that?"

He lifted a shoulder. "Good point."

"Do you have a…a chute and everything?"

"Yeah," he said. "Look, I was ready to leave the rodeo, but I wasn't quite ready to say goodbye to everything."

"Well, I'm appreciative of that."

He got the horse saddled up, and got him in the chute. By then, she could see that he was already agitated, already knowing what was coming next. Callie's heart was hammering hard. She'd had to heal from her broken arm, and she'd been coming up with her plan to get all this going, so it had actually been a few months since she'd been on the back of a horse like this. It made her uneasy. But excited all at the same time.

And then suddenly all her adrenaline went sharp, focused. She lived for this. For this moment. When it all went quiet. When it went calm. When she felt the most at peace with herself and everything in her and around her. In that moment before the chute opened. In that moment before the bunched muscle beneath her sprung into action and she went live.

And then it happened.

She couldn't hear, wasn't aware of anything going on around

her at all except for what occurred between herself and the horse. He did his job, bucking and reeling, rolling beneath her, trying to unseat her.

And she did hers.

Hanging on with all the strength she had in her body, her arms, her legs. This was what she understood. This discomfort. This pain. The cost of success, the sacrifice required to complete the ride.

Eight seconds.

Eight seconds, it was all she needed. And then the horse went right when she expected him to keep going left, and she felt herself losing her grip on the saddle.

No.

She was flying through the air, but she had enough time to try and tuck herself in, to try and roll just right, so she didn't end up with broken bones again. At least, to the best of her ability. Still, the ground was mean, and she heard the horse's hooves connect the dirt right next to her head. She rolled away, getting herself to safety, then stood, stumbling toward the edge of the arena. And that was when she heard Jake.

He was *not* happy.

"Move faster next time," he growled.

"I was moving as fast as I could," she shot back, reflexively brushing the dust off her body, though more trying to brush away the soreness.

It was then she realized he was in the arena, quieting the horse and guiding him out, back into the field.

"That wasn't good enough," he said.

"Yeah?" She spit into the dirt, her mouth grainy. "No shit."

"I thought you wanted to win," he said. "Or at the very least not get your pretty ass stomped."

He was furious.

It wasn't a compliment.

And the aforementioned body part *hurt*.

So.

Pausing at that was stupid. Ridiculous.

She breathed past it.

"I have no desire to get anything on me stomped, my ass or otherwise." He was blazing angry, and it didn't make any sense.

She wasn't hurt.

When she'd broken her arm she'd been unconscious for a minute, and when she'd come to she'd heard someone screaming. It had taken a while to realize it was her. Screaming and screaming over and over. In pain. A blank chunk of time between when she'd been on the back of the horse and the moment she'd come back to herself on the ground.

Jake had been holding on to her, holding her arm against her side, and he'd been cupping her face. Saying things, but she couldn't understand them.

He'd been tender then. Worried.

This time he was pissed.

Hell, most of the time a ride like that ended with the cowboy getting unseated. It was nothing unusual. It was part of the job. The cost of doing business. It was simply the way things went sometimes, and there was no use getting upset about it.

Yeah, she knew it was one reason her dad didn't want her doing this job, but Jake was *not* her dad.

"How many times have you taken a fall, Jake Daniels? Because I think it's been a lot of times. You know that this is just the way things go. Stop acting like I'm made of glass." She took a step forward and jabbed her forefinger directly into his chest. "You have double standards."

"So what? I never said I didn't. You're the one out there trying to pretend like there is no physiological difference between men and women. But I'll tell you what, that's just your inexperience talking."

Anger spiked in her blood. "My *what*?"

"You don't know enough about men to understand how different we are."

Now her anger was a full-blown shot of rage. Her mother was always prodding her, gently reminding her she was a lady. The bargain she'd made with her father and brothers to earn equality was to behave just like them and never show any weakness. And it wasn't enough, it was never enough. And people were always trying to tell her who she was, what she should do and want and be.

And she was done. "I have six brothers, dumbass. I know the difference between men and women."

"You don't have as good of a grasp on it as you need to." He blew out a hard breath. "I'm all for you going for your dream. I wouldn't be marrying you if I wasn't *for* you. But you need to be reasonable. You need… Protection. Protective gear. And you have to be better. You just do. You need to be faster when you hit the ground. You're lighter, so maybe you won't fall as hard."

She crossed her arms and huffed, aware she was starting to sound like a bratty teenager. "It was a pretty good fall, Jake. It's not like I broke another bone."

"But you could have."

She stopped herself just short of rolling her eyes. "Yeah, something could always happen. Were you the one that was just saying that? It could always be something."

"Don't be that cavalier about your own life, Cal. Just don't."

"Oh, only *you* get to be that way?"

His lips twitched and he firmed up his jaw. "We're getting married tomorrow. You need to live to see it."

She forced a laugh out of her lungs. "Yeah, I can't wait. Can't wait to marry a guy who doesn't think I'm strong enough to do what I want, and doesn't think I'm his equal."

"I never said I didn't think you were my equal, Cal. I said we were different. Those are two very separate concepts. And like I told you, the only reason you're resisting it as hard as you are is that you… Well, hell, you don't have any experience with men, do you?"

She closed her lips tight, slid her tongue over her teeth. "Who said I wanted any?"

If she couldn't show vulnerability, there was no way in hell she could… That she could ever…

Not until later. Not until she'd achieved her dreams.

There was no scope for it. No time.

"Hey," he said, putting up his hands. "I'm not judging."

"It's not like that," she said. "It's just that I'm busy. I have dreams. And I don't need a man lying around cluttering them up."

He just stood there, staring, his expression flat stone. Then he spread his arms wide. "I'm sorry, am I cluttering up your dreams, or am I helping you reach them?"

"You know it's not the same."

He crossed his arms then, and gave her a look she couldn't quite read. One that made her skin feel too tight for her body. Made it feel difficult to breathe. She didn't like this. Being at odds with him. And she really hated that the whole marriage thing seemed to be… Making things difficult between them. Though, in fairness, it was probably this whole bucking bronco thing more than it was the marriage. He'd been weird about that from the beginning. Helping, but in a very… Overly concerned kind of way.

And after she broke her arm, he acted like he wanted nothing to do with it. Like a broken bone wasn't just one of those things you had to chalk up to a bad day.

"We're done," he said.

He jerked his head to the left. "Go on home. Clean up."

"I'm not a collie," she said. "There's a difference between a lady and a dog, you know."

"I'm not the one that's confused."

"I'm sorry, did you want me to prove that I know things?

Boys have a penis. Girls have a vagina. There. Do you feel like I gave you enough information?"

Her anger had started to thin slightly, and the redness, the heat that was left in her cheeks, seemed to be the echo of the words that she had shouted at him. Which was stupid. It was anatomy. Who the hell got worked up about that? It was basically like reading a textbook out loud.

She had brothers. So *many* brothers. She was comfortable with men in their bodies, and all that kind of stuff. She was a farm girl. She had seen horses getting it on in the field from the time she was a kid. She…

Suddenly she was very conscious of the fact that she was a whole lot smaller than he was. That he was big and muscular and hard in ways she wasn't.

That he was staring at her with obsidian eyes that glinted in the light in a way that she couldn't decode.

And it made it hard to breathe. Made it difficult to catch her breath. Made it difficult to do anything. So she just stood there, with her boots feeling like they were sinking into the dry dirt, meeting his eyes, and letting those words just kind of hang in the air between them.

"Great," he said. "You know as much as the average kindergartner. Congratulations. But if that's the extent of your knowledge, I'd study up before I get out there in the real world, Callie. That's a problem. You want freedom, but you don't have the knowledge you need to back it up. You don't have any experience. I'm willing to support you, but you need to let your ego deflate a little bit. You're a good kid. And you're talented. But you're not amazing. And you're not going to defy the odds without working at it. You're not bulletproof, you're not made of Teflon. Honey, you gotta get your head on straight. Because what you're doing is damned dangerous, and you're at a disadvantage. You need to be real honest with yourself about that."

"I don't love anything else," she said. "And I don't know…

I've never felt so alive as I do on the back of a horse. Every nerve ending is on fire, every muscle is working for something. It's the only time I'm one thing. Like I'm not being pulled in a hundred different directions. I don't care about how hard it is. I don't care about how risky it is."

"Fine," he said. "You need to say that it's dangerous. You need to admit it."

"Why?"

"Don't push me, Cal. I am not in the mood."

"Maybe I don't care what kind of mood you're in."

He took a step closer to her, and she could feel his gaze somehow. "Listen to me. Listen good. I will stand you up at that altar tomorrow if I think you're just going to take this money and go out there and get yourself killed because you're not taking things seriously enough. So if I were you, I would listen to me. And I would take my friend seriously."

She tilted her chin upward. "Fine. It's dangerous. I did get hurt. It's *still* worth it to me."

"Okay," he said.

They just stared at each other for a long moment, and she had the strangest sensation, like the one she had on the back of the horse. That the air around her had shrunk again, and the biggest thing that existed was the two of them.

"You better not stand me up tomorrow." She turned away from him and started walking toward the house, limping slightly. She was going to have a hell of a bruise on her hip.

"I'm a man of my word. As I think you know."

"Yeah, you're also a pain in the butt."

"No," he countered, "that would be your chosen profession. If you can't stand the heat… Stay out of the arena."

"Buck off." She lifted her hand and held up her middle finger.

"Cute."

"I'm not *cute*," she growled. "I'm a cowgirl. And at the end of all this, everyone's going to know it."

"I'm sure they will." His footsteps stopped. "I have some things to finish up outside. You go have that shower."

"Fine. See you tomorrow morning. At the courthouse."

"See you there."

Tomorrow they were going to get married. Tomorrow, she was going to be his wife.

It wasn't until she was standing in the shower, naked and running her hands over her body, that that word sent a streak of white-hot lightning over her skin, and made her pause. A wife.

Jake Daniels's wife.

And suddenly more memories of her time talking with different women in the rodeo hit, that she really wished had stayed buried.

Stamina.

His hands.

Biggest man I've ever seen.

I think he can hold his breath for at least five minutes.

She didn't know what that last one even meant and it made her skin feel irritated.

No.

It didn't mean anything.

It didn't.

She could lose her focus. Not now. The most important thing was keeping her eye on the prize.

The wedding was just a means to an end. That was all.

CHAPTER SIX

He figured he had to wear his church clothes to a wedding, whether or not it was real. That, for him, meant a long-sleeved black button-up shirt, a pair of black jeans and a nice belt buckle. A black hat to match, and his good cowboy boots.

When he came out of the bedroom and into the kitchen, Callie was there, in blue jeans and a thermal top, looking about the same as she always did.

"I overdressed," he said.

She was staring at him, her eyes slightly rounded.

"What?" he asked, headed toward the coffeemaker. They were having an inhumanely early wedding, since they weren't having anyone in attendance except for the court-appointed witness. So they had taken the free slot that just happened to be right after the courthouse opened.

"Oh, it's just... You look... Clean."

He chuckled. "Thanks."

She kept on staring at him, and he wondered... He had to wonder, just for a second if she was... But even if she was, she didn't know.

Good thing, too.

"Let's go," he said. "Weddings wait for no one."

They loaded up into the truck, and began to drive out toward town.

"This is weird," she said. She paused for a moment. "I didn't think it would be weird."

"You didn't think it would be weird to marry your best friend?" The minute he said that, he realized it danced perilously close to a cliché, and didn't sound as strange as he would like.

She shifted noisily beside him and he was all too aware.

Of her. Her clothes. "I don't know. I thought that... I felt guilty about it. But I thought that because we talked about it, I would be in the right place. We know what this is. I know what it is. I guess..."

"What? Spit it out, Cal. I'm not a stranger. I'm Jake." A reminder to himself, if nothing else. They weren't anything different than they'd ever been. Whatever strange little moments had passed between them over the past week. Whatever electrical currents seemed to fizzle beneath the surface when he got too close to her. She didn't know. She didn't know, and that was what mattered. What he knew or didn't know...

He had too much experience with women. With sex. That was the problem. And it was becoming pretty clear to him that she had absolutely none. Less than he'd thought, if he'd ever let himself think about it. And he tried not to.

But could she really not or was she just...

Denying it.

"It's embarrassing."

His heart hit against his chest, his breath stalling for a moment, and he clenched his teeth, doing his best to hold it together in that moment. Doing his best not to let his mind, his body, race ahead to the question that she might be about to ask.

"Who cares? You shouted anatomy at me last night. We're good."

"It's just... I pretend, right? That I've never once in all my life had a basic… Girly dream. But I thought about it. Getting married. Even though I was never serious about it. Even though there was never… Any one person that I thought I might marry. I thought about it. And I imagined my family being there. And maybe I even thought I'd wear a dress, and I'd be pretty the way that women can be. Right? That's when you're supposed to look the best you ever have. Your wedding. In my head, I thought maybe it would be magic, and I would be beautiful." A minute passed, just the sound of the tires on the road and the engine in the cab. Then she continued. "It's so stupid, because I don't care about any of that. I really don't. But it's this silly corner of my heart that just exists. A thing that I thought once, and then sometimes the image just appears. And this isn't it. Not at all. That's for the best, I think, because it'll get rid of all that for good. Which is really what I want. It really is. But for some reason this feels like some kind of silly letdown all because I don't have a dress and flowers."

He didn't know what to say to that. Her words scraped against raw places in his chest that he didn't want to examine. Expectations for the future. Admissions of dreams. He didn't let himself have that sort of thing, but hearing her talk about it in that way made him feel… He felt like the biggest kind of ass, and he was doing what she asked him to do. The fact that she did, even Callie, tough as nails Callie, who pretended she didn't care about any kind of softness, who acted like she didn't have a whimsical bone in her body, it made him see the world in some kind of bright new way right in that moment, and he hadn't asked for that. She already did that to him, too much already. He didn't want more of it. He didn't want to get down another layer.

Thinking of Callie as the kind of woman who wasn't immune to those secret dreams of romance.

Oh, she hadn't said that in so many words, but wasn't the admittance that you'd fantasized about a wedding close enough?

And suddenly he wanted to do something about it. Wanted to do something *for* her.

Kill a bear with his hands to prove he could protect her and feed her.

Build a cabin right there on the spot to show her he could give her shelter.

Move a mountain, maybe. Just to show she made him want to do the impossible.

It was the strangest feeling.

This deep, driving desire to show up. To make sure that she wasn't disappointed. To make sure that she felt something other than sad right now. Because whether or not it was his fault, he was part of the sadness, and he didn't like it.

And it was met immediately with that violent, gnawing counterweight. That he couldn't fix a damn thing.

That he didn't deserve to try.

But that didn't change the fact that Callie wanted something from him, needed something from him.

Dammit, he would do what he could.

Just then they passed a field, filled with yellow, scrubby flowers clinging to life in spite of the cold. Which he knew damn well meant they were weeds. But before he could stop himself and the impulse to go over, he pulled his truck to the side of the road.

"What are you doing?"

"I'm damn well going to make something happen," he said. "It's November, so… These are sad blooms that are barely clinging to life, but there's something." He opened the door and got out, then rounded to her side of the truck. He opened the door and she simply sat there, looking at him.

"We have an appointment."

"It's Gold Valley," he said. "It's not like people are going to be banging down the door to get married on a weekday morning in the courthouse."

He undid her seat belt and took her hand, and the minute her skin connected with his, a rush of warmth overtook him that nearly made his brain black out. It would be the easiest thing, the easiest damn thing, to chase that feeling of warmth. To pull her up against his body and...

"Come on."

He turned and started heading toward the field. There was a barbed-wire fence that was partly down, blocking them from getting to the rest of the field. "Hang on." He stepped carefully over the fence, then lifted Callie up by the waist, and over it neatly.

She squeaked, and stumbled against him, looking up at him with wide eyes. There was a question in those eyes. And it wasn't about bucking broncos. Or trust funds, or anything of the kind.

And he turned away from that question. Because whatever he could do for her, it wasn't that.

"This seemed important," he said, bending down and scooping up a handful of those dry scraggly weed-flowers.

She looked at him, her expression blank.

"Well, don't get all mushy on me, Cal," he said, handing them to her.

"What's it for?" she asked.

"A bouquet. You ought to at least have that."

And he realized the ridiculousness of it, standing out in a field on a freezing cold morning giving a woman a handful of weeds, on his way to a courthouse wedding. Knowing full well that he was never going to be her husband, not in any real way, and his body pounding against the walls he built up around all the things it wanted, because there was just no...

She'd dreamed of a wedding. A real wedding, and if anything was going to stop him from doing something they would both regret, that should. If her presumed innocence, her naivety, her family connections, didn't do it, that should.

"Thank you," she said, looking away from him.

"Come on," he said. "Like you said, we can't keep everyone waiting."

"Guess not," she said.

They got back in the truck, and she held on to the flowers, dirt coming off a root ball from the bottom of one. She brushed at it idly, and he turned his focus back to the road.

"Just think about the rodeo," he said. "That's the real dream, right?"

"Yeah. It's the real dream."

They were silent the rest of the way into town, and it was probably for the best. He pulled up to the small, brick building, and even though he knew she would protest, he opened her door and helped her out.

"Thank you," she said, surprising him.

They walked into the courthouse, side by side, not touching, because they were just friends doing an illegal thing, and that was it. It was a surprise to him, how perfunctory a marriage could be. Because it wasn't the vows that made it a marriage—you could write your own. It was the paperwork. And the fact that you had to say something in front of a judge and a witness. They elected to forgo traditional vows, because why?

Instead, he made promises of a different kind.

"If you ever need me, I'll be there for you. Whatever, whenever. I'm your go-to."

She nodded gravely. "I'm yours. Whatever. Whenever."

They didn't exchange rings. Rings were an occupational hazard for people who did ranch work or rode rodeo. So there was no reason for those, either.

They opted not to kiss, and not even that was a big deal. Then it was all said and done. They were in a courthouse in Gold Valley, the two of them legally married, and on their way in twenty minutes. They walked out as husband and wife. And it didn't matter that he'd said none of the traditional words, didn't matter that he hadn't kissed her. Didn't matter that it was supposed to be temporary... There was something in him that felt deeply, utterly possessive of her in that moment.

As if you didn't before?

"Well, what should we do?" she asked.

"Get back to work, I guess," he said.

"Yeah. Oh." She pulled a face. "I need to call my parents."

"You don't have to do it today."

She was still hanging on to those flowers.

"I mean, I should," she said. "Because we have to prepare them for the fact that Christmas we're going to show up... Together. Married."

"Right. And so your story is that we fell madly in love at Thanksgiving?"

"You know, feelings brewing before then and things like that..."

"They're going to think you're pregnant," he said. "You know that, right?"

She looked over at him with shocked eyes. "Surely not."

"Honey, why do you think anyone gets married this quick? It's not because of love, not because of lust, even. This isn't the Dark Ages—you can have as much sex as you want without a legal commitment."

"Maybe you're a gentleman."

He looked at her, fire filling his veins. "I am not."

Her eyes widened a fraction and the color began to mount in her cheeks and she looked away quickly. That small moment, that flash of awareness, sent an answering heat barreling through him. "I mean, I know you're not, not in general. Not to the buckle bunnies. But maybe you treated me different."

"I'm not *not* a gentleman to buckle bunnies, to be clear," he said. "What does that even mean? Everybody gets what they came for. You make it sound like I'm using them. And I'm not. I never have. I've never promised a woman something and not delivered it."

She looked exasperated. But still wasn't looking at him. "I guess that's just… How people think of these things."

"Yeah, because everyone thinks about things in this kind of traditional way. I don't. I never have."

Which made a mockery of the feelings that were settled like a weight in his chest right now. Because hell, the fact of the matter was, marrying her felt like something. And for someone who said he didn't give a damn about these kinds of conventions, about traditional values or anything of the kind, he was affected by it.

He shook his head. "I treat people the way they want to be treated. That's gentlemanly, isn't it?"

"In fairness, I'm just saying things other people say. You know, the cowgirls complain about the buckle bunnies."

"Yeah, I'm sure they do. I don't know. I'm not saying any of it's right, it's just the way it is."

"Right. The cowboys get to have all the casual sex they want. And there's a kind of girl for it. But then… You treat other girls different."

He had no idea why in hell she was pushing this now. This was not something they ever talked about. And he'd been more than fine with that.

He didn't need to deal with his attraction to Cal while talking to her about sex.

"It's not that. At least, not for me. Look, I can't speak for my whole gender. And quite frankly, a lot of them suck. But for me it's just… If I'm sleeping with a girl, I don't want to have to see her again when I'm done."

She wrinkled her nose. "That's… Gross."

"It's not. I promise. I don't want messy. It's not… I don't do emotions."

He looked over at her for a moment. The look she was giving him was searing, searching and filled with a dark anger he didn't

RODEO CHRISTMAS AT EVERGREEN RANCH

expect. And it made him feel emotions. Contradicted him again. Made a liar out of him, and he didn't consider himself a liar.

But that was the problem with Cal. She made him care. She made him feel things. Things he wasn't used to. Things he didn't want.

"So, you can't sleep with cowgirls because you have to see them again. And is it because it gets messy, or is it because you're afraid you might have feelings?"

"I'm afraid *they'll* have feelings."

Callie's disgust was like a little tornado whipping around her. "You're such an ass. You're afraid they'll just magically fall in love with you because... Because what? Sleeping with you is *such a good time*?"

He needed out of this conversation. He needed an eject button. And she didn't seem interested in giving him one. She was just going to push and push. And he had to wonder if she really knew what she was saying to him. Honestly, he had to wonder if she was a...

If she was an actual virgin.

Who didn't understand the topic that she'd introduced. The thought of sleeping with someone was this kind of vague and theoretical thing, because he could remember that.

Back when he'd been sixteen, and hadn't got all the way with the girl. Hadn't realized that it was physical and treacherous and intense. And he found ways to make it fun over the years. Fun so that he didn't have those kinds of heartaches and pains and regrets after. And it had become something he relied on to give him an escape from hard feelings. From nights when memories of his family wanted to creep in. Yeah, he could erase all that with the right amount of whiskey and a woman who was looking for a good time. And he'd always figured they had demons they were running from, too. And as long as it worked for both of them, who cared? He wasn't a therapist. If somebody wanted to use him to live in denial a little longer, that was just fine with him. Because he was using them to forget. He was using them to keep his mind from traveling down dark paths. He wanted it. He needed it.

But she didn't know. She didn't know that what she was talking about was physical, downright dirty and just as raw and in-your-face as any rodeo event could ever be.

She was looking at it all through a blurry lens.

And even knowing that didn't help him. Because she was sounding bold when he knew full well she didn't mean to. But it was still hitting him that same way.

"Look, I don't know," he said. "It could happen. I just don't want the entanglement. I use sex to escape for a while. I don't use it to build friendships or connections of any kind."

"Well. Whatever. We don't need to talk about it anymore. Doesn't matter to us. Though you're going to have to try to keep it in your pants while you're married to me."

Lightning shot down his spine. He looked at her. And then her face went red, starting at her cheeks and bleeding down and up, all the way to the roots of her hair, all the way down to the collar of her shirt. "I didn't mean me."

"Just be careful," he said, his throat getting tight. "A man might get the wrong idea."

"We have a marriage license. That's the definition of sticky. Plus we're friends."

He tightened his hold on the steering wheel. "Yeah, thanks for telling me, Cal, somehow I forgot."

"You can't sleep with other women. It's not right."

He gritted his teeth and felt that desire to push her again. And he didn't hold back. She was telling him what to do, telling him who he couldn't sleep with. Why shouldn't he speak some of his mind if she was going to speak hers?

He looked at her sideways. "Is that in the handbook for fake-ass marriages for money?"

"You just can't. It'll piss me off."

"Why?" He didn't look at her, he looked at the road, keeping his hands on the steering wheel. He shouldn't have asked the question. He shouldn't be pushing this line of conversation at all.

"Because it's not...right," she said. "Anyway, if my dad found out..."

"Yeah, it would just add to the list of reasons that your dad might end up killing me someday."

"He's not going to kill you."

"Well, you're going to have to save that bit of certainty for after you call them and tell them that we got married."

"I'll do it when we get home."

"Great," he said. "See that you do."

CHAPTER SEVEN

It wasn't until she had gone into the bedroom, closed the door behind her and sat down on the bed that Callie realized she was still holding on to that bouquet that Jake had given to her. She let go of it like it was a snake, pulling away from it. Like if she got some distance from those flowers it might clear her head up, and make her feel a little less muddled than she had been since he'd handed them to her that morning.

It was *the flowers'* fault.

She had been completely clearheaded about the whole thing until he'd gone and pulled over and got her those flowers. And he'd... Picked her up like she weighed nothing and lifted her over that fence.

She just sat there, staring at the wall. Trying to go over that morning's events clearly. Because she did need to call her parents. And what she really needed to do was figure out a way to relay what had happened this morning in an honest sense, at least honest enough that it made sense. And she was just hung up on these strange little pockets of time where she felt a foreign kind of heat right through her body. Where she'd been held captive by her best friend's gaze in a way that didn't make any sense at all.

She was just going to call her parents. Because she couldn't keep going over and over this. She picked the flowers up off the bed and brushed the dirt that they left behind on the floor. And she felt a little bit guilty, because he'd said that he had somebody who came to clean, and now she'd made a mess.

She stuffed the flowers down into her duffel bag and zipped it up, then took her phone out and hit the button for a video call.

Her parents always liked to see her face. And there was no way she was going to get away with imparting this kind of news without doing it face-to-face. Which really was kind of awful, because it would be great if she could hide her expression.

But she'd known.

She'd known that this was what she was setting herself up for, so she just had to man-up about it now. She was being silly. Sentimental. It wasn't the flowers. It wasn't. It wasn't that moment in the field, or even the way he had lifted her up off the ground. No. It wasn't that at all. The real issue was that she was getting weird and sentimental.

She shouldn't have told him about that memory. Those thoughts that she'd had as a little girl about weddings and all that. She hadn't known what she wanted then. So now she'd had a real wedding day. A real wedding day that had contained weeds and a promise to be friends. It wasn't romantic.

It was reality. She'd worn blue jeans, and he'd worn black. And he'd looked like the outlaw and the hero all at the same time.

It was funny, because in that whole wedding fantasy she'd had she'd never pictured her groom.

And now she'd never be able to picture a different one.

She blinked, her eyes suddenly slightly wet. She needed to get over it. She pushed the button. And she waited. The phone rang for a couple seconds, then her dad answered. He had his tan cowboy hat on, and he was laughing about something. The mustache that he'd had as long as she'd been alive had gone from brown to a wiry gray. His cheeks, which had always been red and round were redder and rounder, and he was beginning to look a little bit like a Western Santa Claus. Her mom, on the other hand, didn't have a single gray hair—though Callie was certain that was with help from a beautician. Her dark hair was still teased out as big as it would go, her face perfectly made up in spite of the hour, in spite of the fact that her parents were at home.

"Callie," her dad said. "Good to hear from you."

"Hi."

Her mom frowned. "What's up, buttercup?"

Callie winced. "Nothing. It's just… I have something to tell you."

"What?" Her dad immediately looks suspicious.

"Nothing bad," she said quickly. "I'm bringing someone with me for Christmas."

Her mother looked like she'd been plugged in. Her whole face went bright. Alive. "Callie, are you bringing *a man* home for Christmas?"

"Yes," Callie said, feeling relieved. Because thank God, *thank God* her mother thought this was a good thing.

Because of course her mom was afraid that she would end up alone.

Now when she found out she missed the wedding she would be mad, and there was nothing Callie could do about that, but she was going to have to count on her mother's relief that Callie had snagged a man to carry her through.

"We didn't plan it or anything, and it was short notice, and I'm sorry I didn't tell you, and I know that you're not going to be happy with me… But… I got married this morning."

Her parents just stared into the camera, completely shocked.

"I know," she said. "But we thought it was… Best… To hurry

up and get married and then we could just come for Christmas. And stay together. And... We wanted to... Be respectful and..."

"Are you pregnant?"

Leave it to her mom to just go ahead and ask.

"No," Callie said, wishing she could physically push back the blood she knew was flooding her face and no doubt making her cheeks bright red.

"I wouldn't have even been mad if you were," her mother said. "At least you're focusing on something other than the rodeo. It's for the best."

Her dad frowned. "I don't much care for the fact that you married some guy who didn't think to ask my permission, but what's done is done."

"Tell us about him," her mother said.

"Well." She coughed, more to give herself time than because of any actual urge. "You know him."

That earned her a sharp glare from both parents.

She pressed on. "Jake Daniels."

"Well, now we *are* going to have to have a chat," her dad said, and she knew that he meant with Jake.

"Dad, don't be mad at him..."

"You just tell me this, Callie," he said, his whole face going deadly serious, "and I won't ask you another thing about your personal life, I promise you. But you've known him for a long time. You just tell me that he never touched you when you were sixteen."

Horror stole through her. "No. It's only that it caught us by surprise. And you know he respects you, Dad, and he wanted to make sure he did the right thing. He wanted to marry me before... Well... Before anything happened."

Horror was the dominant emotion now. Her face was so hot and she could see—thanks to the front-facing camera—that it was the color of a tomato, and she did not want to be talking about this with her parents, but her dad was the one who'd brought it up.

They both had.

Pregnancy and if she'd been taken advantage of, and for a woman who had managed to spend a whole lot of time not thinking about sex it was a whole lot to suddenly have to talk about it as much as she had the last few days.

She didn't like it.

It made her uncomfortable, and she really didn't want to think about it in connection with Jake, because it was… It was wrong. And it had nothing to do with the real reason that she was marrying him. Nothing to do with why she'd chosen him.

"Well, that's unexpected," her dad said. "But I can tell you're not lying to me."

This was an instance where her blushing had probably helped her out. That and the fact that before all this had happened, before her accident and before her dad had come out against her desire to compete in the rodeo, he'd known her better than anyone else.

Had been her closest ally.

She hated now that he wasn't. That she had to lie.

Absolutely hated it.

More than anything, she hated that she'd proven herself right. He had only supported her when she acted tough, unbreakable, and being human had changed things. Having any sort of vulnerability had changed things.

That meant she'd been right all along. That she could never please her mother and gain the support of her father. That she could never wear rhinestones or…

She thought of how she'd confessed her wedding dreams to Jake. She'd wanted that before. Before she'd realized she had to choose.

It was ironic that marriage was the vehicle she was using to get to where she wanted to go. Because she'd written that off when she'd shed as many of her other desires as possible. Anything that didn't contribute to her rodeo dreams.

"He cares about me. An awful lot." That was true, too. If he didn't, he wouldn't be helping her like he was. "And he's a really good guy. Really."

"We'll talk at Christmas," he said. "Or any time you want to come."

"We'll come the week before, just like I planned." She cleared her throat. "His cousin is having a big party. Christmas. This week. And it's important to her that we all go. So…"

"Sure. I can't believe it," her dad said. "I just thought… Of all of you, I never thought you'd be the one to get married first. And I sure as hell never thought you'd surprise me with it."

"I didn't, either," she said. "You know Jake has always been really special to me."

And that was true. The truth down to the bottom of her heart, and the more she could say that was true in this nest of lies, the better. "Then we'll see you at Christmas. And I hope Jake likes to drink whiskey and go shooting, because he and I are going to do both. I have some long conversations about what I expect. He didn't ask my permission. And he's going to have to make up for that."

"I'm sure he will. I am."

And then she had to listen to her mother gush for five whole minutes about how pleased she was that she got married, and how she hoped they'd consider having a big ceremony out of the ranch with all the fixings, because all her mother had ever wanted was to see Callie in a dress.

"I wore what I'm wearing now," Callie said.

"That's ridiculous. Of course you're going to have to dress up."

She got off the phone fairly quickly after that. And she knew that she should feel relieved. Like she'd torn a Band-Aid off. But instead she felt… Well, she felt gross. Because her mom was so happy, so relieved.

Isn't that a great reminder that you have to do this? Because they would rather you randomly marry Jake than be a rodeo rider.

She expected that from her mother. But not from her dad.

When she'd been little he'd been…her biggest support. The way he'd dropped it in the past year, the way he was acting like he'd rather have her married to Jake than following her dream…

It was something she needed to remember. They meant well, but they didn't want her to do this. They didn't want her to be this. They didn't want her to be… Her. And they believed her about the wedding because they wanted so much for her to magically transform into something more traditional that it didn't even matter if it made sense. There was a firm knock on the door to her bedroom and she startled.

"Come in."

Jake was in the doorway, wearing a modified version of what he'd had on earlier. A black T-shirt and a jacket, black jeans, but work boots. He had the same black hat on his head. And there was something about the way the light coming through the window caught his face that made her stop and look at how sharp the edges of his bone structure was. That forced her to examine the way the square line of his jaw met with his strong chin, that made her eyes follow the line up to his lips, nose, eyes. That forced her to take stock of a face that should be absolutely familiar, and see something new in it.

There was something about it that made it difficult to breathe.

If they were really married, what would they be doing right now?

The question caused a pang to shoot through her chest, echoing in her teeth. She gritted them together.

"We have work to do, or did you forget?"

"I was talking to my parents."

"How did that go?"

She crossed her arms. More as a defense against his gaze than anything else. "My dad is pissed that you didn't ask his permission."

"Is that it?"

"He made me swear that you didn't touch me when I was a teenager."

"Hell," Jake said.

"I said you didn't. I said you didn't and he believes me. So… That's it. They're both so glad that I've settled down, Jake. That's all they really care about. I knew that I needed to do this, but I don't think I really understood how much until now. My mom was never going to be happy until I turned into this thing that she…that she thinks I should be. And my dad is just… I don't even know. I thought he really believed in me, you know? But not unconditionally. And I felt kind of guilty for a minute, because they were so happy. But then it went away. It went away because… None of this has anything to do with me. It has to do with an idea of me that would make them more comfortable. And I just can't be that. I can't."

"You know, I think you're both looking at it wrong. You can be a rodeo rider and a wife someday if you wanted to be."

He met her gaze for too long. She had to look away because he wouldn't, and it made her breathing feel shallow.

"It's not that simple, you know it's not. I used to want everything, but I realized you can't do that. You can't be that. My mom wanted me to be more like Sophie. I know she did. Quieter and softer. A replacement for what she lost." She swallowed hard. "But I wasn't happy doing that, and my dad liked having me outdoors with him. But if I…got scared of spiders or complained about the weather he asked if I wasn't tough enough to handle it. Middle ground just doesn't work in my family. In my life."

He cleared his throat and she felt him move closer. Felt the shift in the air. "I know I'm not an expert on dealing with that kind of family stuff. But there are no guarantees in this world.

That's the one thing I'm certain of. You've got to follow your own path, because there's nothing else out there. No destiny. No… There's just shit that happens or doesn't."

She nodded slowly. "I guess. Though that feels…sad. I like to think there's something bigger than just me."

He reached out and put his hand on her face, and she froze, her flowers in her hand, her heart in her throat. "There's nothing bigger than you, Cal. Take care of you."

Then he straightened and walked out, closing the door firmly behind her and leaving her feeling dizzy and confused.

And so, she left her strange feelings about the day back in her room, with those flowers, which were now shoved into the bottom of her duffel bag. And she wouldn't think about it again. Wouldn't think about them again. She knew that she'd done the right thing, no matter how difficult it was. And she wasn't going to second-guess herself. Not now. Not ever.

CHAPTER EIGHT

It was surprisingly companionable to live with Callie.

When she wasn't driving him crazy.

The problem was that prolonged exposure to her wasn't making his attraction to her any easier to ignore.

When he'd been around her all day every day at the rodeo, it had been a little easier to manage. They'd seen each other in certain situations, and then they'd gone away from each other.

Living in the same house meant running into her at strange times. Seeing her just after she'd gotten out of the shower, when her skin was still warm from the water, and he could feel it radiating off her form. He saw her barefoot, wandering around in sweats. Saw her in the morning when she was up and rumpled from sleep, a crease from her pillowcase pressed across her cheek.

Intimate things that he'd never really shared with anyone he wasn't related to. It was downright domestic, and it was playing a weird kind of havoc with his libido. And it was all dumb, because she was his friend. And that was it. But he'd done his damnedest to tell himself that for years now and it hadn't worked. He still thought she was hot. More than that, the chemistry that he felt between them was tense.

And she might not know it, but he did.

She might not understand that the spark between them meant they could light a mattress on fire. He damn well knew. They'd avoided his family over the last couple of weeks, which he told himself was just because they were busy, but in reality it was because having her as even one more part of his life just felt like a potential assault. But today was the big Daniels family early Christmas celebration, and he was thankful for online shopping and fast shipping, because he'd managed to get everybody gifts at the last minute, including Callie. And they'd come gift wrapped. When he took all the packages out of the closet and started to load them into his truck, Callie look chagrined.

"There are presents?"

"You're a guest," he said. "Don't worry about it."

"Of course. I should've brought presents for your family."

"Don't worry about it. We make a big fuss out of this stuff. But I've never really been… Christmas isn't my favorite."

"Oh."

"It just sucks. You know. Dead parents." There were other aspects of it, but he didn't talk about that. Not with anyone. And he wasn't about to get into it with her now.

"No, I know."

"It was happier before. That's the problem."

"Right."

"For the little kids… We did our best. We did our very best to make Christmas memories for them, because for most of their lives, for most of their childhoods, they didn't have parents. They only had what we all put together. And so… We did big gift exchanges, even when we had to make things, or give out hand-me-downs. We made tons of food, and we played music. Saying a lot. Anything to keep it from being quiet. Because how terrible would it have been if poor Rose had to lose her mom and dad when she was nine, and then… Not have Christmas, either? Just because we couldn't get it together. No, none of us wanted that. So… We just have this Christmas tradition. Where we all get together. We have for a long time."

"It's nice. I like it. It makes sense." She looked so young then. Sad and sincere.

"Yeah, I think so."

"Well, thank you. For inviting me. It sounds like it's a really important holiday."

"Yeah, but including people is what we do. We've always been like that. My cousin's wife, Sammy, she moved in with us after… After everything. And she just fit. But having lots of people in the house always made it all feel less like we were missing someone. It was just what we did. What we did to survive it."

For as long as he'd known Callie, they hadn't really talked about this. Of course, he never really talked to anyone about it.

Their relationship had always been based on the way they felt about what they did. Not about talking.

Not about real things. They'd probably covered deeper territory than they ever had before since she'd come here.

And it didn't bother him. Which was maybe the most surprising thing. That he actually…liked talking to her.

Liked listening to her.

"Sounds to me like you did a really good job," she said.

"I don't know about that. We just did the best we could. And if denial was part of it, then we were game for a little denial. I think the girls turned out really good, though."

"Your cousins?"

"Rose and Pansy were really young. Iris was a little older, but still… Not as old as the rest of us. But especially Rose and Pansy. We just wanted to do right by them."

"It sounds like you did."

"Yeah, I hope so. I mean, they turned out all right. Pansy being the police chief, and Rose being the badass rancher that she is."

"They seem really cool."

"They are."

They got into the truck and drove to Hope Springs, and Jake did his best to keep his mind out of the past. When they walked in, he introduced Callie as his wife, which was met with riotous applause from his family.

"Not his real wife," Callie said, her cheeks turning red.

"They know," he said.

"I think you're kick-ass," Rose said, coming up to them both. "You did what needed doing. I admire that. I'm not one to let the grass grow under my feet, either. I like to make things happen."

"And when she says that," her husband said slowly, "she means that she meddles where she's not asked."

"That's true," Jake said to Callie. "Rose is a known meddler."

"Her meddling always works out in the end," Iris pointed out from where she was sitting next to her husband, Griffin, holding his hand. "In fact, it was her disastrous matchmaking that set me on the course to get my bakery, and to meet Griffin."

"Yeah," Rose said, huffing. "I should get a lot of credit for the unintentional results of my matchmaking."

"Why haven't you ever tried to matchmake me?" Colton asked, a smart-ass smile on his face.

"I'm not a miracle worker, Colton."

"Ouch," Jake said.

It was right then that Ryder came through the door, dragging a gigantic Christmas tree behind him, baby Astrid strapped to his chest in a carrier, with West and Emmett bringing up the rear.

"That is an ugly tree," Pansy said.

"Hey, squirt," Jake said. "I didn't see you putting in any of the effort to get that tree. Beggars can't be choosers."

"I could've got a better tree with my eyes closed," Pansy said.

"You know, getting a Christmas tree is not like making an arrest, Pansy," West said. "You don't just apprehend it, honey."

"You don't just apprehend criminals, either. You read them their rights," she said.

"Shoot," West said. "We didn't read the tree its rights."

"I'm *still saying*," Pansy continued, "that your tree selection leaves much to be desired."

"Everyone's a critic."

She crossed the space to give him a kiss and West took a step back. "Come back with a warrant," he said.

Then he relented and grabbed hold of her and gave her a kiss.

It still made him a little bit uncomfortable, the way all of his family had paired off except for him and Colt. Just change. The change of it all was weird.

And then he figured he probably couldn't be pleased, because there was something about the sameness of home that depressed him a little bit, too.

Not because he didn't like it.

Because it reminded him of family. What he'd thought it was. What it wasn't really.

And only Jake knew the truth about his own parents.

But it was Christmastime. Not brood-about-family-bullshit time.

Though he supposed it was often one and the same.

When it was time to decorate the tree, the boxes of eclectic, crappy ornaments got dragged out from the corners of the room, and Colt picked up his guitar, playing a twangy, country version of "Silent Night." Astrid toddled over and started to hit the front of the guitar with her open hand, not on beat at all.

"Well, if anybody can concentrate with George Strait and his band over here going nuts, it's time to decorate," Ryder said. Jake got up and went over to the boxes, starting to dig through them, looking for his dirt bike ornaments, which he'd had since his early twenties. A gift he'd gotten at some point, to go on the infamous Daniels Family Ugly Tree.

Some people had ugly sweaters, they had an ugly tree.

Full to the brim of hideous decorations—the worse, the better.

"I've never decorated a Christmas tree," Callie said.

"What?" he asked. "You're joking."

"No. My mother takes her tree very seriously. She decorates it to a theme every year, and we are not allowed to touch it under pain of death."

"Wow. We go out of our way to make ours as terrible as we can. We absolutely pile on the crap."

"Yeah, those are ugly ornaments," she said, looking at the dirt bikes.

"They are," he agreed. "That's the fun of them."

Pansy was hanging her police cars, while Ryder had his Santa cowboys and Sammy her peacock feathers, which Astrid was placing in a bunch all in one spot. Logan was watching Rose hang her own ornaments, and Elliott was helping. Iris and her husband, Griffin, hung back, and after a couple of minutes, both of them went to the kitchen. Nobody in this house was inexperienced with loss. Griffin had lost a daughter tragically several years before, and from what Jake knew about him, this was his first Christmas back in the real world, so he had to wonder if holidays dredged up even more what-ifs for him. That was the kind of thing that...

Well, Jake just never wanted to have anyone in his life to care about like that. The world was too random. Life was too... Too much of a dick.

Even as happy as Griffin was with Iris, it wouldn't make that kind of pain go away. How could it? But in only a few moments they were back, and holding hands. They went over to the ornaments box, and began to sift through it. And they started hanging them up with the rest of the family.

It didn't take long, with all the manpower they had working, for the tree to be done. And when they stepped back, it was a thing of beauty. Well, a thing of ugly beauty. All tinsel and colored lights and glittering, mismatched ornaments that looked like someone had vomited Christmas spirit all over everything.

It was their way. Messy, outlandish, a little bit tacky. But theirs.

"This is incredible," Callie said. "I've never seen anything like it in my life."

"And you never will again. Every year it takes on a unique shape. As you can see, we have many unused boxes. We just kind of dig through the mountain and hope for the best. Though I always use my dirt bikes."

After that, it was time for presents, and they all moved them into a big pile at the center of the room. And with very little ceremony, they fell upon them.

Callie only had one, and it was from him. He found it, and held it out to her.

"Oh, no," she said, looking worried. "I didn't get a gift for anyone. You can't give one to me."

"I can do whatever the hell I want. I wanted to give you something."

She narrowed her eyes, looking at him skeptically, but took the small gift from his hand. She opened it slowly, and then stopped when she lifted the lid on the box. "What is this?"

"Well, now I know you're not allowed to decorate your family tree. But since... Well, since you're getting emancipated and everything with your new trust fund, you might be able to put this to good use."

She lifted it up, and he was relieved to see that it was even nicer in person than it looked online. It was a cowgirl, sitting on the back of a bucking bronco, fully rounded and trying to shake her off its back. And she was hanging on, one hand on the reins, the other one flung up in the air. Her hair was wild and free, a red hat on her head.

"It's incredible," she said. "I didn't know they made things like this. With tough-looking cowgirls."

"Well, this is clearly the ornament you should've had all along. And hey, if you ever come back here for Christmas… You're welcome to put it on our tree. Everything matches our tree. Because nothing does."

"I like that."

He looked at her for a moment, and he wished… He really wished that her family did more to support her. To give her what she wanted. Because she was amazing, and she was strong. And she deserved this cowgirl ornament, as much as she deserved to feel like she was that cowgirl. And just for a moment, everything in him went still. Tight.

She licked her lips, and a slug of lust hit him down low in the stomach. Made it difficult for him to breathe.

Right here in the living room in front of his family, because he was watching the girl get a Christmas ornament. This was stupid. Ridiculous.

And he couldn't turn away from it or her any more than he could stop reading.

"Thanks," she said. "I mean it."

"Well, you're welcome."

"Chicken oven mitts!" Sammy had the gift from him on both of her hands. "It's perfect," she said laughing. "Thanks."

"I'm knocking it out of the park today."

And he was grateful for the distraction, because God knew they needed it. Because there was something about this moment that was edging way further into domestic than he would like. Something about this whole thing with Callie.

And it was the domestic that made him start to feel a little bit claustrophobic. He knew why. It didn't take a rocket scientist to sort through it.

He didn't need to think about that. Not now. It was stupid to start thinking about it just because he was sitting here in this house. Where he spent Christmases as a child. Where his parents had handed him his gifts. He gritted his teeth and stood.

Then walked out to the front porch. He just needed some air. Just needed a minute. He shouldn't have been too surprised when the door open behind him, and loud footsteps followed. Of course it was Cal.

"Yeah?"

"What's wrong?"

"Who said anything was wrong? Is just hot in there."

And it was freezing out here. The air had a biting quality to it, and it was welcome. Anything to distract him. To get his mind more firmly in the present. But then, this was the problem. It only worked for a minute, and then he was cast right back to another winter. All those years ago.

When things had seemed like they would be okay. Finally.

And it had all fallen apart.

"I don't buy that. Don't BS me. We're friends."

"It just gets to be a bit much sometimes. That's the house I grew up in with my parents. It wasn't the same for the rest of them, you know. It wasn't where they spent their childhood. I mean, we all spent time together there, but it wasn't where they lived with their parents. It was where Colt and I lived with ours."

"I'm sorry."

"It doesn't matter now. It doesn't. Except…when you're a kid you believe. That things will be okay. That they'll turn out all right. That the good guys win. That love wins. And I had that taken from me. It's okay, it is. I learned. Some people never have to, and good for them. But that's the truth of it. That's life."

"You don't believe things will be okay?"

He shook his head. "I don't believe we can know if they will be or not."

"So why…why keep going at all?"

He cleared his throat. "Because the other option is dying, I guess. And I've seen what that's like, too. So I just go on living."

"Without hope?"

There's you.

He didn't say it.

He'd found some hope through that scrappy girl he'd met all those years ago. In her optimism and fire.

"Turns out you can go on breathing just fine without it."

"I'm really sorry. I'm really sorry that… That it's like this for you." And she did a very un-Cal thing.

She reached out and put her hand on his.

And all those little broken fragments of feeling that had been weighing down on him, that had created the crisis that he just experienced in the living room, suddenly solidified into one. Focused. On her.

His wife.

Callie was his *wife.*

And for a moment all he could do was stare. Stand there and look at her, really look at her. And see not just the determined cowgirl that he'd known all these years, but the woman that she was, as well. Her brows creased, the corners of her lips turning down, confusion etched across her features. She looked down at their hands, where their skin met, and then back up at him. And then she pulled away. Sharp. Fast.

"I'll let you have your time."

"Great," he said, his voice rough. But Callie turned and disappeared back into the house, and he was left alone on the porch, which was what he really wanted, after all. Wasn't it?

The door opened again, and this time it was his brother.

"Hey. I haven't got a chance to talk to you much since I've been back."

"Yeah," Jake said.

He and his brother got along just fine, but they weren't exactly known for their heart-to-hearts. Because there were things that he just didn't want to discuss with Colt, things he never had wanted to discuss with Colt. And maybe that had driven kind of a wedge between them back in the day.

But he was supposed to be the older brother, and then Ryder had been the one to step up. To step in.

Jake felt like he'd kind of dissolved there for a while.

Sunken into his own pain, and he'd felt a little bit guilty about it. Until guilt had become so typical a thing he barely registered it. Because he should've been there for Colt more than his cousins had been. But that was the thing. They'd always been separate in their way. And he couldn't help but feel separate from each other, which he knew no one else really saw or understood. But he felt it. All the same.

Because you don't really know how to be close to anyone. And the person you're closest to is a woman about seven years younger than you that you can't let yourself have.

No. Because every relationship he had was dependent on clear, defined boundaries. He got along great with his brother as long as they were drinking and bantering. As long as they were talking about the rodeo. And their relationship had skimmed along just fine that way. Everything was great with his family as long as they were eating and laughing and talking. And nothing ever had to get serious.

There were lines. There were lines and he'd begun redrawing them these past few weeks with Callie, and he didn't like it, not at all. It was throwing off the balance of everything. Absolutely everything.

"Yeah, how's the rodeo?"

"Are we ever going to talk about why you left?"

"I told you. *I'm old.*"

Colt snorted. "Like eighteen months older than me, Jake, it's not convincing."

"It was just time for something different."

How could he tell him that he'd realized it was the minute Callie had hit the ground. That he'd understood that he'd gotten himself into an attachment that he didn't want, and that that attachment had followed him home, and now he was testing the lines of it here, there and everywhere.

"Be straight with me," Colt said.

"Why?" Jake pressed. "We don't do straight, Colt. We do shots, and then we talk about bull riding. We do shots and we check out hot girls in the bar. We don't do... This other shit."

His brother leaned back against the wall. "Don't you ever want things to change?"

"No. I don't."

He looked wholly skeptical. "So what are you doing with Callie, then?"

"Nothing. I'm helping her out."

"It's plain as day that you are..." He paused and redirected. "That girl has you by the balls, Jake, and I've known it for years. You're closer to her than you are to me."

Why the hell was his brother choosing this moment for a heart-to-heart?

"She's like a sister," he said.

This time Colt laughed. Out loud. "She's not. You love her."

The word hit him like a punch. "Yeah, not like that."

"What does *like that* mean when it comes to a woman? It just is, right?"

"Like you'd know?" Jake asked.

"Nah. But I don't have any nonfamily women that I love, either."

"I have never touched her." His skin still burned where she put her hand against his. "Not like that. I never will. I could. I mean, don't get me wrong. She's... She's beautiful. But... She's not into it. Hence a good thing. Because what the hell can either of us offer a partner? We can barely have a conversation with each other."

"Yeah, because a conversation with each other is always going to lead back to a bunch of roads neither of us want to go down. That's the problem. We've never dealt with them dying. Or with how it was different for us. They lost…well, hell, the rest of them lost their perfect family, didn't they? What about us? What about what we lost?"

"There's no dealing with it," Jake said, actively trying to ignore the memories that had been pressing in on him all night. "It's shit. It's shit and it just sits there. It doesn't go away."

"I guess so."

"Do you actually like Christmas?"

Colt laughed. "I don't know. It's a thing we do. Anyway, it's better than sitting around being drunk alone."

"Is it?"

"I don't like being drunk by myself," Colt said. "There has to at least be a naked woman."

"Yeah. Fair."

It had been too long since Jake had seen a naked woman. Maybe that was his problem. He was fixating on Callie because he was attracted to her. Because it was a preexisting situation, and on top of that he was in a bit of a dry spell since he'd left the rodeo and bought this ranch. Normally, he had a pretty steady stream of women throwing themselves at him, and here you have to go out and look for one. And it was entirely possible he would've gone to high school with her, and that did not appeal.

"What?" Colt asked.

"I was just thinking that coming home again has been detrimental to my sex life."

"Another reason I'll probably never come home, then," Colt said.

"Well, definitely something to keep in mind."

His brother leaned forward on the railing and looked out into the darkness. Jake followed suit.

"Do you ever wish that you got in on the ranch? Dad was the one who worked it."

"And Ryder was the one who kept us together. He worked the ranch all those years. We left it behind."

"But do you ever wish this was your place?"

"No," he said. He pushed away from the edge of the porch. "I don't want to live in a mausoleum. And that's what it amounts to, to me. A tomb for all of our great childhood memories."

"Yeah, that's what I think, too. But I wondered if you did. And we've never talked about it. You know, we don't really talk about much of anything. None of us do. I mean, Ryder's had Sammy all this time, so I think he's always shared with her. The girls have each other. Logan used to be our friend, but I feel like he sort of lumped in with Ryder in the end, probably because he was afraid he'd get kicked out since he wasn't family. And then… Whatever the hell with him and Rose. They all have someone, and we don't. We don't talk." Colt paused for a moment. "Why did you really come back?"

Jake looked back toward the house, his chest getting tight. "I think you know why."

"You didn't do a very good job getting away from her."

"No. If I were someone else I might take it as a sign."

"Oh, no, not you. You think everything is bullshit."

He nodded. "Especially signs. The universe doesn't give a damn, Colt. Not a single damn. We're on our own." The words scraped heavy past his throat.

"I don't think that," Colt said.

"No? You still think there's some kind of greater purpose?"

"I have to. I wouldn't get out of bed, then."

"I think it's even worse to think that. If someone's in charge… They've made some pretty big mistakes."

And with that, he left his brother standing out on the porch, and went back to join the party. Because sometimes the less said, the better. And he'd already said too much. Already dug down deeper into things than he wanted to.

And his hand still burned.

CHAPTER NINE

Callie was nervous about Christmas at her parents' ranch. To top it all off, she couldn't sleep.

She was practically hog-tied by her sheets, from all the twisting and turning she'd been doing, trying to find a comfortable spot. Trying to get herself settled down, and she just flat-out couldn't.

What had happened at Hope Springs Ranch kept on playing in her head in a loop. The present he'd gotten her. The way she'd felt when he'd given it to her.

Understood. Seen.

And then… Then he'd gotten up and left.

And she'd touched his hand, and something had happened when he'd looked at her.

She felt *changed* by it. Not so much that it was decisive. No, nothing quite that helpful. She was a little bit the same, and a little bit different. Like he was a little bit her friend, but a little bit a stranger.

Or her husband.

It had made her want to cry. She didn't know why. She didn't like it. She didn't like her body doing unfamiliar things. Her body was a tool that she used, one that she often had to fight against to do her rodeo events. Honing it into something fiercer, something harder, than it was born to be was a point of pride for her. Pushing herself past her limits. But she felt everything in her go soft when she touched him. When he looked at her. And she just didn't like it. Not one bit.

So she got out of bed and got dressed again. Hoped to leave her tangled thoughts behind with the bedsheets.

She tacked up one of the horses and started riding. She ran a barrel racing routine without the barrels until her face was freezing and her nose was running.

When she'd been in her cast, she'd been limited, and she had hated it. She had no limits. Not now.

Then she started running laps on foot. Run to one side of the arena, touch the fence, drop in the dirt and do a burpee. Up and down and up and down, punishing herself. Her skin slick with sweat in spite of the cold. Because she just didn't want to go to her room and think. She didn't want to sit in what had happened tonight. And she didn't want to think about what was coming. What she wanted to think about was the rodeo. Because it was easy, because it made sense. Because it was everything that she needed it to be and nothing more. And yeah, it was a struggle. A challenge. But it was one that she appreciated. One that made her feel good. Or at least made her feel something she recognized.

And so she ran.

"Cal," she heard his voice say, echoing across the arena. "What the hell are you doing?"

"Working out," she shouted back, going down for another burpee.

"It's late."

"I know it."

"Is this what you do? You just… Push yourself all the time?"

She ran back toward where he was standing, and then dropped

in front of him, doing another burpee, refusing to slow down just because he said to. "I have to," she said, her lungs burning. She turned to start running another sprint, and he grabbed hold of her arm. "Why?"

"Because I have to," she said, wildly wiggling to get out of his hold.

His hand was so hot—he'd been hot earlier, too. What was it? It was like he was a damn furnace. She didn't like it at all. It was unfamiliar, and it was... Not Jake. Jake was safe. Jake had always been safe. The person who listened to her. The person who believed in her. The person that she had driven to see. The person that she'd known would marry her so that she could get what she wanted. Except now he was her husband, and there was something different about it. Something strange. And it made everything feel unfamiliar, including the skin on her body.

"What are you running from?"

"Don't ask me that." She was sweaty and furious.

"What's your goal? I mean, I know you want to ride in the rodeo, but what do you want to get from it?"

"I want to do it. I want to show that I can. And if I'm not... If I'm not sore, then I'm not working hard enough. If I'm not out of breath, I'm not running fast enough. And tonight was really fun with your family, but I'm distracted and I haven't been doing the work that I need to do."

"You work plenty hard."

"We did *one* ride together, and I fell. And now we have to go visit my family." Panic was rising up inside her and she didn't know why. That same panic that had her twisting and turning in her sheets. That same panic that made her feel like she was turning into someone else.

Or she and Jake were turning into some other people.

Like signing a legal document made their friendship change and it shouldn't.

It's not just that...

She couldn't lose focus. This was about her. About finding her place, making her place. Forcing them to…to accept her.

"This has nothing to do with what happened earlier tonight?"

His voice was low and smooth and far too calm. And damn him for asking that.

"Nothing happened earlier tonight." She stared at him, and she felt her face getting hot. She was grateful for the cover of darkness, because she was absolutely sure that she was blushing.

"Oh, is that right? Nothing happened earlier?"

"We went to your family's house," she said stubbornly. "You gave me a present."

And that was when he reached out and grabbed hold of her hand, almost like she'd done earlier, but different. Assertive. He kept his eyes on hers, glittering in the darkness. He slid the tips of his fingers along the inside of her wrist, down her palm, all the way to her fingertips. His skin was rough. The hands of a man who did ranch work. Familiar hands. Because she knew men like him.

Cowboys.

But they didn't touch her like this.

Like this.

He was her friend. He wasn't supposed to touch her like *this*. *Like what?*

She knew. That was the problem. She'd been trying to pretend that she didn't. Trying to pretend that the small moments of eye contact, these moments that left her insides shaking, weren't something mystifying. Something that was maybe nothing. A disturbance in the air, rather than a disturbance coming from the innermost core of her being.

And why was he…?

He liked those shiny women. Those pretty women.

He liked easy sex—he'd told her that.

Just then, an arrow of awareness shot right between her thighs.

Because she was looking at him, and he was touching her, even if barely, and she had just thought that word.

And about him. Having it. And she'd said all kinds of things about sex and what-have-you earlier, but they hadn't been touching. And she'd been pretending that...

It was too much. It was overwhelming. And yet, she found that she couldn't move. He turned his hand, and laced his fingers through hers, tugging her closer. There was still a healthy amount of distance between them, but he was hanging on to her, and he was looking at her. Like a dance that was frozen, neither of them willing to be the one to make the next step. The breath in her lungs was frozen solid. She wanted to run from him, but she also didn't want to move. Because she didn't want the moment to pass. She didn't want now to become later. She just wanted to sit in this. Because it was dangerous, enticing, but also one of the nicer things she'd ever felt in her life.

It made her body feel less like an enemy, this moment. Less like something to be subdued. She had been trying to teach her body all kinds of tricks. All kinds of things over the last few years. Make it stronger. Make it faster. And this... She didn't know what to do. She didn't know what any of it was about. She didn't know what any of it meant. But her body seemed to know what to do.

This felt like instinct.

The rodeo might be in her blood, but this felt like it might be coming from her very bones. From her soul. And it was the strangest sort of right, and at the same time it felt outrageously, dangerously wrong.

Jake.

It's Jake.

And that jolted her. Brought her back to reality. Because she was standing there, touching her best friend. Like that. And he wasn't pretending, and neither was she. And it had to stop. One of them had to be sane.

She jerked her hand away. "No," she said. "It doesn't have anything to do with that."

"But it's there," he said.

She shook her head. "It doesn't matter."

He took a step away. "You're right. It doesn't matter. But to be clear, we are about to go see your family, who does think this is a real marriage. So it's not like being with my family. I'm going to have to touch you. Because that's what I would do with my wife."

She shivered. And then she found she couldn't stop shivering. Because her sweat had cooled off, and now she was freezing. And that was why. It wasn't because of anything else. It wasn't because he'd touched her hand. It wasn't because he was making her question all the things she thought she knew about herself. It wasn't because she was afraid. Because she couldn't afford to be afraid. She had to be stronger. She had to be better and faster. She had to be fearless. And one... *Dang stupid cowboy* couldn't make her afraid.

"Doesn't matter to me."

"You can't even handle holding my hand," he said.

"I'm not used to it. That's different. I'll be able to do it when it's time."

"You have a lot of confidence, Callie Carson, and I have to tell you, it seems to be misplaced."

"Misplaced?"

"You think you know everything. You think you know a whole hell of a lot. But at this point, you're just writing checks your ass hasn't even tried to cash. You think you can do saddle bronc because you've done some practice runs. You think you can pretend to be my wife just because you do."

"Fine. If you need me to prove it."

And she took two big steps toward him, flung her arms around his neck, went up on her toes and planted a kiss on his lips.

CHAPTER TEN

Callie had never been kissed before. And she'd been about to lay one on his mouth and pull away. But then his arm went around her waist like a vise, and whatever control she had slipped away. Because he put his forefinger underneath her chin and held her face steady as he angled his own, changed the slant on their mouths and slid his tongue past her lips.

She gasped, because it was so strange. So slick, and it made her... Everything in her body went tight. Muscles that she'd never been aware of before—and she was pretty sure she was aware of all her muscles before this moment—rippled. And she could feel the moment spiraling away from her. Turning into something she didn't recognize. Turning into something she didn't understand. She could feel the control getting farther and farther away from her grasp. As he kissed her, took it deeper. Took her to a place she hadn't known existed.

Jake.

Jake's mouth. Jake was kissing her. Really kissing her.

And she was letting him. She didn't know what to do in return, so she was just letting him. And suddenly she realized her face was wet, because tears were streaming down her cheeks, and she didn't even know why. She didn't understand what was happening.

And she couldn't breathe past it.

There was something bright and hot burning down between her thighs, and then he shifted, and brought her body close to his, and he was like a wall of rock. She knew that he was big. She knew that he was muscular. But he was so...*so hard.*

Everything about him was hard.

His chest, his stomach, his thighs—and for all that bold talk she'd made about anatomy, she could feel that the most male part of him was hard, too, and that scared the hell out of her.

And she was the one who wrenched herself away. She was the one who proved that she couldn't handle it. She was the one who ended it, because it was way over her head. And way above her pay grade.

Because he was right. It was a check her ass did not know how to cash.

"You won't have to kiss me *like that,*" she said, stumbling back with big steps.

"You're going to have to not freak out if I do."

"Is that just how it is for you? Is it just how it is for men? You grab ahold of a woman, any mouth will do, and you get all excited?"

He chuckled. But there was no humor in it. It was hard, and she didn't like it at all. Because he was like a stranger, and she just wanted her friend back. This man...this man that was her husband... She didn't know if she liked him.

"That's what you think? That's the only thing that you can come up with to explain it? That any port will do in whatever storm I'm going through? That I'm basically no better than an inexperienced teenager? Anything female will rev the engine?"

She sputtered. "Well nothing else explains it."

"Except that maybe I want you." His gaze was unflinching. His mouth set in a flat line.

Nothing about him looked like a man who was telling a joke. But she laughed.

Because there was no other response to that.

He didn't want *her*. He was…he was like a whole other species. A… A god of that kind of masculine beauty that all sorts of women wanted to worship, and she was…she was just *Callie*.

The only sin she'd ever enticed a man to was anger.

She was not a…a…fantasy object of any kind. And that was just for a start.

She was younger than him, and she didn't know how to kiss. She didn't understand any of that stuff. He could have any woman he wanted, and as far as she could see he had. So it didn't make any sense that he wanted her and he just…

No. He couldn't. He didn't. "Stop it," she said.

"Stop what?"

She took a step toward him, planted her hands on that hard chest—which she was more familiar with now than she had been a minute ago—and shoved him.

"Don't make fun of me on top of everything else."

"Fuck," he said. "I just kissed you, and you're not an idiot. You're the one that was telling me all about penises, so it's not like you don't know mine was hard. And now you're trying to tell me that I'm lying to you?"

"Well, it's not true," she said. "I'm not special. I'm not… I'm not like that. And anyway, we're friends."

"Yeah," he said. "We are. So maybe you should think about that. Maybe you should think about what that means. Do you think I'm lying to you? Or do you think maybe I just decided to use a little restraint with you because I do care about you?"

He shook his head, dragged his hand over his face, then looked at her, straight on. "Here's a couple things that are true, Callie Carson, and you can go ahead and sit with them ahead of our big long trip over to Lone Rock. It'll give us something to have an awkward silence over in the cab of the truck tomorrow. I want you. And you know, I made it clear these past few days that was the case. Do you think I touch my other friends on the face? Do you think I look at them the way I look at you? Hell. I want you. But I care about you. And the bottom line is those two things do not go together in my life. Because I'm not gonna fall in love with a woman, and I'm not going to give her a home in a house. As far as I'm concerned, that's the first step on the road to death. Domesticity might as well be dying. That's how I feel about it.

"You want to know why Christmas is so hard for me?" he continued. "Because it's like suffocating to death in that house. On family. On this bullshit bond of grief that we all share but can never really talk about. Because we have to pretend like everything's fine when actually everything sucks. Yeah, we had each other, and I'm grateful for that. But I couldn't stay in it. I couldn't stay in that monument to death. That's what it is to me. It will never be a celebration of the life that we all share, because that life came out of something that I wouldn't wish on anyone.

"So yeah." He breathed out hard. "Caring and wanting are two things that just don't mix for me. So I chose my path with you. But you're the one that came here and made it like this. You're the one that kissed me. You're the one that had me marry you, so dial your outrage back a little bit, and quit accusing me of things when you're the one that put us in the situation. And recognize that on the person that understands this."

Her teeth were chattering. His every word had shaken loose something inside her and now it was all rattling around in there, rocking her from the inside.

He wanted her.

Jake wanted her.

Callie Carson, who didn't fit in any costume she'd ever put on, not really. Because to be the kind of cowgirl she thought she had to be she could never be anything else, couldn't feel half of what she felt. To be the kind of daughter her mother wished she was she'd have to leave behind the rodeo.

And Jake wanted that Callie, who didn't know how to want anything other than rodeo dreams.

Don't you?

"You don't know what I know," she said, the words a shiver.

"You're a virgin, right?"

She had never, ever once been ashamed of that. She'd never given it a lot of thought. As far as she was concerned, if she'd ever wanted to not be one, she wouldn't be. It just wasn't something that bothered her right now. Wasn't something that concerned her. But the way that he said it…the way that he said it *burned*. The way that he said it made her feel like she was small and silly. And somehow something less than him. And it made her angry.

"It's none of your business."

"So you *are*."

Some sort of unholy noise came out of her mouth and she knew she sounded like a wet cat. And she couldn't stop it. "What does that have to do with anything? It's just a choice *not* to do something. I could if I *felt* like it." Her tongue was moving faster than her brain now. "You cowboys are such unholy sluts. I could have had…well, apparently, I could have you if I wanted. What's to say I couldn't push you into it?"

For the first time, he looked taken aback. For the first time, in all the years she'd known him, other than that time she'd fallen off the horse, she thought she might see fear in his eyes.

"Although that's the real issue, isn't it? You need to piss me off because you know I could push you. You know that if I wanted it, I could get it. From you. So you have to dismiss me, and talk about being a virgin, and talk about how I don't know anything. Because if I wanted to lose it with you, I could, couldn't I?"

Fear and adrenaline rushed through her in equal measure, and she felt like she was on some wild trajectory that she could no longer control. Because she'd found a way to poke at him.

She found a way to feel like she had the upper hand, but it was like playing with matches near a tank of gasoline, and she well knew it. It might explode on her at any minute. And she could feel that. She could. But she couldn't stop herself from pushing, either.

"Be careful."

"I'm right," she said. "Oh, I'm right. You're afraid of me. Because you're afraid I'll push you, and you might want me, but you also don't."

"It's for your own good. Trust me." He reached out and grabbed her chin. "Callie, I can sleep with a woman and never think of it again. If you wanted to play around for a bit, I could do play with you. And I could walk around with you any time after and forget it happened. Sex is common. It's cheap. Our friendship, that's not cheap. That's real."

"I don't see how one cancels the other out," she said, not sure why she was pushing. "We just vowed to be friends forever, didn't we?"

"I could walk away," he repeated. "And pretend nothing happened. You couldn't, though, Cal. That's the thing. I know well enough to know that. That's the real reason I avoid the barrel racers and the rodeo queens. It's not because it would be complicated for me. It's because it would be complicated for them. In terms of women I speak to, women I associate with, there's more of them that I've slept with than not. You're the only one I have this with. So sure, I want you. Sure. I could be the guy to take your virginity. I'd do a good job. I'd make you understand what all the fuss was about. And then when we were done, we'd be done. For me. For you, I don't think it would be that simple. So I'm protecting you."

"So you get to be an asshole?" she said, enraged now. "And pretend that you're doing it for my own good?"

"It is. Trust me."

"You came out here. You pushed me. You touched me. You

made us have to talk about this. And now you just… You're gonna push me and act like I'm a stupid kid? You're going to act like I'm the one that caused the problem? Well, don't get worried about me begging you for sex. I think I'm turned off permanently. Thanks for the awakening, and for the permanent deep-freezing of my libido one sentence later."

She pushed past him and stomped into the house. And she didn't stop moving until she was reasonably certain he hadn't followed her. She went into the bedroom, slammed the door and locked it for good measure. She had kissed him. And he had made her tremble. It had made her cry. And all for what? It wasn't worth it. He wasn't worth it. She hated this. This… Whatever it was that had taken their friendship and twisted it into something sharp and mean. That had taken one of the most important people in her life and made him an adversary.

And they were driving to her parents' house tomorrow, and they were going to have to pretend to be a couple. A few weeks ago, that had seemed easy. But now…

Now she didn't even know if they could pretend to be friends.

And the trouble was, she had gone and married the man.

For the first time, she seriously doubted her plans. Because for the first time, Callie Carson doubted absolutely everything she'd ever thought she'd known about the world and herself.

CHAPTER ELEVEN

The next morning he got up early to do the chores, and did his best to push aside the events of the night before. He'd been an absolute asshole, it couldn't be denied.

He wasn't even *looking* to deny it, not really, but he would like to forget that the entire thing had happened. She'd kissed him. And then she'd taunted him, and the real problem was that she'd been right.

If she pushed him, he wouldn't be able to deny her. If she tried to seduce him he wouldn't be able to say no, and nothing that he said about her lack of experience or skill would amount to a whole hill of beans. What the hell was wrong with him? He didn't particularly know.

In his world, attraction and feelings were two separate things. He felt attraction to Cal. But he also cared about her. And those two things were a whole canyon that there was no crossing with him. What he'd said to her was true. He would have no problem exploring the attraction between them and going back to the way things were. It was her that he worried about. And rightly so.

Whether she thought that or not. He was the one with the experience.

And when he'd been young and stupid, and out all on his own without Ryder hanging around to talk about *morals* and *ways to treat a lady* and whatever other things his cousin had said when he'd been trying his best to father-figure an angry teenager only one year younger than him... Jake had burst into the rodeo and felt...well, free. Eighteen and with so much anger to burn that it turned into alcohol and a voracious sex drive once he'd been on his own.

He'd slept with every pretty cowgirl who'd winked at him and had made a really awkward situation for himself right at first. He'd broken hearts he hadn't meant to break and he'd had to see those women frequently after, and they'd acted like it was something he was doing to them personally when none of it had felt personal to him at all.

Either way, he was in need of the punishing workout that came with that morning's chores. And in need of some distance from Callie, considering the two of them were going to spend a few hours in the cab of the truck together today. His words from last night came back sharp and clear. About making sure the ride was full of awkward silence. Yeah. Felt good to get in her face like that last night. To pour out some of the frustration that had been churning inside of him for months. It was a lot less fun today now that he was facing down that car ride.

He was already heading back to the house by around 7:30 a.m. when the front door opened. Callie's duffel bag exited first, making a loud thunk on the wood planks.

He'd thrown all his stuff in his truck earlier in the day.

He was grateful now, because he didn't want to walk up onto that porch and past the snarling bobcat that he had a feeling was about to make her way out.

Cal's appearance a moment later confirmed his bobcat hypothesis. She had a black cowboy hat pushed low on her head, her hair back in a messy braid, and she looked red-cheeked and sweaty. Which was not a good sign for this hour of the day.

"Good morning," he said, stopping by his truck and leaning against it.

"Good morning," she said.

She didn't look at him.

"Better get a move on," he said.

"Let me get coffee," she said. She picked up her bag and began to walk to her truck.

"We're not taking that," he said.

She looked over at the big green beast. "Why not?"

"Because it's a piece of shit."

"*Your* truck's a piece of shit," she said.

"No, it's not. My truck is great. Yours is a hand-me-down of the hand-me-down that went through your brothers before it went to you, and I don't want to drive a long distance in it."

"It's how I got here."

"Yeah, but it's not how I'm getting there."

"You're a dick," she said, picking up her duffel bag, slinging it over her shoulder and walking down the stairs.

He grabbed it up off the top of her shoulder and pulled it out of her grasping, angry fingers as she tried to follow the path of it upward over his shoulder.

"Such a dick," he said, hefting it up and wandering over to his truck.

Callie's hands were clenched into fists at her sides, and she stomped over to his vehicle.

"Knock it off," she said, getting in the passenger side and shutting the door.

"Thought you wanted coffee," he said, poking his head through the driver's side.

"You can buy me one on the road."

"Anything for my darling wife."

There was that word again. He had to be careful using it.

Even as a joke. Especially as a joke, because that was when it came around to bite him in the ass.

He did his best not to linger. Not to look at her face. Not to remind himself of what had happened the night before. He got in his side of the truck and started the engine.

"All right. One word."

"I was promised awkward silence," she said, staring straight ahead. And that was when he found he couldn't help himself. He found he had to stare. Her nose was just perfect. A little slope, her lips full and inviting. And he'd had a taste of them. She was glorious. All strung out and wired like a filly that hadn't been broken in yet. But warm like the summer sunshine. Sweet like the smell of grass and hay. So many of his favorite things rolled all into one package.

Good thing he was an experienced man who'd had a lot of sex, or thinking of her that way might get him hard. In the cab of his truck. And nobody wanted that. Least of all him.

He reminded himself repeatedly as he fought against his body's natural response.

"Well, you're going to have to give me your coffee order before you get your awkward silence," he said.

"A mocha."

"A mocha," he repeated. "Cal, I didn't take you for a sweet drink kind of girl."

"Maybe there's a lot you don't know about me."

She looked at him out of the corners of her eyes.

That was the problem. There was a lot he didn't know about her. And he thought against listing the things. The way her bare skin looked against his sheets being one of them.

He drove a little faster on the road that led into town, and parked his truck in front of Sugar Cup.

"After you," he said when he killed the engine.

"Not going to open the door for me? Have I gone to the level of a buckle bunny now that your tongue's been in my mouth?"

"You're a brat," he said. "Do you know that?"

"Yep."

She got out of the truck and headed toward the coffeehouse, and he got out, slammed his door and followed behind her. They went inside, and he could see the moment that Callie's anger faded a little bit as she took in the atmosphere of the coffeehouse. The roughhewn wood floor, the exposed brick walls and the glory of the chandelier that hung in the center of the place. All a bit of hipster nonsense for his taste, but he could tell that she was charmed. And he took a small amount of satisfaction in that, because he knew she was trying to be angry. So any sort of charm—even if it didn't come from him—felt like a victory in his corner.

"I'll have just a black coffee," he said, walking up to the counter and making his order a greeting to the sullen-looking girl behind the register. "*My wife* would like a mocha."

He could practically see a plume of smoke erupt over Callie's head.

"We're newlyweds," he said, grinning.

"Congratulations," the girl said, not smiling.

"Thank you," he said, intentionally using an overly bright tone. "We're going back to her parents' place for the holidays."

"I'm sure that's very romantic."

The whole performance would've been more fun if he would have had someone at the register who actually cared to make small talk. But still, it was making Callie angry, and as long as that was working, he was enjoying himself.

Why exactly?

He didn't know. Except that she had kissed him. And it felt like a violation of a great many things. She was acting like she had punched her own face, and blamed him. That was the problem. So really, if he could make her mad, or happy against her will, he would take it. Because he was mad. Pissed off. He had gone years wanting to kiss her, and not doing it. She had blown all that to hell. She had proven the thing that he had never wanted proven, which was that they had chemistry. And if she was a little ruffled by it so be it.

Actually, he would really like it if she was a *lot* ruffled by it.

When their drinks came out, he turned to her and smiled felicitously. "Here you go, *sweetheart*." He handed her the drink and gave her his best grin.

And the way she looked at him wasn't all that fun. Because her cheeks went pink, and her eyes went wide, and there was nothing like a performance in the few seconds that passed between them then. Instead, he felt something that arced through him like an electrical current that passed through the air and went straight down his spine. And he didn't the hell like it.

"Let's go," he said, taking his own drink and putting his hand on her back, propelling her out of the room.

"Knock it off," she said when they got outside. She shook away from his hold, and got in the truck.

And they went ahead and embraced that awkward silence from then on until they were out on the highway, driving the long, winding route from Northwestern Oregon to Eastern Oregon. It was a nice drive. He couldn't complain.

The thick, dense trees were beautiful, and then they slowly changed, growing a little more sparse before the ground became rife with volcanic rock. More and more scrub brush began to appear, large gray mule deer milling about and eating the sage off in the distance. He let Dierks Bentley and Tim McGraw provide a buffer between the two of them, but then some of the songs got a little bit sexy, and he turned the radio off, because that wasn't helping anything at all.

Then they really did have silence. And it really was uncomfortable.

"When you get up here, take the sign that says John Day Fossil Beds," she said.

"Okay," he responded.

They'd left cell service behind a little while ago, the terrain around them wild.

"You ever been to the Painted Hills?"

"No," he said.

"We need to stop there."

"Do we?"

"Yes," she said.

"Well, since you're speaking to me again…"

"I just feel passionately about where I'm from," she said. "And think that everybody should experience the natural beauty."

"Now you just sound like a really angry tour guide."

"I kind of am."

He drove on, following her instructions, and the more words they said to each other, the easier it got to just keep talking. And maybe, if they said enough words, they could erase everything that had happened this morning, and the night before. It was wishful thinking on his part, but out there in the middle of nowhere, with the wild closing in around them, it seemed possible at least. And it made him feel a little bit more ready to let go of his irritation. A little bit.

"Turn up here."

The road moved from pavement to dirt, and the side around them was like an alien planet. Rounded slopes of fine dust that moved in stripes. Red to white with inky black that looked like brushstrokes mixed in between.

"No points for guessing why they call it the Painted Hills."

"No," she said.

"Where do we go?"

"Pull over here."

It was freezing out, but they pulled over and got out, putting their coats on. Callie led the way over a wooden walkway that wove through the scenery. He had never seen anything like it. He didn't know there was a place like this out here. He'd been to Eastern Oregon plenty of times. To Pendleton for the roundup, and to Sisters for various events. But he hadn't been out here. Hadn't seen this strange, cold desert space that looked like an artist had physically painted it.

"Up here's the viewpoint."

He followed her up the hill that overlooked a vast expanse of these painted mountains. They were so bright and rich and strange. And he had the weirdest sensation of being small. He had felt jaded for a long damn time. Like the mystery and magic of life had been drained away when he'd lost his parents. And there was something... Gut punching in this moment, to stand there and look on something in his home state that he'd never seen. To feel like he was seeing the world with a fresh set of eyes. It wasn't anything he'd expected, wasn't anything he thought was even possible.

"It's incredible, isn't it?"

"Yeah. It is," he said, his chest feeling tight.

"I love it out here. It's honest. It's not... I love the rodeo. But I have to play a part in it. I have to be as tough as the cowboys, right? If I want to do what they do."

"You just have to be you. If you, Callie Carson, are capable of competing against them, what the hell do you care if you're like them or not?"

Her lips twitched, her eyes fixed on the horizon. "I have to be taken seriously."

"Why?" he asked.

She looked away from him and he could see her working on the words. "I don't know. Because I have to be."

Her words were stubborn and confused all at once.

"Look, Callie, let's call a truce. We can't go walking into your parents' house acting like we hate each other. And we've known each other a hell of a lot longer than it took us to kiss. It was just a kiss."

"Right."

"Proves my point, though," he said, his voice low.

"Oh, what? That I'm a virgin who would be forever ruined by your magic hands?"

He cleared his throat. "Just saying." He tried not to let any of that penetrate deeper than the surface. Because he didn't need to go overthinking it.

"I don't want any of that. I don't. It's… It's embarrassing. Have someone say that kind of stuff to you. I was mad at you. You were an ass."

"Sure," he said. "I can't deny that."

"Because you were the one that was shaken."

"Callie…"

"No, listen to me for a minute. Out here, there's no one to hear us, and we can have our truce after. I promise. I have to be better than my brothers. I have to be flawless. I have to be… I don't know, I just feel like I'm the replacement child, and I can't measure up so I have to make a whole new metric. And I haven't been exceptional. I fell. I hurt myself. I broke my arm."

"Don't tell me Boone has never broken his arm."

"It doesn't matter. I can't. I need to somehow be more invincible. Because I have to prove to them that I can do this. I'm lost in this family. They're all… Rodeo royalty. Superstars at what they do. They're bigger and stronger and my dad is so proud of them. And I've just never been able to… To do the right things. I thought I could. I thought I did. But then…this proved I didn't. It's like I was born into the wrong… Everything. I don't fit. I need to find that place that I fit. If I don't… Well, I can't think about it. So, as nice as the kiss was, everything around it was terrible. And I don't want another one. And I won't be ready for one from anyone until… Until the rest of this is handled."

"Well, sorry that all the rest of it was terrible."

"I forgive you. Because you're right. We've been friends a long time. And that was just… What, six seconds?"

"Yep."

"Shorter than a good ride."

"Shorter than a good ride."

But the world was alien around him, and Callie felt similarly alien next to him. And it wasn't all that simple. But she needed it to be. And he knew that it had to be. So he just had to get it together. Get it together and deal with himself.

"How much farther to your folks' place?"

"About an hour."

"It's really out there in the middle of nowhere, isn't it?"

"Yeah. It is. Lone Rock is a… It's a quirky town. Not much to do. Except go to the Thirsty Mule for a beer."

"If the mule is leaving thirsty, I'm not sure that I'll fare any better."

"I mean, that is a worry."

"Thank you," he said. "For taking me out here. It's really something. It's really something special, Cal."

"You're welcome." And for a minute there, things felt almost normal. They walked back to the truck in silence, but this time there was an ease to that silence.

"So, your dad didn't make it sound like he had any plans to kill me?" He asked that question when they were back on the road.

"No," she said. "Like I said, they just seemed happy."

She didn't look thrilled about that.

"Look. You may never get them to feel the way that you want them to about it. But… Do you need them to?"

"I'd like them to. I mean, who doesn't want their parents to be proud of them?"

Would his parents be proud of him? Or would his dad just be off in Southern California, living a new life, while his mom stayed on the ranch bitter as hell. Would they have sold the ranch?

Would his mother have hated who he was, how he drank and how he slept around?

He'd never know the answer to any of it.

"I suppose everyone does," he said.

"Yeah," she responded. "I just want them to understand. And I don't know why it's so important. But I wish that... I wish I was impressive rather than disappointing."

"You're impressive to me."

He kept his eyes on the road, but he could feel her looking at him. "So impressive that you think I need a lot of extra training."

"I just want to make sure the rest of the world knows how impressive you are." He cleared his throat. "And that you're safe."

"Well. Thanks for that. I'm not a kid, though."

"It's safe to say that I know you're not a kid."

And that brought a little bit of tension back into the cab, though it wasn't the same as the awkward, angry silence that had rested between them most of the way. It was something else, and it wasn't a something that he particularly wanted to deal with. Wasn't a something that he was all that happy about.

He shouldn't have said anything. But he'd been baiting her since they'd gotten up. Pushing her again.

And he couldn't help but wonder if it was because of what had happened when he'd pushed her the last time.

No.

He wasn't going to go there. Not again.

Not again.

CHAPTER TWELVE

The road to the ranch had tall, sparse pines and flat ground all around. The rocks that rose up behind the trees had sharp, stone peaks, markedly different to the lush green that he was accustomed to. It was beautiful. Though in a different way than he was typically drawn to. But he could see how this rocky environment got underneath people's skin. The cold, on the other hand, he found less appealing. And less understandable. The air here was dry and frigid. And if you breathed in too deep you ended up coughing. Not his favorite.

But Callie looked rapturous. Like she was enjoying the scene. Like she was enjoying the place. He did like that. Thought it was sweet. Thought she was sweet, come to that. He tightened his grip on the steering wheel and turned his thoughts away from that. She wasn't sweet.

She was a bona fide firecracker, and he would do well to remember that. There wasn't a damn thing sweet about her.

Yeah, that's why you like her.

He pushed that aside, too. He didn't need to go dwelling on that kind of thing right before he met up with her family.

This would be interesting. He knew her parents, vaguely. He

knew her brothers, as well as he knew any of the cowboys that he circled around the circuit. But hadn't been to their house. Certainly didn't know them in this context.

And he would be doing it while pretending to be married to Callie. Which, hell, he supposed he could be grateful they were pretending to shack up. The odds of him keeping all of his body parts in place were much better this way.

The sign for the Evergreen Ranch that hung over the dirt drive was bigger and grander than the sign at Hope Springs, but then the house that was maybe a mile down the road from that sign was something more than grand. In the early sunset, the floor-to-ceiling windows glowed orange, showing off the warm, inviting interior. But just because it was warm and in-viting didn't mean it was simple. The whole place practically reeked of money. Unlike any place Jake had ever been. It was difficult to reconcile this place with the rugged terrain and liv-ing that came with the rodeo and the way these people lived when they were out on the road.

"What?" Callie asked.

"This place is… Something else."

"Yeah, it is. They just had it redone a year or so ago. And when I say redone, I mean completely rebuilt. But you know, they like nice things. Even though they spend a lot of the year practically camping."

"Sure. Though I've seen your dad's RV. He definitely does it in style."

"My dad does everything in style."

He had to laugh at that, because it was true.

"Am I going to where we're staying first or…"

"No. We'll stop at the house first. I'm sure that Mom has dinner for us."

He'd faced down angry bulls. The family of his fake wife shouldn't be that big of a deal. Of course, it would've been better

if he hadn't just kissed her last night. Except they weren't thinking of that. They'd made a truce. Left it up at the Painted Hills.

He tried to feel that.

He parked the truck right in front of the porch, and this time
he did go and open the door for her. And he took her duffel bag.

"You can leave that. We'll have to drive over to the cabin."

He nodded, putting it back in the car. Then since his hands
were empty he... Reached out and took hers.

She looked up at him, her brown eyes serious. "I..."

"Newlyweds," he said.

She nodded. "Right."

He tightened his hold on hers as the two of them walked up
the porch and to the front door. She had calluses on her hands,
like any person who did work outdoors, who rode horses like she
did. But her hands were still undeniably feminine. Fine-boned
and delicate, with elegant fingers.

Elegant fingers.

He'd never thought of something that way in his whole life.
It was weird. And still, he stood by it.

Callie was about to knock when the door opened. And there
was her mother, looking between the two of them like she was
inspecting something closely.

"Well," she said. "Well, well. Callie Carson. Aren't you a dark
horse." Then she reached out and hugged them both.

Jake was... Stunned. He hadn't been hugged by someone who
wasn't family in a long time. Longer than he could remember.
And this was... Maternal. And he didn't like it.

But it was over before he could get too restless, and he found
himself being ushered inside along with Callie.

"Your daddy half didn't believe it," she said. "I half didn't
believe it. No offense, Jake," she said.

"None taken, Mrs. Carson."

"You can call me Mom," she said.

He stood there frozen to the spot. Because he didn't say that word. Didn't have a reason to.

"I…"

"Better if he calls you by your first name," Callie said, nodding.

"Okay," her mother said with a look that promised to get the rest of the story later. But he was just glad he didn't have to tell it now.

Grateful that Callie really was his friend, for all the marriage was fake, because she had understood what he was thinking effortlessly.

"Dinner's about ready. Everyone's at the table," she said.

And when he was ushered into the big dining room, he knew… Well, that hadn't been an exaggeration. Because there everyone was. From his new father-in-law, down to each and every one of his new brothers-in-law, and they were all staring at him.

"Boone, Chance, Flint, Jace, Kit, Daddy. You all know Jake." She tightened her hold on his hand, and the two of them walked down to the two chairs at the end of the table, where they sat together.

"Sure do," her dad said. "Though I have to say, I didn't expect to be welcoming him as a son-in-law. Especially not with such little warning."

"Sorry about that," Jake said, giving his best, charming grin, because he knew he could be charming. But whether or not he could be charming to the man whose daughter he'd up and married without permission, he didn't know. "Callie came to visit me for Thanksgiving. You know we've been friends for some time. Change in our relationship threw me," he said. "I didn't expect it."

That much was true. He certainly hadn't expected to be marrying her.

"And as much as I would've liked to do things properly in

that regard, I also wanted to make sure I was right and proper with her."

Yeah, he knew what he was implying. At the damn dinner table. But he had a feeling that if he was going to pick a route, the one that suggested he hadn't had sex with their sister and daughter until he'd made vows to her was the one that was most likely to win points.

"Old-fashioned," he said. "Appreciated. Your daddy must've raised you right."

Damn family stuff. This was the second mention of his parents in the minutes since he'd walked in the door. This was why he didn't like this sort of thing. At least with his family there was shorthand. At least with them there was an inbuilt knowledge of their past. They didn't have to explain things to each other. And if someone needed to leave the room because things had gotten a little too heavy, nobody had to ask. Just like how it had been for Griffin back at their Christmas celebration. He might not have the shared grief the rest of them did, but they all understood grief. And that sometimes you didn't want to talk about it. You just had to feel it.

But these people were all relative strangers to him, and they didn't know about his life. And so it required a little bit more explanation. And he didn't particularly want to give explanation.

"To the best of his ability," he said. Because that seemed a safe an answer as any.

"Callie mentioned you did Christmas with your family before you came here." He chuckled. "Right after Thanksgiving?"

"My cousins are big on holidays. We grew up together."

"That's nice," his mom said. "I've always liked big, close families."

"Yeah. It's… It's a good one."

"I guess we know how you met," her brother Boone said, giving him a hard look.

"Yeah, guess you do," Jake said. And he probably would've

been a little bit more circumspect if Boone were his actual brother-in-law. But he wasn't. And this wasn't going to be a situation Jake had to deal with for the rest of his life, thank God.

"You ever been married before?" That question came from Flint.

"No," Jake said.

"Any kids?" This one from Chance.

"No."

"Criminal record?"

"None of the above."

"You have to forgive us," Boone said. "It's only we got robbed of torturing you before you married her. We didn't think Callie would ever get married. But she is the only sister we have, so you know we've been saving up a lot of torture for the man who thinks he's good enough to steal her away."

"Nobody stole me away, bonehead," Callie said. "I'm still Callie Carson."

"You're not taking his last name?" That deflated question came from her mother.

Callie recoiled. "Why would I do that?"

Boone chuckled. "Good for you, Callie."

"I'm a Carson," she said. "Just the same as any of you. Why should I become less of one just because I got hitched?"

"Fine by me," Jake said. "Wouldn't want to change her," he said, meeting Boone's gaze. "I like her just like she is."

"Another good thing," Boone responded.

Dinner was served, and there was less chatter, because there was homemade pasta, and Jake felt like it might've been worth the whole trip just for that. Really, all the inconvenience was a washout because the pasta was that damn good.

After that, the chatter turned back to the circuit, different scandals that were happening in the rodeo, changes to event rules. And he noticed that Callie tried to chime in, but she often got talked over. It was definitely clear that her father deferred to the expertise of his sons, and was much more interested in their opinions than the opinion of his daughter.

And he could see Callie getting more and more frustrated. Could see the family dynamic that had pushed her into the corner that she was in.

"So how about it," her dad said. "You want to go shooting with the men tomorrow?"

"Sure," Jake said. "I didn't bring my rifle."

"We've got plenty. We're going to blow up milk jugs."

"Possibly some C-4," Boone said.

"I don't want to hear this," their mother said.

"Nobody's lost a limb yet, Mom," Jace pointed out.

"How did I raise such a pack of rednecks?"

The boys just shrugged.

"Shooting, huh?" Callie asked.

"Callie, I need you to stay to help make cookies," her mom said. "You know how much fun it is for us to decorate Christmas cookies."

Callie look tortured. But this was her show, and she didn't give any indication of what she wanted. He could certainly lobby for her to come, and hell, if he were her actual husband that's what he would've done. But he was here to help facilitate whatever she needed in terms of easing things with her family, easing things with the rodeo. So he didn't want to go make a mess of it by intervening now when he didn't have the full scope of what was going on.

"Right," Callie said, looking angry and flat with it.

"Well, that was a right good dinner," her dad said. "I think I'm ready to go take a drink in the study, if you boys want to come."

"I think Callie and I better head on to our cabin. It was a long day," he said, because he was ready to make the call now.

He lifted her up from her chair, and ignored the wide-eyed look. "Come on, darling," he said. "I feel a might tired."

And then her cheeks went rosy red, and he smiled. Slow and deliberate.

And he didn't really know what he was trying to accomplish with it. Except... They ought to know. They ought to know that she was something more than special. They ought to know her.

He did. And it wasn't that they didn't treat her like she mattered. They did. They were all genuinely happy to see her, and he could tell that they loved her. But they seemed determined to write her into a different role than the one she wanted to put herself in, and that was what bothered her. He knew it.

And he was disrupting what they'd decided about her. So he figured... He might as well go with that.

And as they walked out of the dining room, he bent down and kissed her lightly on the cheek. Her skin was so damn soft, and he hadn't counted on the lightning bolt of desire that would overtake him at the casual contact. Callie had her hand on his back, and her fingers curled into a fist, grabbing hold of his shirt. They walked out the front door, and once they were on the porch, she moved away from him.

"What was that about?" she asked.

"You're right. They do treat you like a kid. Like... A kid that you're not."

She was mad at him, and hell if he knew why. He was backing her up.

"So you thought making it sound like you were taking me back to the cabin and... Somehow you thought that was going to help? You might have insisted I get to go shooting instead."

Damn. He had missed a trick there. "I didn't know what you wanted. Honestly. I'm not here to stir shit up. I'm here to help you. Do you want me to go back in and say that I want you to come with me?"

"That won't help."

"I can say I can't bear to be without you. Even for a few

hours. I cannot go. We can stay in the cabin, make them think that we are—"

"No," she said. She let out a long breath. "My mom likes me to do the cookies with her, anyway. There's not much I can do about that. I can't... Not do it. You know how it is."

"I don't," he said, the words sounding flatter than he intended.

"Sorry. I'm sorry. I'll tell my mom about... Your stuff. So that she doesn't... So that she doesn't say anything else."

"I can take care of myself, Cal. I'm a big boy."

"You're here taking care of me. I might as well do my part to minimize the crap my family says to you."

"Come on," he said, wrapping his arm around her as they walked to the truck. She was warm and soft. And he knew he probably didn't need to touch her like this. But she didn't push away again.

They got into the truck and he started the engine. "You're going to have to give me directions."

"Yeah, I will."

She let out a long breath. "It's just up the road." Her voice sounded small, shaky. And he had to wonder if she thought he was actually going to take advantage of the situation.

"Chill out," he said, reaching across the space and putting his hand on her thigh. Which he realized too late wasn't helpful for either of them.

"It's just my family," she said. "I love them. But..." She looked over at him. "They are the reason we're in this situation."

"Noted."

"Turn left just up here."

The cabin was hardly that. It was much larger than he'd guessed it would be, with large windows and a roof with a deep peak.

"Wow, this isn't exactly the close quarters I was expecting."

"I told you. They've got... Lots of space here."

"You weren't kidding."

They got out of the truck, and he hefted their bags inside.

"There's at least four bedrooms in here. Feel free to choose which one you want."

"Sure."

"The fridge should be stocked. And there should be coffee and everything. So... When you get up to go shooting with the boys tomorrow you should be well caffeinated."

"Important," he said.

"Yeah. So I hear. There's not enough caffeine in the world to do cookies with my mother."

"You don't like to bake?"

"No. And more to the point, I'm terrible at it."

"You're terrible at it because you don't care about it."

"Oh? And you know that for sure?"

"I know you. If you care about something you're going to become good at it. So, I assume you just don't care about baking."

"No. I don't. But my mom does. So..."

"I get it." A memory whispered at the back of his mind, and he blinked. "I used to make cookies with my mom sometimes. Logan's mom... She made the best oatmeal chocolate chip cookies. My favorite. But my mom made the best sugar cookies. The crispy kind. I don't like them chewy."

"Well, you'll have to be disappointed. Ours are chewy."

"That's okay," he said. "I'd rather have them different than... You know, almost the same but not quite right."

"Yeah," Callie said. "I'm sorry. It must seem really ridiculous to listen to someone complain about baking with their mom when they can bake with their mom."

He shook his head. "No. I don't think of it that way. I can afford to. If my parents were still here... They'd drive me nuts. I'm sure of it. You're allowed to be irritated by your parents. Just because somebody else doesn't have them, doesn't mean you don't have problems with yours."

"Thank you."

"No problem." And there was something about the way the night had fallen outside the window that reminded him of last night. That made him think of the way they'd kissed then, and the way she'd felt his arms. And his memory was all too willing to cut out the fight they'd had surrounding it. And just imagine that kiss. The way it had felt to slide his tongue against hers. To hold that soft, strong body in his arms.

He took a step back. "I'm bushed. I better head to bed."

"Okay."

"See you tomorrow, Cal."

"See you tomorrow."

And he walked down the hall, toward the bedrooms, without looking back. Because if he looked back, there was no telling what he might do.

CHAPTER THIRTEEN

Callie woke bright and early, and irritated. Jake was already in the kitchen making coffee, and she found her eyes glued to the sight of him. His broad shoulders and back, his narrow waist. His muscular thighs.

And his... Well, his ass.

She had never really been transfixed by a man's body before. But she couldn't really move for all the effort it took to take him in. She didn't like it. It made her feel exposed. Like when he'd kissed her that night, he'd peeled back a layer and left her damn near naked to everything around her.

It was *terrible*.

And when he turned around, and offered her a cup of the morning brew, she did her best to look casual. To look like she wasn't just taking a visual tour of his every muscle.

And then a smile curved the corners of his mouth, and her stomach did something weird.

He was beautiful. He was really beautiful.

"I expect you're about to head out for the shooting."

"Yep. C-4 is involved."

She rolled her eyes. "If Boone's around, it usually is."

"Why exactly?"

"I don't know. He likes blowing shit up."

"I mean, I don't *not* like blowing shit up."

"Who doesn't like to blow shit up?" Callie asked. "It's one of the great joys in life. I have to make frosting instead. That is not as much fun."

"I'll enjoy eating it later."

"Bullshit," she said.

But he smiled, and there was something wolfish about it, and it took that twisting feeling in her stomach and ramped it up even more. And she couldn't even say she disliked it. Because it was strange and intense and made a pulse echo between her legs. And it felt... Good. Dangerous. Interesting. It was like getting on the back of a horse, not knowing how hard the ride would be. Not knowing how rough. That moment before everything went live.

It was like that, but different. More. Frightening and intimate and... There was something sort of shameful about it, and she found that made it a bit dirty and heated and bright. And she shouldn't find that to be true, but she did. She nearly didn't recognize herself. And that made her feel like she was drowning, right there on land, in a kitchen, staring at the man who was supposed to be her best friend in the whole world. Because there was suddenly something more exciting than rodeo. And it was something she shouldn't even want. And it was something that wouldn't go anywhere or get her anything. She blinked, and breezed through the moment. Made a conscious decision to let it pass by.

They rode back to the main house together, and she didn't bother to greet her father and brothers as he went over to them. She just went straight into the house, straight for the kitchen. She was too irritated by the fact that they were having a man-only shooting party, and too irritated and thrown off-balance by the way she had been looking at Jake this morning.

"Hi, sweetheart," her mom said, smiling.

And then she felt guilty, because her mom was so happy. So happy that Callie was with Jake, and so happy that she was here baking cookies. And Callie was lying.

"Hi."

Her mom handed her an apron, and Callie put it on without complaint.

"Already have the sugar cookies ready to go. Some of them have already been baked and are ready to frost. And here we have the frosting colors." She put them in front of Callie, her eyes shining. And Callie knew she was supposed to try and look excited.

"Yeah," she said.

"Now," she said. "I want to hear some details about this man of yours. And if you're pregnant—"

"I'm not," Callie said.

Her mom was still staring at her.

"I'm not." Her voice went up half an octave that time.

"I just have a very hard time believing that he up and married you so quickly because he is that traditional."

"He's *traditional*," Callie said.

"So you said. So he said. But it's my experience that rodeo cowboys rarely are."

"That's a little bit too much information about you and Dad," Callie said.

"Don't get me wrong. I don't mind it. I just… It's not my experience."

"Family is important to him," she said, seeing it as a good opportunity to push into the conversation about Jake's family. "So I guess he's traditional because of that."

Her mom handed her a plate of sugar cookies and began uncovering frosting bowls. Callie started mindlessly slapping icing onto the precut cookies.

"He doesn't want to call you Mom because his mom died," Callie said. "Both his parents did. It's painful for him."

Her mom's face contorted with sympathy.

"Oh, dear. I wish I would've known. I'm so sorry. I didn't mean... I can understand that. How he doesn't want to feel like he's replacing them."

"Well, maybe you can tell Dad. Because the subject of his family is going to come up, and I hope he doesn't get interrogated up there shooting today. But hopefully it'll just all be too loud and filled with explosions for any talking to happen. It was a long time ago, but I know it still bothers him."

"Well, we don't want to hurt him by bringing up old pain. I know just how that is."

There was such a depth of sorrow to her mom's voice, and Callie felt immediately... Uncomfortable. Wounded. She didn't like that the subject of her sister always made her feel this way. But it did.

"Callie Patrice. Please pay attention to the frosting. You're the only one who does this with me. And you know how much I like the cookies. If you're just going to slap it on like a coat of paint..."

"Sorry," Callie said.

But she couldn't get away from the feeling that her mom had suddenly gotten irritated with her because she had imagined the daughter who should be here in her place. And what might've been. Her mom had never said anything like that to her. Not outside of her sixteenth birthday, and events surrounding it. And Callie had been...

She knew she'd hurt her mom. She did.

But she'd been hurt, too.

It had happened once. Only once. But the wound it had left behind had been so deep that it had never fully healed. Not between either of them. She knew her mom felt bad about it. She knew her mom regretted saying it.

She also knew that her mom believed it to be true.

And there was no amount of "I'm sorry" that could make it different.

But Callie couldn't be sorry for the way she'd been born. And she couldn't feel the same grief for someone who had died years before the fact, either. And it was one of those islands that stood between her and her mother, and kept them from really understanding each other. Kept them from connecting.

"Anyway," Callie said, clearing her throat. "He's a good guy."

"I'm so pleased for you," her mom said, clearly taking the olive branch, and deciding to restart. "I hope that you start a family soon."

Guilt tensed her stomach and she knew she couldn't let that go. She couldn't go pretending she was on the verge of giving her mother grandchildren.

"Well, I'm not finished with the rodeo. And Jake doesn't expect me to be. He was my friend for a long time. He understands how much it matters to me."

"Oh, honey," her mom said. "But his expectations will change now that you're his wife. If he's traditional like you said, then he's going to want you at home taking care of him. And you can be angry at me all you want for forcing you to learn to cook things, but I know that's what he's going to like. You'll get to give him the kind of family life he didn't have."

"Oh, I... Mom..."

"You can't honestly think that you're going to keep riding when you have a husband at home. I know he's not in the rodeo anymore."

"Well now, he's got his ranch, but we don't mind spending a little bit of time apart."

"That's just not responsible," her mom said. "You have to be there for your husband. Your marriage is more important than riding horses."

"No," Callie said. "Riding horses has always been important to me."

"Callie, you have a husband."

"And if… If Boone gets a wife, does he have to quit?"

"It's different," her mom said. "It's different, and I think you know that."

"It's different," Callie echoed. "It'll just always be different for me, won't it? You're never going to be proud of what I do."

"Callie, what you do is nice, but it's not—"

"They all make their careers out of the rodeo. And nobody questions it. It's all fine and dandy when it's them. I thought that at least when Jake and I were married, and you knew that he didn't mind… Well, I figured you would see that it's a valid thing to want. That I'm serious."

"I believe that you're serious," her mom said. "I just also believe that I have more of an understanding of what's really important in a woman's life."

Frustration filled Callie, and she let her frosting knife clatter onto the counter, uncaring about the mess it made.

She felt sixteen again. Sixteen and opening a box with a necklace in it, rather than the hunting knife she'd wanted. That she'd been expecting. That all her brothers had gotten.

She'd realized then. That it didn't matter what she did. That it was all playing to her mom. That she just needed to grow up and be a woman the way she recognized it.

She hadn't shown her disappointment, not then.

It was what had happened after that that had caused problems, and Callie could regret those, and still be angry at the situation.

"It's not fair," she said.

"You know what isn't fair?" her mom asked. "I want just a little bit of time a year with you, where we do the kinds of things that *I* want to do. Not just sitting in a dusty arena watching you ride. I want you to frost cookies with me for an afternoon and not have a fight. Can you do that?"

Callie was stricken. Because this was the closest they'd come to that kind of fight they'd had all those years ago. To her mom outright saying she just didn't like the way that Callie was. The way that she'd turned out.

Totally different to how Sophie would have been, she was sure.

And her mom didn't have to say that for Callie to know it.

"Fine," she said, picking the knife up from the counter. She ran her finger through the frosting, wiping it off the granite, and then she lifted it to her lips and licked it right off. "Let's frost some damn cookies."

Going up in the hills with his father-in-law, his brothers-in-law and weapons was something that Jake hadn't fully thought through. And they all looked at him with a kind of keen interest when the targets were set up and they were all in position. They had driven all the way up to the snow, the white-capped mountains around them majestic, and the sheer cliffs steep, so if they wanted to dispatch him and get rid of his body handily, he could see multiple ways for that to happen.

"Frankly," Boone said, slinging his gun down from his shoulder. "I'm surprised that somebody was able to tame her."

Jake chuckled. "Well, I wouldn't go that far."

"It's a damn good thing," her father, Abe, said.

"What is?" Jake responded.

"Callie having something, someone, in her life other than the rodeo. Poor girl feels a little put upon, I know, but there's a limit to how far women tend to go." He shook his head. "I'm not sure I did her any favors. I indulged her for too long."

He felt like a turncoat, standing there listening to that. On some level he realized he hadn't really believed how deeply Callie was right about her family. He hadn't really…understood that her father fundamentally didn't believe she could do this because of her gender.

And it was...

Well, hell, he'd faced a lot of uphill in his life. Had been through enough crap to defeat most people. But no one had ever told him he couldn't do something because he was a man.

"I don't know," he said. "I was doing some reading about a cowgirl with a diamond tooth who did bucking broncos way back in the early days of the rodeo."

"The sport was different back then," Abe said. "Now it's extreme. Everybody always pushing the limits, the animals pushing the limits, the breeders pushing the extremes. Just not the same. Anyway, everybody has to find a life after the rodeo, as you well know."

It was tough to argue with because he did know that. But the thing was, he'd done his riding. And she hadn't.

"You're right," he said. "There's more to the rodeo. And there's life past it. But I got to live my life in it. I got to win a championship. And I got to quit when I was good and ready. But Cal doesn't feel like she's done, and I'm going to support her until she makes that decision for herself."

Her brothers looked at him with a measure of respect that surprised him. Callie might have more allies than she realized.

"She's lucky," Boone said.

He shifted uncomfortably. "Oh, I make sure she knows it. It's too bad she doesn't feel it more from the rest of you."

"Let's see if you're any kind of a good shot," Jace said.

Boone chuckled. "I think he's a good enough shot. I love Callie. We all do. But we worry for her."

"Sure. But she can't live any life but her own."

He had trusted Callie when she'd come to him saying that she needed to get married in order to do this, but he hadn't really understood how deep it all went until now. The way that she got forced into the roles that they wanted her in. The way that he raised his rifle, fitted against his shoulder and lowered his head so that he could look at the scope. Then he squeezed the trigger, and the bullet unerringly hit its target.

"What blows up, though?" he asked.

Her dad clapped him on the shoulder. "We're going to have fun with you."

And suddenly his skin felt like it was too tight. Because for all the irritation he felt on behalf of Callie, this was... A family. A real family. And the way her dad was touching his shoulder was like...

Like a father.

He swallowed hard, and Boone rescued him with C-4. And they spent the rest of the afternoon blowing shit up. Which was infinitely preferable to conversation.

CHAPTER FOURTEEN

Callie was restless and pacing and so completely stirred up by what had happened earlier between herself and her mother. And she was… She was thinking. About the implications of it all, and everything that went with it. And then he walked in. He walked in looking beautiful, and she… She could scarcely breathe around it. And she didn't know what to do about it. He'd done this thing to her. He'd made her want something other than her deepest, most real goal, and she…

And she thought that she… She thought that if she focused, if she didn't even try to be at all like her sister, her sister who was gone, who she would never be… Who she would never be as good as. She thought that if she just put all that away, that her parents would see. That she was different. But that she was special all on her own.

And she… She was standing here, twenty-four years old and completely without experience with men, having these feelings about one for the first time in her life, all because she had shoved it down so deep for so long in the name of… Trying to be like her brothers. Trying to be something special. Trying to be… Anything but what she'd been born as. Anything but wanting.

Compared to her sister, who had apparently been the princess dream of both of her parents. A poor, innocent child that she resented, even though she was dead.

And she didn't like thinking about it. Not this much. Because it was a weird grief mixed with a strange sort of resentment, and it didn't feel fair or right or even real half the time. And all she felt was tired. Tired of trying so hard. Tired of wanting. He'd made her... He made her feel things. And that was so awful to her. And he...

Maybe it's not him.

Maybe any man would do. You're just hard up.

And the real tragedy was that she was married to him. Married to him, and staying at her parents' property and about to peel her skin off.

"I take it you didn't have a very good day baking?"

"No, I didn't have a good day baking," she said. "I would think that it'd be obvious."

"What's wrong?"

"I want to kiss again," she said, the words tumbling out of her mouth.

"What?"

"You heard me. I want to kiss again."

The demand shocked her as much as it seemed to shock him, and excitement broke out over her skin in the form of a cold sweat.

"Cal..."

"I can't win. I can't win, Jake. I'm... They're never going to see me as a son, so why bother? I'm a woman. I'm a woman who wants to ride saddle bronc, and I don't care if it's crazy. But I am a woman." Her eyes felt wet, and she hated it, and she couldn't stop it, either. "And I... I like men. And I've had to pretend I'm just one of them. One of the guys, so that I could... So that I could maybe... I thought maybe I could compare to my brothers. Because there's no way in hell I can compare to a dead person. A dead person who had limitless possibilities, who never disappointed anybody, who never even got the chance to. How can I live up to that? At least Boone is an asshole sometimes. So maybe I can be as good as Boone. Just maybe. And I thought that I had to be just like them in order to do that. Except better. But it's not ever going to work. Because my mom just keeps talking about how I have to understand that the rodeo isn't the important thing. And it's not what I want. It's not good for me. And… So forget it. I'm tired of it. I held myself back because of it. But I'm not going to do that anymore. I'm all in. So… Show me what it's all about, then."

"Callie," he said. "I am not kissing you just because you're pissed off at your parents."

"Why?" she asked, knowing it was silly to push. No, more than silly it was…tragic. Like she had no pride. "You married me because I was pissed off at my parents."

His hand curled into a fist, like this was costing him. Like she was a bother to him. "I'd like to still be friends on the other side of this."

She was so…so angry. So helpless feeling, and she hated it. She was sick of being stuck in the middle of no-win situations.

Couldn't be as good as her brothers because she wasn't a boy. Was never going to live up to her sister because she was the wrong kind of girl.

Got a necklace, traded it for a knife. Broke her mother's heart when she was just trying to please herself.

Couldn't kiss Jake. Couldn't stop thinking about kissing Jake.

And why couldn't she kiss him? Because he said so?

It was always because someone else said so.

And no one *listened* to her when she said what she wanted. "You're the one that made me feel these things," she said. "Man-up and do something about them."

"It's a bad idea."

And that was just it. She lost it. She was so tired of everyone telling her what she wanted, everyone telling her what she should do.

"Fine. I don't need you. I just need another cowboy for the night."

"Hell, no," he said. "We agreed none of that."

"Were not really married, Jake, as you well know. And if you won't give me what I want, I'll find someone who will. I can get myself a buckle bull if I damn well feel like it. And I aim to do just that."

She walked right out of there, without getting dressed up, without *anything*. Because she was going to show him.

There was an old work truck sitting there in the driveway with the keys on the seat, and she gave thanks for the ample vehicles on the property and lax security.

Then she started to drive toward the main street of Lone Rock.

It was a Wild West town. Nothing quite as quaint and civilized as Gold Valley. The old wood buildings were painted bright red, mustard yellow and emerald green. White pillars and balconies added a nice contrast to the color.

And among all that, the Thirsty Mule stood out. It was all brick with a white sign that had a hazy-looking mule on it. He had his tongue hanging out and a bottle of whiskey beside him.

Without even thinking about it, she parked right in front of the bar.

She knew that Jake was pissed, but she didn't care. She didn't care about anything. She was desperate to prove that it wasn't just him. It couldn't just be him. Because he was denying her, and it was just kissing. So would probably be the same with any guy. She was pent up in all that. Since she'd never had a chance to let herself go like this before.

She got out of the truck, her stomach fluttering slightly as she put her hand on the door, then pushed it open. The place was packed full.

The lighting was dim, strips of neon running along the ceiling and signs proudly proclaiming different brands of booze lit up on the walls. There was a pool table and a dimly lit dance floor where people were less...*dancing,* more *swaying and groping.*

Cowboys and cowgirls drinking, dancing. She was not going to dance. Anyway, the dance floor was packed, and she couldn't see well enough into it to get a bead on whether or not there was anybody she wanted to dance with.

She hung back by the door for a few minutes, looking around. And then she spotted a particularly tall, well-built cowboy by the bar. He was closer to her age than Jake, she guessed, which was good. He wouldn't have that paternal vibe. That overprotective crap that Jake tried to pull on her. So she walked up to the bar.

"Hey," she said. "Can I buy you a drink?"

He arched a brow. "I could buy you one."

"That works, too," she said. "Works nice, in fact." She stuck her hand out. "My name's Cal. Uh, Callie."

"Dan," the guy said, grinning. "Come here often, Callie?"

"I think you know I don't," she said. "Unless you don't come here all that often."

"Matter of fact, I do. So yeah, you're right. I know you don't."

"That's all right," she said, looking at him critically. "I don't need you to be smooth."

He chuckled. And she felt like she was winning at a game she didn't know the rules for somehow. And she was thrilled about it.

"What do you need me to be?" he asked.

She tried to think of something that a woman with experience might say. Or at least what Lara might say, the shiny, bold barrel racer who spoke her mind and never seemed to regret it.

"Easy," she said.

That earned her another chuckle.

"I am that," he said.

Thank God.

Although when the drinks did get set down on the bar, she

realized that she had basically propositioned the man for sex. And she didn't feel a whole lot of anything but angry. She certainly didn't have that crackle under the skin that she felt when she looked at Jake. Didn't have that twisting sensation, that about-to-ride excitement. She lifted the beer to her lips, and tried to look...seductive or something. She genuinely didn't know how. Then she realized that she just needed to quit playing games.

So she took a step toward him, and she felt herself resist. She didn't want to kiss him. She stared at him, studying the planes and angles of his face. He was handsome. More than handsome. He was hot actually. A good-looking guy close to her age, and there was no reason she shouldn't want to... Put her lips on his.

She'd kissed Jake, and it felt good. Kissing felt good.

Kissing Dan should feel just as good.

But no matter how much she told herself that, she couldn't bring herself to take another step forward. Maybe it was because she had a husband.

And no matter that it was fake, everything in her resisted the idea of kissing a man when she was married to another.

Maybe it's just Jake...

No, it couldn't be Jake. Because he was just like everyone else. Telling her what to do. And there was no point wanting him, because he'd said himself they wouldn't be able to be friends after.

Oh, she hated Jake right now. She really did.

"What the hell is this?"

She turned slowly, and think of the very devil.

And good grief, he looked like something devilish, too. His eyes were a storm, his jaw set hard like granite, his mouth a firm line.

She was...in trouble. And something in her was anticipating it.

"How did you know where I was?" she asked.

"You mentioned the Thirsty Mule when we were driving out here. And there are, like, two places open in town at this hour. Didn't take rocket science to figure it out."

"Excuse me," Dan said. "Who are you?"

Jake practically growled.

"Her husband, you weedy bastard," Jake said, taking a step forward.

Jake really was much larger than Dan. Taller, broader. And everything.

And she felt…

Like she'd been invaded by some creature she hadn't known existed. Because her whole body went soft when he stepped forward, all rage and possessiveness and a hundred things she would never have said appealed to her. A hundred things she would never have said her friend had ever exhibited on her behalf.

"Husband?" He looked at her. "You trying to get me skinned?"

"No," Callie said, scowling. "He's being dramatic. Anyway. He wasn't *in the mood.*"

Jake wasn't looking at Dan at all, and Callie wished he would. He was looking at her. All laser focus and rage. "I'm *in the mood* for a hell of a lot now, Callie Carson, and you better pray you survive it."

The sensual threat in his voice was not lost on even her, and it made her whole insides go giddy. Spiked with her anger, it was a strange and intoxicating combination.

Only an hour or so ago she'd been shouting at him about how she was a woman. Even though she wanted to ride, even though she liked jeans and didn't get all fussed about makeup and frills.

And she had to wonder if this swirling, dark need inside of her was another of her contradictions.

And if she had to be made of contradictions, why not this one, too?

"I—"

"We're leaving," Jake said. He looked at Dan. "Buy the lady's drink, would you?"

"Sure," he said, holding his hands up. "She didn't say she was married."

"*She is,*" Jake practically snarled. "To *me.*"

They had drawn a few stares from around the bar and Jake, to her horror, turned to address them all. "This is my wife," he said. "If she comes back, just want to make sure you all know that."

Then he took her hand, and dragged her out of the bar.

"Jake, *what the hell?*"

And she found herself being pulled up against his hard, broad chest, his lips crashing down on hers. And he was kissing her. More than kissing her. He was devouring her. Doing exactly what she had begged him to do earlier. But he was… Oh, he was mad. Madder than he'd been the other night. Madder than she'd ever seen him. Ever.

Mad because she…

Was it because she had almost kissed someone else?

But then she couldn't think, because his big rough hand came up to cup her cheek, and she felt reborn. Remade into something completely different than she had ever imagined she could be. Because she knew how to punish herself. And she had a feeling that this was Jake's punishment. But it was something so much more than she'd imagined it could be.

"Jake," she whispered.

And he kissed her deeper, biting her bottom lip as he did. Sensation shot through her, an arrow right between her thighs.

"Don't you ever do something like this again," he growled against her mouth.

And in that moment her friend was gone.

Replaced by someone more feral, more primal, than she'd known existed inside that body. Inside that skin.

You've seen him like this before.

She remembered. The day she'd fallen off the horse. The day she'd broken her arm. The sound he made.

It had been from this part of him. This wild, frightening part of him.

But it didn't repel her. It shook her up inside. Woke something up in her. But it didn't scare her. It was scary, but that was different than being afraid of it.

Instead, she clung to him, and she kissed him back.

And something felt uncaged inside of her just then.

Because this was for her. She didn't have to stop. This wasn't for anyone's approval, it wasn't for show. It wasn't for anything but pure want. And everybody was going to be so disappointed when they found out this marriage was fake. And they'd be even more disappointed if they found out she'd slept with him knowing it was going to end.

And she just didn't care. Her entire family could take a long walk off a short pier as far as she was concerned. Because she just wanted. She was hungry. For Jake. For this. And why couldn't she have him? So she kissed him back, and dimly, she was aware that tears were falling down her cheeks again. That she was hanging on to fistfuls of his hair, but she didn't care. Not only had she never been kissed like this, she wasn't sure anyone had. With so much fury and passion and everything in between.

And she would've said… Well, she would've just flat out said she didn't understand it only a few months ago, but she understood now. That there was nothing to understand. It just was. This thing just existed between them. They hadn't chosen it. They couldn't rationalize it. Any more than she could force herself to kiss Dan back in the bar. She couldn't make herself want to kiss him any more than she could make herself not want to kiss Jake.

Maybe they could do this.

Maybe she could. He'd said that the problem was she wouldn't be able to go back to being friends if they did this. But she could. She knew that she could. It was just that he was wrong about her. He thought that because she didn't have any experience it meant that she couldn't handle it. But she could. Because for whatever reason this was what was happening. And she didn't particularly believe in fate, or put much store in it, because if she did, then she would have to also acknowledge that fate could be a particular kind of bastard.

Giving her parents a girl after all those boys, then taking her away. Then giving Callie as a replacement who would never quite be able to replace anyone or anything. Callie, who could never be her brothers, but could never be her sister, either.

But this felt just about right. And maybe this was part of it. This growing. Because he'd asked her… Couldn't she just do it for herself? And if she could… Oh, if she could, the possibilities that opened up. Because then maybe she could have this, too. Just for a little while. Just for fun. Why couldn't she? Because the cowboys did it—they'd talked about that. And she wasn't looking for love and marriage or any of that sort of thing. So why couldn't she do things the way that he did? And what better person to test it out on than Jake? He was the one that she'd gone to. He was the one that she trusted. She still trusted him, even furious at him. That was the thing. No matter how irritating he was, he was Jake. And there was no one else like Jake. He'd taught her to ride a bucking bronco. Maybe he could teach her this, too. Maybe it could be part of it all.

They pulled away, and they were both breathing hard.

"Jake…"

"Get in the truck," he said.

"But I drove," she said.

"Oh, I know. We'll sort that out tomorrow. But right now, you're coming with me."

"I don't think—"

"I don't want to know what you think. This was stupid. Now get in the truck."

"Fine," she said.

She got into his truck, and he didn't speak again until they started driving.

"Were you trying to punish me?"

"You're giving me too much credit. I wasn't trying to punish you. I was trying to prove to myself that I could kiss someone else and enjoy it."

"And?"

"I didn't kiss him."

"Because I came in?"

"Maybe." She let out a long breath. "No. I wasn't going to be able to do it. I just wasn't. I tried. But I… I don't want him."

"Good," he said.

"Jake…" She reached across the space and put her hand on his forearm.

He made a sound, halfway between a breath and a tortured growl. "Be careful."

"I don't want to be careful. That's the problem. I squished myself into a box for my whole life. And there's a reason that you're the person I came to when I was ready to be free. There's a reason that it's you. And there's a reason that this is you, too."

"Because you—"

"Don't say because you're the first man I kissed, because that was the point of coming out tonight. To prove that wasn't why. But it is. I trust you, Jake. If I didn't trust you I wouldn't have come to you with all of this. You taught me how to ride. You taught me how to be a cowgirl. Really. Can you teach me this, too?"

"You want me to teach you to be a buckle bunny?"

He asked the question in a scathing tone. Unkind. But she didn't flinch. Because that was what he wanted her to do.

"If that's what you need to tell yourself, sure. But you're the one who said that I couldn't handle it, so why are you acting like you're the one with the issue?"

"I already told you. For me these are two separate things. They don't cross. They don't meet. Feelings, sex. Not the same."

"Okay. How do you know it won't be that way for me?"

"Because it won't be. It just won't be, Cal. You're not like that."

"How do you know?"

"I know your family is difficult. But you have them. They're just... There were things in my life that broke apart certain bridges inside me. That's the only way I can describe it. Things inside people that connect up, they just don't for me. Now, on the other hand, I've lost enough. The relationships I do have are very important to me. I can have sex with anyone, but I can't have what I have with you with anyone else."

"Oh." It was difficult to be mad about that, because it was a nice thing to say. Except... She still felt hurt by it.

Because it still made her feel like there was something about her that wasn't quite right. And it made her sorry for him.

"I just need you to trust me," she said.

"It's not you I don't trust. Well, I guess it is. But I don't think you're lying to me. I think you just don't know."

"That's what everyone thinks," she said. "That I don't know what I'm getting myself into. That I don't know what I want. Everybody thinks that I'm not as smart as they are. And everybody wants to keep me from having all the life experiences that they have. What's the worst that could happen, Jake?"

Right then, they pulled up to the cabin again. He turned the engine off, and the sound of the heat popping against the hood was the only thing that remained.

"I could hurt you. That's about the worst thing I can think of. Even if you could put on a brave face, even if you... I could hurt you, Cal. And that's not acceptable to me."

"News flash, Jake. I'm hurt already. I'm hurt because I want to be something to my parents that I'm not. I'm hurt because trying to be...what I want hurt them and they've been hurt enough already. I don't know how to get what I want, while keeping them from… I don't know. I'm hurt because I want you and I'm basically having to beg you over it. Because we're friends, but this thing that I instigated between us pushed us into a weird zone and I don't know how to get us back into a better space. There's just going to be hurt. It's life. It's like the bucking bronco. I got bucked off, and I broke my arm. But it healed. I'm going to have to do this sometime, with someone." She turned to face him. Stared him down, even while he refused to look at her. "Wouldn't you rather it was you? Wouldn't you rather that you were the one that was there? Making sure that everything was okay?"

She could feel it. She could feel all the tension inside of him snap. She could feel him give in.

"Dammit."

"Jake…"

"Inside."

She didn't need to be asked twice. She hightailed it out of the truck and scurried into the house. She heard his heavy footsteps behind her, and stopped. Then strong, firm hands were on her shoulders, and she was turned to face him. He looked down at her, something in his eyes that she couldn't read. But he wasn't angry.

"I don't know what that's like," she said.

"What?"

"Kissing you when you're not angry."

He closed his eyes, and groaned. Then he cupped her face with rough hands, and kissed her. It was gentler than all the other kisses they'd shared. Softer. But no less devastating. He tasted her slowly, deepening the contact with each firm press of his mouth against hers. Then he parted her lips, his tongue sliding between them, and she trembled. Trembled as the slick friction worked its way through her body. As it turned her one-quarter liquid, and made it so she could scarcely breathe.

She clung to him. She had never held on to anyone like this. She had never felt quite so dependent on another human being. Like if she didn't have him right there she would just melt into a puddle on the floor.

When they parted, she was breathing hard. And that giddiness was back. That rush of adrenaline she felt out on the street in town.

"We're really doing this, right?"

"I'm sure as hell not stopping now."

"Good," she said.

She felt drunk with power. With freedom. And it wasn't until this moment that she realized just how many strictures she'd put on herself. How many limits.

"I built a fence around myself," she said.

"What?"

"There just wasn't... There wasn't anything stopping me from doing this the whole time. With anyone. I mean, not that I want to do it with anyone. I'm glad that it's you. I just mean... There's all these fake rules. And all these... Fake lines. Kinds of women you could be, ways to be taken seriously and all these things I told myself. About how I can't let myself feel good because if I did that I was being a wimp, like I've been afraid my dad thinks I am. That I wasn't working hard enough and... I am. It's not bad to do this. To let you make me feel good."

"Wait a minute. Are you telling me that you didn't like to let yourself feel good because you thought it meant... That you weren't working hard?"

"It's just that when my muscles are sore I know I worked out hard enough. When I can't walk after a good workout, I know that I'm on the right track. That night when you kissed me, when I was doing the burpees out in the arena... Part of why it made me so upset was that I just... Sometimes I just want to punish myself."

The admission felt so heavy. So, so heavy, but it was real. It was true. "I'm…not who I'm supposed to be."

He frowned. "How could you not be who you're supposed to be?"

"I…" Anguish escaped her chest in a gust. "I should have either been born a boy, or not at all. Sophie should still be here. The daughter they wanted. I'm like a consolation prize. A bad one."

He gripped her arms, his eyes fierce. "Don't you ever say that. You are like nothing and no one. And you are the best woman I know, do you hear me?"

She did. And she…she found she really wanted to believe him. Really wanted to believe this. She wanted…she wanted so much to be the best woman. At least right now.

At least for Jake.

"I'm not that great. My mom… It's… I just didn't know." She tried to breathe deep, but it caught in her throat and shuddered. "For our sixteenth birthdays…well, for my brothers' sixteenth birthdays, my dad got them this special hunting knife, and then they'd go away on a hunting trip. Well, you know that my sister… Sophie…she was sickly."

He nodded slowly. "You said she wasn't very strong."

"No, she was born with a genetic heart defect. My mom… she tried so hard to protect her and it didn't work. It didn't…it didn't work, so when I was born, and I was checked over head to toe and proclaimed healthy, my dad wanted me to experience everything. He wanted me outdoors. He wanted me to get tough, to be raised outdoors. To be treated like the boys, and I was." She sighed. "And I thought I was really like them. But when I turned sixteen…my mom gave me a necklace. There was no knife. No hunting trip." She still got angry. Because it was a small thing. Because she could have ignored it. Because it still hurt. "Well, I was… I was so mad. I realized it was fake. I wasn't one of the boys. I wasn't the same. I was an experiment.

Kept outdoors till it was time for me to be domesticated." Her lips twitched. And she didn't go on.

"If they don't see what I do, that's their own problem."

"But it's why," she said. "It's why I have to win. And it feels like the only way to make myself strong enough is to...ignore everything about me that's...female. That it's the only way to become the thing that I have to. But I don't... What if I don't have to become anything? What if I can just be me? And that doesn't mean I don't have to work hard. I know that I do. Because you're right—for all that I'd like to pretend that there's nothing that's going to make being a saddle bronc rider more difficult for me, I know there is. So yeah, of course I have to stay in shape. I get it. But it doesn't have to be all that. And I thought that it did. I thought that I had to be all one thing. And I..."

She put her hand out, touched his chest. Worked her fingers beneath the collar of his shirt. "I just... I know that I can stay on the back of a bucking bronco for eight seconds. And I know that I can complete a great barrel racing run. But I don't know what else I can do. I don't know what else I can feel. I want... I want to feel...more."

He kissed her again, and stole her breath. Kissed her until her knees were weak, until her heart was racing so hard she could scarcely breathe. Kissed her until she was lost to everything that was him. Everything to this.

And then she found herself being gathered up in strong arms and carried down the hallway.

It was an out-of-body experience... When Jake set her down in the center of the bedroom and closed the door behind him.

She *never* felt nervous around Jake. He was her friend. And suddenly the enormity of what was happening threatened to overwhelm her. He was her friend, and changing this, knowing this about him, was going to change that.

But she felt like *she* was changing.

The minute that she had decided to get married in order to

get her trust fund, to achieve her dream no matter what, she had begun to change. It was no longer about making her parents proud, whatever she told herself. Because she was an honest person. Because she did care about doing what was right. The minute she had found something bigger than truth, she had begun her metamorphosis. She had prioritized her dreams. And it was more about that than making her parents proud of her in any way. And this was part and parcel to that. To the...*growing*.

And maybe she and Jake would never be able to be friends in the way they had been after this.

But right then and there, she thought that it might be a reasonable sacrifice.

No. It wasn't even that.

It was just that it was too late. Because she could see now. That he was the epitome of masculine perfection. That all the reasons he was big and hard were the reasons she was smaller and softer. That everything in her responded to that masculinity at his core. That she was created for it.

She had put on blinders, and she had decided not to see it, but it was there all the same. And she couldn't make it... She couldn't make it *not* be.

And she didn't want to. It was like going your whole life not knowing what chocolate was. Hearing that it was a bean and having a vague understanding of what that might be, based on previous experiences with beans.

And then getting served the most beautiful, decadent flourless chocolate torte imaginable.

You could never really just see it as a bean. Not after that. Even though it was true.

Because you'd seen the potential. You'd seen what it meant.

And it was a silly analogy, but it was true. Her best friend was a man, and she'd always *known* that.

But this, right now, was really knowing that *her best friend was a man.*

And that she was a *woman*.

She was going to start crying again, and she hated that. Because she didn't really cry. And it wasn't that she was afraid or sad. It was just that the feeling was so big that it needed somewhere to escape. Or it would overwhelm her. So it started leaking out of her eyes. And she didn't particularly care for that at all.

So she took a deep breath, and she closed the distance between them, kissing him again. And then she took a step back, pushing her fingers beneath the hem of his shirt. He grabbed it from behind his head, finishing the job for her as he jerked it up over his head.

"Holy shit," she said, looking at him.

"What?"

"It's just that you…"

He grinned. The bastard. He smiled at her.

"Is that your way of saying that I'm hot?"

"I… I need to sit down." So she did, on the edge of the bed.

"What's going on, Cal?"

"I don't know how I didn't see you."

Those words, that moment, stretched between them.

"You didn't want to," he said. "That's not a bad thing. You could just only see the thing right in front of you."

"Yeah." She shook her head. "I'm tired of that. I'm tired of squeezing myself down. Squeezing my life down. It stops now. It stops at this." She reached out and put her hand on his stomach. It was rock hard. Ridged with muscle. Rough from the dark hair that dusted him. He was incredible. She wanted… She leaned forward and kissed him. Right there on his abs. She felt his body tense, his muscles jump. She looked up at him from where she sat on the bed, and started to work at his belt.

"Careful," he said, warning in his tone.

But she wanted to know. She really wanted to know. Because she'd spent all this time deliberately not wondering. About men in general, about him specifically. And now she just felt like a deep well of wonderment. And she wanted to reach the bottom. Wanted to find the end of her curiosity, which she didn't think she was even close to at this point.

She undid his belt. His button on his jeans, his zipper. And quickly pushed the denim, and his underwear, down his legs. And there he was, thick and proud and strong, standing out from his body. And she felt like she'd been punched in the solar plexus.

She could only stare at him.

"Callie…"

"You want me," she breathed.

Because she might be a virgin, but she knew that much. She knew about the mechanics of everything. Knew that this meant he was hot for her. The same as she was for him.

She reached out, curving her fingers around him. He was so hot. Soft and strong all at the same time. She moved her fist up and down, stroking him. And he groaned, his head falling back. And something inside of her shifted. Because he was teaching her. She'd asked him to. But it mattered to him. It meant something. He felt something. She was holding him in her hand. The most intimate part of him. And it felt right, because it was Jake. Because Jake had been there for her all this time. Because he was…

Her trust in him was limitless. There was no one else on earth she could've gone to and asked to marry her.

Only him.

So it stood to reason that he was the one to experience this with.

She leaned forward, and before she could lose her nerve, she flicked her tongue out over the head of his arousal. She had heard the girls talking about this. In fact, she'd been scorched in the ears hearing one of the barrel racers talking about getting on her knees in the horse trailer and doing this with one of the champion bull riders from Brazil. She'd said he was worth it. Much more so than the garden-variety American cowboys. But Callie didn't see how anyone could hold a candle to Jake.

His hand was suddenly in her hair, pulling. "You don't have to do that," he said, his voice rough.

"I want to," she said.

And she tasted him again. He was salty, and she liked the smell of him. It was so… Strange to think that. So strange to want it. But she did.

She parted her lips, and took him into her mouth. And she lost herself. And suddenly she was shaking all over. Because she never felt more powerful in all her life. And she wasn't on the back of a bucking bronco. She wasn't proving her strength. She was being intimate with a man. She was letting herself be a woman. And she'd been certain that there was nothing but weakness to be had there. Certain that there was nothing but breakable vulnerability. In failure.

Oh, she'd been sure there would be failure.

But she wasn't failing. Because he was trembling. A man who by his own admission had had a whole hell ton of sex was trembling with her untried mouth on his body.

So she couldn't be bad at it. She had to at least be okay at it. She had to be.

There were so many things tumbling in on her at once. A whole lot of new. And a whole lot of emotion.

And suddenly he was moving her away from him, and she fought to get back.

"No," he said, his voice hard. "Not like this, sweetheart. Not like this."

He sat her back on the bed, pulled her top up over her head and unhooked her bra quickly. His gaze was hungry. And she felt undone. Because again, he was just admiring her, just the way she was. And she didn't have to do anything or be anything or try to win at something. He was just there. Wanting her. Without any clothes to cover her.

He undid her jeans, pulled them down her legs, took her boots along with them. And then they were both naked, and he pushed her back on the mattress. Tangling his limbs with hers. It was like flying. This freedom. Touching him like this, with no barrier between them. It was the thing she hadn't known she wanted. She had cared for Jake for a long time. But this was like a missing piece. And she hadn't meant for it to be. It just was.

He put his hand between her legs, and started to stroke her. Stoking a fire there that made it impossible for her to speak or think. All she could do was gasp with pleasure as he pushed her to the brink over and over again. Then he kissed her neck, her collarbone, down between the center of her breasts. She'd never thought much of her breasts, except that they got in the way, and she had strapped them down really tight with a sports bra to keep from being uncomfortable when she was getting tossed around the back of a horse. But he made her appreciate them. Because they didn't feel uncomfortable or in the way now. They felt worshipped. And they felt pleasure. So much pleasure. As he toyed with her nipples, with his fingers, his tongue, his lips. And she wasn't embarrassed. Not at all.

How could she be?

She had asked this man to marry her. She had yelled at him, kissed him, stamped her foot at him. She had cried in front of him.

She had fallen off the horse and broken her arm in front of him.

What was this but just right next to all those things?

He kissed his way down her stomach. To the tender skin of her inner thigh, and then he put his mouth on her there.

And she ignited. He pushed her, higher and harder than she ever thought she could go. And everything in her was tight, drawn like a bow. Like that moment before the gate opened and she and the horse exploded into the arena. But he kept going. On and on, like she was poised on the edge of a massive explosion, and she couldn't think. Didn't think she could handle it. And then he pushed one finger deep inside of her. And she released.

Her head fell back, and a hoarse cry escaped her lips. He was up her body quickly, catching her cries with his mouth. She rocked against him, and she felt him against the entrance to her body. Hard and heavy. Stretching her.

"Dammit," he said. He moved away from her, and she grabbed at him, trying to bring him back to her. But he was down on the floor, grabbing his wallet off the ground. Taking out a condom and rolling it over his masculine length.

And she was grateful for that.

Because she would've forgotten. She just would've damn well forgotten. But he hadn't. He protected them both, and then he pressed himself to the entrance of her body, his lips against hers. "This might hurt," he said.

"It's okay," she said. Right before he breached her, right before he pushed inside of her. She gasped.

She felt like she was being split in two, but it ended quickly. It was just such a foreign sensation. And he was so big. She arched against him, and he went deeper. And she nearly pushed him away, but he pressed forward, and then it started to feel… Oh, then it started to feel good. Really good. He withdrew slightly, then flexed his hips forward and she groaned, grabbing hold of his shoulders. She rocked against him, chasing his every movement. Luxuriating in his every thrust.

This was something deeper and more connected than riding on the back of a horse, which, until this moment, had been the most spiritual experience of her life. But this was something else. *Jake.*

Above her. In her.

And they moved as one. It wasn't hard. It was perfect. Right and brilliant. And much to her surprise, pleasure began to build inside of her again. Higher and higher. But this time, she didn't fight it. This time, she chased it. She arched her hips in time with his, the friction of him being deep inside ramping up her pleasure. They pushed each other. His forehead pressed against hers, his breath and hers mingling together. And then she broke. Shattered completely in his arms. And she didn't feel weak. She felt strong. And he did the same. Shivering and shaking as he found his release. In her.

With her.

And nothing had ever seemed simpler than it did in that moment.

Man and woman.

Jake and Callie.

Husband and wife.

And she was desperate to keep the moment frozen. Because it wouldn't stay simple. And she knew that. Because she'd made all kinds of bargains with herself before going into this. Because she'd told herself it was okay if things changed. Because she told herself they didn't have to. And right now, she was afraid that if she stepped outside of this room, if she had to separate from him, if they had to get out of this bed and put on clothes, nothing would ever be okay again.

And that was when she realized that all the things she'd yelled at him hadn't really been fair. Because yes, the people in her life often told her what she wanted. And she never thought that any of them were right.

She'd never thought for one moment that Jake might be right.

But lying there in bed with him, with him still buried deep inside of her, she was desperately afraid that he might be.

And that the consequences of this night could destroy her.

CHAPTER FIFTEEN

Jake could hardly catch his breath. He couldn't believe it. Years of restraint, completely undone. He'd... He'd made love with Cal.

Had taken her virginity. Everything he'd ever wanted to not be, he'd become, with her, just then. And he found he had a hard time regretting it. He should. But maybe that was part of that disconnect. Because he'd been with her, and the world had caught on fire. And now he was lying there and she was... Callie. But Callie like he'd never seen her. Warm and rumpled. Her hair was still in a braid. And she was naked.

She had a beautiful body. And everything had gone so fast... Yeah, he'd indulged himself. Tasted her, kissed her. Touched her. And now he was just... Staring. She was his best friend in the whole world. The closest person to him of anyone. Closer than his family. Closer than his brother. This was uncharted territory for him. Being with someone that he knew this well. Being with someone that he felt this kind of way about.

So, he pushed his feelings to the side. Because that at least was something he knew how to do. And he looked at her. At the gentle curves of her body. Her soft skin, with muscle definition just beneath. She was a fine-tuned little package. Feminine and strong all at once. So much more than she let herself be. Than she gave herself credit for.

And if nothing else, he wanted to make it his mission for her to feel all of that. She told him that she felt like she was stuck in a box. Like she was limited.

He didn't want that. She was too incredible to live her life with limits. He'd known that from the first time he'd met her. That she was something else. That she was something special.

He reached out and took the rubber band off the end of her braid, slowly weaving his fingers through her dark hair.

"What are you doing?" she mumbled.

He smiled. She was sleepy. But then, she'd come pretty hard, so he imagined she was halfway to knocked out. Normally, he would be, too. Normally, he would be getting his ass out the door, or sending his partner on her way about now so he could get some sleep. But he couldn't do that with her.

He'd never slept with a woman before. And there were other bedrooms in this house. But he didn't... He couldn't make her go. He wanted to shield her. Protect her.

The strangest surge went through his chest. An expansion that felt like air, but was just her. Her and some emotion he couldn't pin down. Like trying to catch light and put it in a jar so he could examine it.

He didn't want to examine it. He wanted it gone.

He should go. Right now.

But it would hurt her.

And he wanted to keep on touching her.

"I want to see your hair down," he said.

"Why?" She turned over onto her back and started to rub her eyes. But his focus was stolen completely by the sight of her bare breasts. She looked at him, bemused. "What?"

"I can't remember. I'm distracted," he said. "You're hot."

She locked her brows together, her mouth stretched into a flat line. "I am?"

"Callie," he said. "I've wanted you for a long time."

"You've...wanted *me*?" She sounded genuinely confused.

"Yeah," he said. "But I knew there was no point to it. I had to keep my hands to myself. At least, that's what I told myself."

"Why?"

"We've been over this."

"Right. Feelings and sex and friendship, and none of it shall meet."

Which was one reason he was being so careful now. Callie was his friend. Bottom line. This was the only woman he'd ever cared about that he wasn't related to, and that mattered. So this…this couldn't go past tonight. "That's how it has to be."

"Yeah," she said, a slight note of wonder in her voice.

"What are you thinking, sweetheart?"

She frowned. "You never call me that."

"Yeah, don't worry, though. I never ask women what they're thinking, either. So it's not like I'm using a generic line."

It was true. He never asked. Because usually it was just over by now. Orgasms and done. That was what sex was to him. Physical. Not emotional. But Callie was still Callie. She hadn't transformed into a stranger just because she'd taken her clothes off. And it was… It was a hell of a thing. To actually know the woman he was lying beside. To know the woman that he was naked with. And to care. Really, deeply care. That she was taken care of. That she felt good about what had happened. That she felt safe and protected, and confident.

It was a weight, a responsibility, he couldn't carry long term.

"I'm thinking… I don't know how this is my life. I don't know how three weeks ago I asked you to marry me, and now we're married, and in bed together. I don't know a whole lot of anything actually."

"Yeah." He cleared his throat. "Life is weird."

"To say the least."

"You still want the same things, right?"

"Yes," she said. "But I need to figure out what it means to want for me. I've been so… Obsessed with having all this stuff to make my parents understand me, or see that what I do matters. But this wasn't for anyone but me." She put her hand on his chest, her expression adorably filled with awe. "This was just for me." Then she looked up at him again, this time a hint of fear on her face. "Jake, please tell me that we'll be friends after this."

"I told you," he said. "That was my worry."

"I care about you," she said. "About what we have. So much. You're the most important person in my life. You've been there for me... Through everything. And this is another way you've been there for me. I just don't want to lose you because of this."

"I told you. You're not going to lose me. I promised."

"Pinky swear," she said.

A bubble of humor erupted in his chest. He stuck his hand out, and extended his pinky. "Pinky swear."

Her expression was serious, grave, as she locked her pinky with his. Then he wrapped his arm around her and pulled her up against him, crushing her breasts to his chest. "I have never pinky swore a woman anything. Much less naked in bed."

He kissed her then, because how could he not. He'd wanted to kiss her for so long. And he let this be about her. He let it be about teaching her things and taking care of her, and the knowledge that she would go out and find another man if he didn't damn well do the thing. And he couldn't stand that, that much he knew. Seeing her with that guy tonight...

He'd been full of murder. And that was damn telling. Because he told himself all this time it was just that he thought she was sexy, and he thought a lot of women were sexy.

He also didn't care if they kissed other men.

But if Callie—his Callie—had kissed that fool at the bar, he couldn't have been held responsible for what happened to the poor son of a bitch.

"Better cool it," he said. "Two times in one night is not going to work for you."

She frowned. "Don't tell me what I want. You know I don't like it."

"I know you don't," he said, kissing her again. Just for him.

Just because he wanted to. And he enjoyed that kiss. He enjoyed it a hell of a lot.

"Then why are you?"

"Just trust me, Cal."

"So...we get to do it again?"

He hesitated. He was... He needed to get his head on straight because this was something he'd told himself he'd never do.

Ever.

"Don't worry about it. Sleep."

She fitted her body against his, and he held on to her tightly. And a strange sensation bloomed in his chest. But he pushed it away. He focused instead on how soft she was. On the curves of her ass against his dick, because that was something he was familiar with. It might be more intense than what he was typically accustomed to, but he knew sexual arousal. He knew sexual desire. Because it was safer than acknowledging anything else.

Jake wasn't a man given to deep thought, and he wasn't going to start now.

The most important thing was their friendship. In the end, that was the thing that mattered.

He was a man who rode bulls for a living, but the thing about that was, there was a time limit. The time it would end. And that was why the danger was acceptable. Because it was fleeting.

This wasn't any different.

He waited until her breathing was even, and then he pulled himself out of her arms, and put a pair of jeans on. He didn't want to sleep. He'd never slept with another person.

He wandered out into the living room, discomfort settling over his skin.

He'd made love with Callie.

Cal.

Regret rolled over him in a wave. Now that she was sleeping and he had distance from the pleasure, he was clearheaded enough to know it was wrong. That it couldn't happen again.

Because things were too messy between the two of them.

He sat down on the edge of the couch and closed his eyes, doing his best to banish images of what had just happened.

Because if he knew one thing, it was that it couldn't happen again.

And it wasn't because she wouldn't be able to handle it. It was because he couldn't.

When he woke up he was freezing. Lying on his back on the couch with nothing covering him but a pair of jeans. But it wasn't the cold that woke him. It was the pounding on the front door.

He jackknifed into a sitting position and stumbled to the front door, spotting Boone through the window.

Guilt just about sliced him in two, but he opened the door, anyway. "Can I help you?"

"As a matter fact, you can." Boone's eyes glittered with the kind of anticipation he'd seen in the other man's eyes just before igniting some C-4. That…did not bode well. "You're just the man I was hoping to see."

Well, he didn't like that at all.

"Yes?" It was cold outside, but it was either invite Boone in, and potentially wake Callie up—who was naked in his room—or step out into the cold shirtless. He opted for the cold.

He might be married to Callie, but he still felt caught, and he didn't particularly like it.

Because you are caught, you dick.

You slept with her and you never should have. You can't even handle round two, much less anything deeper.

"What the hell is going on with you and my sister?"

And now he felt really caught. Except he was married to Callie as far as Boone was concerned. And they were legally married, anyway.

"I'm her husband."

"Don't give me that shit. What's going on?" Boone looked like he'd have no trouble getting neighborly with violence right at that point. "You never acted interested in her at all. And suddenly you're here and married to her? *You. Married.*"

He rocked back on his heels. "Plus, I saw her down at the Thirsty Mule last night. I saw the both of you. She was chatting up some other guy. And you were pretty pissed off about it, I'll give you that. But if you're married to my sister, why is she chatting up some other guy? Either you're up to something or the little brat is trying to teach you a lesson for some reason. And if my sister is legitimately married to you, and hitting on another guy, you must've done something really stupid. And if you did something really stupid while married to my sister, let's just make it very clear that I am willing and ready to emasculate you."

"Calm the hell down, Boone," he said. "We had a fight, that's all."

"Again, my sister wouldn't be chatting up some other guy unless it was a real serious fight."

The door opened behind him, and Callie, who looked rough after a night of doing… Well, exactly what they'd been doing, stepped out wearing his T-shirt and a pair of sweatpants. Her hair was sticking out in every which angle because he'd taken her braid out, and he knew that they unambiguously looked like they'd been at it.

"What are you doing here, Boone?"

Boone looked at her, then at him. "I want to know what's going on," he said.

"Nothing," Callie said. "I married him."

"I was at the bar. So cut the shit, Callie. Why were you trying to pick up some other guy if you're married to him?"

"You can't tell," Callie said, her expression going fierce. "You should understand, Boone. I need you to understand. You have to. Please. Just don't tell Dad."

Jake groaned. Because this was going to get him killed. She might not be aware of how clear it was that something had happened between them last night, but Boone sure as hell was. And now she was about to admit the marriage wasn't real.

"What?" Boone asked.

"I need my trust fund," Callie said.

"Oh, dammit, Callie, are you serious?"

"I want to ride saddle bronc, Boone. I *need* to. You know that. You know how it is. You know what it's like when it's in your blood. I know you do. And Dad was putting up barriers. Making it so that I couldn't... That I couldn't do it. So I asked Jake to marry me. I asked him to help me out."

"Dad is going to kill you," Boone said. "To say nothing of what he's going to do to *you*." He directed that last part right at Jake.

"Yeah, I figure I'll be back in Gold Valley by then," Jake said. "Though don't think I didn't think about that. But she is my friend. And she asked for help."

"Why couldn't you just talk to them?" he asked his sister.

"He wouldn't listen. I did talk to him. I'm not going to be able to have what I want unless I'm free. I can't be free without that money."

"That's some stunt," he said. "Really."

"Have you ever had to fight Dad to get what you want?"

Boone just looked at her for a long moment. "No."

"Then you can't judge me. Not for this. I'm trusting you, Boone. I'm trusting you to please be on my side."

"I'm on your side," he said. "I am. I promise. And if you want to I can even do better at talking to Dad on your behalf. But you're going to have to be more careful. Because it was obvious to me something wasn't right when I saw you in the bar. And you're really lucky Kit or Jace wasn't there. Or any of the others. Because I don't know that they would land on your side here. They don't particularly want you putting yourself in dan-

ger like that. And I can't say that I do. But I know how important it is to you. And I respect that you're good. That you work
hard to make it as safe as possible.

"Your secret's safe with me," Boone said. "I promise."

She shifted uncomfortably, and he could feel the exact moment she started to feel exposed standing out there in her pa-
jamas.

"I just need… Coffee," she said, turning and going back into
the house.

Boone's eyes locked on him. "I'm not going to embarrass my
sister. I won't. She's one of the most important people in the
world to me. And she hasn't had it easy. But I can tell something is going on between the two of you. Not just because I
saw you grab her and kiss her last night outside the bar. So you
can't pretend that this is just platonic. If you're sleeping with my
sister, I swear to God, you'd better not hurt her."

"I won't." That was a vow. He was going to make this right
with her. He would.

"It wasn't necessary, though, was it? She needed your help,
and now you're…"

Even feeling as pissed as he did at himself, he couldn't let that
go. He'd never, ever taken advantage of Callie, and he never
would.

"Give me more credit than that, Boone. I know we don't
know each other all that well, but you know that I care about
her. Hell, I wouldn't put myself in this position if I didn't. It's
for her. It's not for my benefit. I'm not going to be able to offer
anything beyond this. But this is what she wanted. She needed
someone to marry her, and I stepped up to do it. And I submit-
ted myself to being at this family Christmas nonsense, when I'd
frankly rather stick my dick in an anthill. So, you should know
that whatever I do, she's at the center of it. You can't actually
be a hell of a lot more protective of her than I am."

"I'm her older brother," he said. "I assure you I am more protective of her than you'll ever be. And if my sister cries for any reason at all, I'm going to be there to make sure that whoever caused those tears is punished. Don't be the object of my punishment, Daniels. Because you won't like it."

"Noted. But just so we're clear, your brand of protection doesn't seem to be what she wants. At all. In fact, the whole lot of you seem to be protecting her as long as it's on your terms. You may not like what I'm doing here, but everything I've done, she's asked me to do. Everything I've done, she's wanted."

Boone frowned. "I mean, good. But I don't need to know about the intimate details of your time with my sister."

"No, I don't suppose. Because then you'd have to acknowledge that she's a grown woman and a whole person, not any different than you. She should get what she wants, because she's worked for it. And she should sleep with whoever she wants—God knows why it's me, but it is. I respect that—you should work on that."

"It's not about respect," Boone said, "whether you believe it or not. I lost a sister that I loved very much. She was sick. No one could keep her safe from that. I can keep Callie safe. So I have. If you fail? Well, I wouldn't want to be you."

And just like that, everything was beginning to feel like it might be falling apart. But when he went back in the house and closed the door behind them, Callie was sitting at the dining room table with a cup of coffee, staring straight ahead. And he knew that he couldn't show any of the negative feelings he was having, because she needed to feel comforted right now. And he was going to have to be the one to do it.

"It's fine," he said, sitting at the table across from her.

She looked up at him, her eyes glossy. "Is it?"

"Yes, Callie. It is. Because I've got you. I promise. I do."

She laughed, a watery sound. "You know, I need to talk to my dad. About... The trust fund. I mean, I have to make sure that I get him our marriage license and all of that. And it's uncomfortable, because I don't want to draw attention to things, and now Boone knows and—"

"Boone's not going to make any trouble." He put his hand out and covered hers. "We got this."

"Do we?"

"Yes."

And this, at least, he knew how to do. He knew how to be Callie Carson's friend. So today, that was what he would be. And he would worry about the rest later.

CHAPTER SIXTEEN

Callie knew she needed to talk to her dad. But she felt like a jumbled-up mess. And honestly, if Boone hadn't come busting in this morning, demanding to know what was going on, she would've put this conversation off for longer.

Except… This was the point of the whole exercise. To make sure that she got the trust fund money so that she could compete in the saddle bronc event. To make sure that her future could go ahead exactly the way she wanted it to. It wasn't about this thing happening with Jake, and the fact that sleeping with him had left her raw and uncertain, and that irritated her. Because she couldn't afford to be distracted, least of all by her escape hatch. That's what he was. He was a means to an end. He wasn't the end. He wasn't the thing.

The rodeo was the thing. Her path to showing them that she was talented and special. That she had drive and determination spare few people out there did. And this was what had always worried her. That if she took her eyes off the prize, that if she let herself feel these other things, then she would forget what she really wanted.

And right now, her clear and present vision that she always

had of arena dust and horses was clouded by visions of muscle, memories of pleasure…

She had never fallen asleep in the arms of another person before, and sleeping with him had been… Even pushing the sex part aside, sleeping with him had been something really special. And it was all she could think about now, when what she needed to do was not think about Jake.

She took a deep breath and walked into the den, where she knew she would find her father, seated in his favorite chair. A wingback made out of a cowhide. He had the football game on, unsurprisingly, and was deep in what he called his relaxation mode. Likely, he didn't want to talk about this with her now. But that only made it better. She needed to claim the advantage. And she needed to focus. Not on Jake, but on this.

"Hi, Dad," she said.

"What's up, munchkin?"

"I just… I needed to talk to you."

"Sure. Sit a spell."

He muted the TV, and she took a seat on the couch across from him.

"It's just… I got married."

"Yes, I know. And quickly."

He was eyeing her keenly.

"Don't do that," she said. "I already told you and Mom that I'm not pregnant. I'm not lying. What would the point of that life be?"

"All right," he said. "Then go ahead and tell me what's on your mind."

"The trust fund. It's just… I got married, and you know, a certain amount of time into the marriage, my trust fund opens up to me, right?"

"Yes," he said slowly. "Why are *you* acting like you don't know exactly when it opens up to you."

"I'm not acting like anything."

His lips twitched. "All right."

"Jake's got a ranch, Dad," she said. "And he's getting it off the ground, and I just want to make sure that I can contribute."

"You're BS-ing me, Callie. I'm not a stupid man. And I should have realized. You're…you've been piss, vinegar, hell and high water from the time you were a little girl, and I should have known that would never change." Her dad's eyes were hard, assessing. But not without love. "If you want your money, you'll get your money. At the end of the sixty days."

"Dad…"

"Are you planning on entering the saddle bronc event?"

She looked away. "I'm married now."

"Yes. But what does that have to do with your plans?"

"Nothing. Yes, I'm planning on entering the saddle bronc."

"And is Jake supportive of that?"

"Jake has been teaching me. Jake always was the person who taught me. He's the one who helped me with my barrel racing, and he's the one who's helped me with this."

"There's not much I can do about that. Whether I approve of it or not. He's your husband."

"Yes," she said.

"And I happen to know, probably, a bit too prideful of a man to take any money from his wife. So next time you try to spin me a tale, you might want to make sure it's a little bit believable. If you want your money, you're entitled to it. The rules are the rules. Whether or not you're doing something I want you to do with it or not."

"Dad…"

"It's just worry," he said, his eyes suddenly growing grave. "It's worry that I can't undo, Callie. And I understand you don't think it's fair. I understand that to you this doesn't feel just. But I lost your sister."

Callie's heart thundered in her ears, her breath stalling out.

They talked around this tragedy plenty in their house, but they didn't mention it directly.

Sophie was a ghost that whispered in the halls, not a person to be spoken of in conversation.

But he'd said it. And he kept on going.

"I lost your sister, and I'm not going to get over that. It doesn't matter that it was so long ago, and I think no amount of time will ever heal it. When you know the world can take a child from you, you don't take anything for granted. I lost my little girl once. I can't lose you. I wanted to teach you to be strong but there's a limit. Because I'm not strong. I am not strong enough to lose you. But I can't control you, either. And now... You couldn't have made it clearer that you're a grown woman. I sure as hell can't direct what you decide to do with your grown-up years. But I just want you to be safe. More than you can possibly know, I need you to be safe."

Her heart twisted.

"Dad, I want to be safe. But I don't understand how you can be okay with the boys doing it and not me."

"Because I've never lost one of my sons. I had a little girl, and she was precious to me." Her dad's eyes glistened, the pain in them making Callie feel a deep sense of...of shame. That she knew full well they grieved, but that she didn't respect how sharp it still was. "She was a miracle after all those boys. And we didn't have you to replace her, I hope you realize. We didn't. But after her, you seemed to be a double miracle. Another girl—I was afraid I wouldn't be allowed to keep you, either. And how can I cope with that? How can I cope with it twice? It's impossible. So you just promise me that you'll keep yourself safe. You hear me?"

Her heart felt bruised. She'd felt like her dad was smothering her because he didn't trust her. That he was too hard on her because she was a girl. But it wasn't her. It was life. He was afraid the world would be harder on her, and so he acted accordingly. It wasn't her—it was what might happen to him if he lost her.

And she had a feeling her dad was far closer to the truth of what was happening between her and Jake than she wanted him to be. Although… She wasn't exactly sure what was happening between her and Jake. And she hadn't had the time to reflect on it. But that was the problem with being here. She was either with him or she was with her family. And there was spare little time to sit in her own head and process exactly what had gone on. The only thing for it was to head out to the stables. What she needed was to go for a ride. It was bitterly cold outside— this December weather in Eastern Oregon bitter and biting. But she didn't care.

This was her home. There was clarity out here. She'd spent a lot of her childhood and her adult years on the road, but her family ranch had always been her touchstone. She tried to ground herself on that now.

She went down to the end of the stable, and retrieved her favorite mare. Queens Are Wild was a retired rodeo horse that her parents had had for six years. And she was the one that Callie favored when she came home for a visit. For leisurely rides around the place, rather than for athletic pursuits. She had just gotten Queenie tacked up when she heard the sound of boots behind her. She felt a low growl rise in her throat before she could do anything to stop it.

"Easy there, Cal."

She turned quickly, and saw Jake. And felt herself blush all the way to the roots of her hair. He was wearing clothes now, but it didn't matter. Because she could vividly picture him naked. And she was still sorting through the events of this morning and last night. She didn't think he'd stayed in bed. But she wasn't completely sure. When she'd woken up, he was out on the porch with Boone. But she couldn't say for certain when he left the bed. At around three in the morning she rolled over and found an empty space where she'd expected him to be. But she wondered if he'd gone to the bathroom or something. She'd drifted off before she could verify his whereabouts.

"I thought maybe you were one of my brothers. I am not in the mood."

"I figured I would see about having a ride. Your dad said I could use one of the horses."

"You were talking to my dad?"

"Just briefly. He mentioned you'd been by to chat with him."

"I had to talk to him about the trust fund. He didn't seem that surprised. And honestly, he knows what I want the money for."

"Is he going to keep you from getting it?"

"No," she said. "He said..." Restlessness built up in her chest, frustration. "I can't talk to you right now, because I've seen you naked. And I keep seeing you naked."

He arched a brow. "Excuse me?"

"I really need my friend Jake. I'm going crazy, because I'm stuck here with my family, and I can't get a second to myself. And if I can't get any time to myself, then what I want is time with you. You're the person that I talk to. Well, what the hell am I supposed to do when you're part of the problem?"

"I see. I mean, I told you, Cal. I told you that I was worried about this being a problem."

"Yeah, well. I want you to stand there for a second and be the guy I didn't see naked, okay?"

"I'm not doing anything different one way or the other. The question is if you can stand there and not picture me naked."

"Are *you* picturing me naked?" she asked, her eyes wide.

He laughed, but it wasn't light or easy. The sound was rusty.

"Here's the thing. Let's... Let's tack up and go for a ride. Okay? Because I don't want to stand here and talk about this in a place where your family could walk in at any moment."

"Fair enough."

She waited while he got his horse ready. And then the two of them mounted up and started to head up one of the trails that wound its way into Evergreen Mountain. It was notably greener than all the surrounding landscape. More blue spruce than scrub brush. It was lush even now, here in the dead of winter when everything else was scraggly.

"All right," he said, his voice coming from behind her. "Yeah. I can talk to you. Go ahead."

"He told me that it's not me he doesn't trust. It's the world. He said I'm not the one who isn't strong, it's him." Her voice broke, her heart along with it. "I don't know what to do with that, Jake. I don't know how to live in the shadow of someone who died that I never even met. Everyone in my family was so affected by the loss of her and I don't even know who she was. And sometimes I get angry that she ever existed. Because she's had more to do with my life than I have in some ways. More to do with the way my parents see me. I can't be mad about it. Not really."

"But you are."

"Yes. I am."

"Callie," he said, his voice rough. "Anger is part of grief. You can't escape it."

"But I'm not grieving."

"You're upset about the life you could have had. And that's grieving the loss. Whether it's about your sister specifically or not. It's grief all the same."

"I never thought of it that way."

"Well, I've had a lot of time to think about grief. I get angry sometimes. At my parents. At the pilot of the plane. At my aunt and uncle. God. I get angry as hell all the time. It's just part of living. And that's the thing about grief. It comes for those of us who live on. So… They're not here to see if you get mad. Might as well feel everything that you feel."

"My parents don't deserve it."

"Grieving or not. Your parents have done a pretty decent job of messing you up. And I don't mean that in a cruel way. It's just that's what parents do."

"Yeah," she said, trying to laugh.

She felt safe there, on the back of the horse, in this densely closed-in grove of trees. Felt safe because she couldn't see him. And she could just hear his voice and think of him as Jake, her friend. Not Jake, the man she had kissed and touched and tasted.

Jake, who she had seen naked.

"We have to talk, Cal," he said.

"I don't want to," she said.

"Like you said, I'm the person you talk to. Well, you're the person I talk to. As much as I talk. And I need to make sure I get said what needs saying. We can't do that again."

She could hardly breathe. "What?"

"We can't do it again, Callie. That has to be it."

"Oh." It felt like being punched in the stomach.

A million thoughts ran through her head. That she had messed it up somehow. That she wasn't really this great, feminine goddess like she thought she was when it had been happening.

But he'd…well, he'd seemed to like it a lot.

But maybe that was just how men were. Maybe there was no particular kind of achievement or skill in making a man tremble if you put your mouth on his dick.

Maybe that was just how it was.

And she didn't know enough to know that.

What she hated more than anything was that he'd been right. Because she felt shaken. Undone by what he was saying to her.

Wounded.

And that made it seem like what he'd said about how affected she would be by it was true. That he really had known more about her and her inexperience than she had.

Oh, that made her *furious*.

And at the same time she was… Relieved. Relieved because it was all too much. Because she'd spent half the day thinking

about it and him, and how could she do that if she was still figuring out what she wanted? If she needed him to be her friend,
and she couldn't even have a conversation unless they weren't
looking at each other because she couldn't stop herself from picturing him naked.

He was right. He was. But she was her all the same.

And upset and sad and a million other things that she shouldn't
be.

"Yeah," she said. "Okay."

"You're not upset, are you?"

She'd upgraded from feeling punched to feeling as if she'd
been *shot with an arrow.* But no. Not upset. She couldn't be. And
she would never show him that she was anything but okay. Because she couldn't... Suddenly she felt small and foolish. Because she had tempted him and taunted him, and told him that
he wouldn't be able to resist her. Because she'd laughed and told
him that boys had penises, and claimed all manner of nonchalance when in reality she'd felt *none.*

When she felt younger and softer than she had for a long
damn time.

When she felt silly and undone.

She wanted to slap the girl she'd been just a couple of days
ago. For kissing him out of anger. For treating such a deep, intimate thing like a sporting event she had to learn how to do.

And this was why they couldn't do it again. This was why
he was right.

And this was why it made her feel like a hollow, scraped-out
pumpkin.

"Yeah." She cleared her throat ostentatiously. "Thanks for
teaching me."

"Don't say it like that," he said.

"Why not? That's what it was. A lesson."

And he would always be the first man.

Maybe someday she would think there was something special about that.

That the first man had been her friend. A guy she still had
a relationship with, even. One that she could always have fond
feelings for. That was a gift, wasn't it? One that *later* she would
appreciate. That her first time wouldn't be with someone she
couldn't even bear to think about because he broke her heart,
or something.

She decided then and there, on the back of her horse, that she
didn't have a heart that a man could break. Because she didn't
want forever. And she didn't want a real marriage and children
or anything like that.

So how could it break her heart?

The thing with her and Jake was that their only option was
going deeper into something neither of them would be able to
take all the way. And that's really where someone could get hurt.
She didn't want that. She wanted it to be good. Always. So that
was what it had to be.

"Now we just have to get through the rest of Christmas,"
she said.

"Yeah," he said, chuckling. "Christmas."

"You really don't like Christmas."

"Christmas got increasingly tense with my family. And that
last one…my parents were in a bad space and my aunt and uncle
were planning this Alaska trip for all of them to go on. They
couldn't even be in the same room together. Except when we'd
have the whole family over and then it was all these bright, tense
smiles I thought would break their faces."

"Oh."

"Yeah. And then…they fought about the trip and my mom
wasn't going to go, and then she decided to, and I… Well, it
looked like things would be okay. I remember feeling this incredible sense of hope. Like it would…all be okay. And then it
wasn't."

His voice was hollow and so were his eyes. And she could see it, right there, the death of hope. That moment it had all gone out for him.

"And you know that it was terrible that they died," he said. "But...after. In my dad's things I found a plane ticket. Just one. Los Angeles. One way."

"Oh... Jake..."

"I don't know if he would have gone. If he was saying good-bye to my mom by going on the Alaska trip with her. If he'd changed his mind and decided not to leave us, after all. If he was really leaving us. All I know is I thought everything was finally going to be good. But not only...not only was it not okay, it never was."

"Jake, I don't even know what to say."

"So yeah," he said. "I don't like Christmas."

"I'm sorry," she said. "I'm sorry that because of me you have to have two."

"Hey," he said. "It's worth it. I promise."

Really. Was it worth it? The two of them treading around the weird, broken territory of their friendship thanks to all this. Thanks to the way she'd... Used him. She had trusted him so much. Except... It wasn't even that.

What she had done was give herself complete and total tunnel vision when it came to what she wanted. And she'd been so sure that he could help her. That he *would* help her, that she hadn't even thought about what all this meant for him. She hadn't given any thought to the potential issues he might have with Christmas.

Hadn't considered him at all when she'd made her move on him. She felt so misunderstood by her family. She was so wrapped up in this idea that she was fighting against something, fighting for the greater power of getting what she really wanted, that she hadn't realized how... How little she thought of Jake's feelings. She claimed he was her best friend.

"I'm a bad friend," she said.

"What?"

"I haven't considered how this affected you enough. I thought about me and what I wanted. And I didn't ever think that this time of year might be hard for you. I didn't think about the way that it might change things for you if I kissed you."

"Don't worry about it," he said, his voice rough. "I already told you. Sex isn't a big deal for me."

"You didn't stay in the bed, though, did you?"

"I don't sleep with women."

The way he said that. The way he closed the door on the conversation, it stung. And she wished… Right then, she wished things could be different. But she couldn't go back and remake his life, any more than she could go back and remake herself. They just were the kind of people that were going to have something else. They were the kind of people who were never going to have conventional, or normal. Those weren't her dreams. And his pain… It had been cemented inside of him a long time ago.

"Someday, you have to let me do something for you," she said.

"What does that mean?"

"Well, you're doing this for me. You've done a lot for me." She looked around at all the trees. "I let you be my mentor. And that's how our friendship has gone. But it shouldn't be that way. I can't just take from you."

"Callie, I care about you almost more than anyone in the world. I don't care about a hell of a lot. So for someone like me, that's a gift. Remember that."

She nodded, swallowed hard.

"Tomorrow's Christmas Eve," she said. "You're almost liberated from this."

"Yeah," he said.

"And then we just have to stay married another month. And it will be over. Like it didn't happen." She laughed. "Except…" But she wasn't going to say anything about sex. Her being a virgin, or anything like that. "Except I'll be rich. And I can do whatever I want."

"Yeah. But hey, holiday or not, I say tomorrow we have you go for a bronc ride."

"Here?"

"Yeah," he said. "Here. Because I want your dad to see it. I want him to know how good you are. And we need to keep that end of the bargain up."

"I just told you, you need to quit doing me favors."

"I don't need you doing me favors. I'm the one that said I wanted to train you. Because I want to make sure you're safe."

"Yeah." And she understood, in a new way, how he felt like he needed to keep her safe. How this man who said he didn't believe in much of anything struggled with whether or not anything was truly good.

Jake had given her so much, and he had no hope. He didn't believe things would be okay. And that felt wrong. She wanted to fix it. To give him more.

That was another thing about them sleeping together. He felt like destiny in a way she could hardly explain now. In a way she didn't want them to be. And right now she felt closer to him and farther away from him than she ever had. Because now, she wanted something from him that she didn't think she could ask him for. Because now, she was just so sorry about her own behavior. And she didn't...

Maybe this was growing up. And the very idea made her frown deeply. Because she had felt grown up. She was twenty-four, after all. But over the past few weeks, she had come to know Jake in a way that she hadn't before. She'd met his family. She'd gotten an inside look at his pain.

And her father's.

She had come to understand people in a different way than she ever had before. And it was harder and harder to keep her focus narrowed on her goals in the rodeo. Not that they didn't matter. But they felt a little bit less like life and death. And she felt like a little bit more than a cowgirl. She didn't know why that felt sad. Somehow more dangerous than riding bucking broncos ever could.

"Are you ready to head back?"

"Yeah," she said. "I'm ready."

CHAPTER SEVENTEEN

It had to be done. He'd had to put an end to the thing between him and Callie, but it had been difficult when they'd gone back to the cabin that night. He'd gone straight to his room and shut the door, locked it for good measure. Not against her, but against him. And now it was Christmas Eve, and he had it on good authority that they would be spending the day on various family pursuits. And Jake had decided it was time for Callie's family to see her ride. She had fallen at his place, but she hadn't fallen badly. She did know what she was doing. And maybe this was more for him than it was for her. To prove to himself that she could be safe, because since he'd given her the path to doing this, he had to make sure she could do it safely.

He didn't know why the hell he'd told her about the plane ticket. Nobody knew about that. Not even his brother. What had been the point of sharing that? That their dad wasn't who they thought?

Colt had his own guilt and issues surrounding the situation and Jake hadn't wanted to make it worse.

But he'd done the right thing, pulling away from her. There

was nothing else to do. He could give her this, though. He could give her this.

She emerged from her room, looking freshly scrubbed and young, a long-sleeved white top and tight jeans her uniform for the ride.

A kick of lust burned through him.

He still wanted her. He thought back to what she said to him yesterday. About how she couldn't unsee him naked. He was familiar with the problem. Because every time he looked at her, he saw those gorgeous breasts, totally bare. Her pink nipples. Before, that had been theoretical. The color of her nipples. Now it was a reality, and it was one that he couldn't stop imagining.

"You ready?"

"I was born ready," she said, taking her black hat off the peg and pushing it down hard on her head. He fought the urge to tug on one of her braids. He couldn't just touch her like that. Not anymore. Not for a while. Because he lost all the control that he had around her. And he might be able to talk some kind of big game and say that they were done, but his body was having a tough time recognizing it.

It was time for them to see what she was made of.

"I'm more than ready. It's everybody else that seems to be worried about it."

He chuckled. "True enough."

He had the horse in the chute ready to go. And his cowgirl was ready to ride. And he couldn't... He wanted to do something. Wanted to touch her. Squeeze her, kiss her before she got on the back of the horse, and he couldn't. Because it just wasn't what was happening now. Wasn't what could happen. Though her brother Kit was already out there, his boot resting on the bottom of the fence. So he probably should give her a kiss. He leaned in, and dropped one on her cheek, and her skin turned scarlet.

"You should try to look more used to that," he said, looking over at Kit, who had been joined by her dad. Just like he figured.

"I'm not used to it, though," she said. She looked away, and he felt a heap of regret about being the one to hurt her.

That's how it is. That's how it is for you.

He pushed that to the side, because it wasn't time for him to get all sorry for himself when Callie was about to get on the back of a horse.

"All right, princess. Show them what you're made of."

Callie climbed up the side of the chute, and dropped on the horse. He began to jump, to kick back against the metal railings. And she looked up at him, her expression determined.

This girl.

She was far too stubborn by half, and too full of piss and vinegar for her own good.

And he... He could only respect her. Stand in awe of her.

"You make sure to man the stopwatch," she said.

"I will. I'm not going to let you get shorted on your ride."

"Good. When you're ready."

He could see that she was ready. Her arm was poised, her body falling right into position. She'd punished herself, and she'd worked harder than any one person should. But he could see that it was worth it. That this place she'd gotten herself to made it worth it.

It humbled him. Because he'd never worked so hard for anything in all his life. Never. He decided to jump on the back of a bull, and the rest was history. No one had stood against him. No one had tried to stop him. Muscle built easily for him, and the strength that it took to stay on the back of the animal was easy. He looked the part, so everyone assumed he had it.

Callie...

She had to work so hard just to get here. She married him just to get here.

"Go," he said. He pushed the button, just as he let the chute fly, and the horse went sailing out the front.

He was a spinner, moving in circles in one spot, around and around and around. And Callie was leaned as far back as she could go, her arm working in time with the up and down of the animal. Her entire family was out there now, standing against the fence.

Her mother had her eyes covered, and that was all that Jake could take in, because he had to put his eyes back on Callie. Eight seconds. It was all she needed. But eight seconds felt like forever in a moment like this.

And then the clock rolled over.

"You did it," he said.

Callie shifted on the saddle, and timed her dismount, hopping down off the animal. And then he ran forward, urging him back into the enclosure. Her brothers were already there, ready to get him out of his gear. And everyone was hollering.

"That was amazing," Boone said, hopping the fence and clapping around the back. "A good ride, Callie."

"Incredible," Kit said.

"You about gave me a heart attack," said her father, taking a step forward and grabbing both of her shoulders. "But you're damn good."

"Thank you," she said, her cheeks coloring.

"I'll try to be stronger," he said. "Okay?"

"Don't worry about me. I'm strong."

"I've always known that."

Callie walked to where her mother was, her expression guarded.

"I might not understand why you love it," her mom said. "But I can see that you do. And I can see that you're good at it. Callie, I... I don't want to have distance between us. I don't want to fight."

Her mom wrapped her arms around Callie, who stood stiff

for a moment, before curving one arm around her and patting her on the back. "It's okay, Mom."

And it made Jake's chest go tight. All of it. Because this was the kind of family togetherness, the kind of parental...stuff, that he just didn't quite know what to do with. And it wasn't his to witness. Wasn't his to be a part of. He'd taken that. He'd taken it from everybody in his family, and he...

He shoved all that to the side. None of this was about him. And he was doing a pretty champion job of making it about him.

"Were going out to dinner tonight," her dad said. "Why don't we head over to the house until then?"

"I'll need to change for dinner," Jake answered. And not only that, he needed just... A little bit of time. A little bit of time to himself. Hell, he'd done his part, of all this. And that made him feel good. He had gotten Callie what she needed, and on top of all that, it seemed like she might even be able to find some kind of acceptance with her parents. But there was no place for him in the middle of it. He had just been a catalyst. That was all.

He turned and started to walk back toward the cabin, and Callie shouted from behind him. "Wait," she said.

Her smile was wide, her cheeks red. Her hat had fallen off her head, and was hanging down her back. Her braids were loose and flying away. "Where you going?"

"I'm heading out," he said. "Your parents said that there is dinner tonight. So I ought to get looking good, don't you think?"

"You look plenty good to me."

He looked down at his blue jeans. "Where do you usually go out for Christmas Eve?"

"All right. It's fancy a lot of the time." She waved a hand. "I just usually wear a pair of black jeans."

"Well, I should at least go get some of those, then."

"All right. I'll see you later."

Everyone was watching, but he couldn't bring himself to kiss her. Just for some reason, it didn't feel right. The game was almost over. After Christmas, they would go home and finish this out on the legal end, and then Callie would be free. Though he had a suspicion that after this, she might already be. But she wasn't taking anything for granted, so neither was he.

At least it was almost over.

He just had to complete the ride. That was all.

Callie's brothers practically carried her back to the house and foisted beers on her. They were laughing, treating her like one of them, and it was... Everything she'd ever wanted.

They'd never seen her ride a bucking bronco before. She'd shocked them. Impressed them. And she was elated.

They weren't acting like she was a kid. They were acting like she was an honest-to-God rodeo queen. Oh, not the kind with sparkles and sequins or anything like that. Just the queen of a real rodeo event.

Exactly like she'd always wanted.

But she wished that Jake were here. And it made her chest sore that he wasn't. He had said that he just needed to go back and change, but he hadn't reappeared. And his extended absence made her think that there was something else going on. But she didn't feel like she could leave her family to go after him. Not when they were finally... She was finally getting what she wanted. And all of this, the whole thing with Jake, was about her family. Except sometimes it started to feel like it was more and more about him.

She was just getting all mixed up again.

"Are you going to wear that out tonight?" her mom asked.

She didn't look as disapproving as she often did, but it was definitely a question tinged with a little bit of concern. And her mother had said she was proud of her, and that she thought she'd done a good job. And maybe...

Maybe it wouldn't be the worst thing in the world if she gave her mom a little something. If she... Dropped her guard a little.

"No." She hesitated. "Actually, can you help me find something to wear?"

Her mom's eyes widened. "Of course I could. I just... You don't normally ask me for help with that."

"I know. But I might want to wear a dress."

And if part of her wondered what Jake might think if he saw her in a dress...well.

But she'd slept with him.

And he'd seen her naked.

And he made her feel more like a woman than anyone or anything else ever had.

Proving to her family that she could ride saddle bronc, actually having them be impressed with her, rather than worried or doubtful... All of it was coming together and making her feel like she didn't have to hold on to these things quite so tightly. Like maybe she could wear a dress tonight. And put on jeans tomorrow. That actually letting her mom dress her up wouldn't signal to the other woman that what she wanted was to assimilate, but just that she wanted to try that, too.

Because she was the same woman who wanted to ride horses as she'd been before she became the woman who had touched Jake Daniels's body. She was the same woman as the one who had kissed him in a fury, right after she had been killing herself doing burpees. Sweaty and gross and not at all someone he should find attractive or compelling.

She was all those things. So she could be this, too. Or she could try at least. She never had before.

"I have just the thing," her mom said. She took her hand, and led her to the polished oak staircase. The rich red carpet depressed beneath their footsteps as they went down the hall, toward her parents' bedroom.

Her mom had a massive walk-in closet, but Callie had never

looked inside. It was full to the brim of clothes. And her mom went unerringly to the back, and found a crimson-colored dress. With the V-neck, and a close-fitted skirt that flared out at the bottom. It looked like it would land just below her knees.

"Oh," Callie said. "I've never worn anything… I haven't worn a dress since you put one on me for Easter Sunday when I was ten. And I tore the crinoline and you never made me wear another one."

They didn't talk at all about the necklace that she'd bought her for her sixteenth birthday. The one that Callie had never worn.

The one she had traded at a pawnshop for a pocketknife.

Where is the necklace I bought you for your birthday?

I… I lost it.

Callie Patrice. Where is it?

That fight, when the truth had come out, was when she'd decided to quit trying. She'd hurt her mother, horribly, and she hadn't meant to.

You don't care about me at all! And you don't know me. I wish you'd just stop. I don't even like being around you. I just like being with dad—at least he listens to me!

But her mother had hurt her. She'd disregarded who Callie was. She'd made it about what she'd hoped Callie might be. The memory of a child who'd died superimposed over the reality of the child she'd had instead.

It was the first and last time they'd let those resentments out into the open.

And that had been when Callie had met Jake. Jake, who had accepted her just as she was in fostering her interest in barrel racing. In the rodeo and in horses.

Jake, who she was beginning to see wove into different areas of her life in deeper, more meaningful ways than she had previously realized.

He was her friend. That was how she thought of him. Her best friend.

But that wasn't all. It wasn't.

It wasn't that simple. Wasn't that shallow. He was like a part of her.

Standing there, that realization washing over her as she stared at the dress, she found it difficult to move.

"Try it on," her mom said.

Callie closed the door on the closet, and stripped off quickly. Then she eyed the dress with suspicion before undoing the zipper in the back and tugging it on over her hips. She zipped it, doing a bit of a contortionist act to do so, but the back was a V, as well, so it didn't go up very high. And she felt exposed. Her whole chest felt exposed. When she looked down, she saw cleavage, which was not anything she ever tried to foster.

"I can't wear this," she said, opening the door.

Her mom's mouth dropped open. "Callie," she said. "You look beautiful."

"I look naked," Callie said, stepping out cautiously.

She never wore things so tight. This clung to every inch of her body, and the fabric felt so *thin*.

"What's the point of being in such great shape if you don't show it off?" her mom asked.

Callie looked down at her body, then into the mirror. Trying to see what her mom had just said. Until Jake, her body had been utilitarian for her.

A pocketknife, not a necklace.

Something to use, not something to look at.

She frowned. "To ride horses. My muscles serve a purpose. It's not to look good in a dress."

"But the side effect is that you look very good in this dress," her mom said.

She pushed Callie over to the full-length mirror, and held her there. "Look at you."

Her stomach rolled over. She looked… Like a woman. Like a very pretty woman actually. It made her whole body look different. Not strong so much as soft. She noticed a different shape to her legs than she ever normally did. Noticed an extra curve to her butt that she certainly hadn't noticed before. She wondered if Jake would notice.

"That husband of yours is going to like this dress," her mom said, as if she could read her mind.

"Mom," she said, her face getting hot.

"You want him to like the way you look, don't you?"

"I haven't had any complaints," she said, mumbling.

"That Jake is a stunningly handsome man. It wouldn't hurt you to gussy up for him sometimes."

As she said that, her mom removed the two rubber bands out of the ends of her braids and loosened her hair. Callie dodged and moved away, but her mom followed, still fussing with her hair. "Makeup next."

"Makeup?"

But it wasn't a discussion. Callie was attacked with cream and blush and something shimmery on her cheeks. Followed by a crimson lipstick. "You look fantastic," her mom said. She was beaming. "And you made me so happy."

"Well, I'm glad I could make you happy," she muttered. She looked in the mirror, and the person she saw there was a stranger. Her cheeks looked hollow, her cheekbones sharp. And the emphasis on her mouth felt obscene, especially when she thought of...

The way she had put it on Jake just a few days ago. And she did not want to be having those thoughts in front of her mom.

"Can I... Can I borrow a necklace?" Callie asked, looking at the bare expanse of skin displayed by the neckline of the dress.

Tears pooled in her mom's eyes. "I... Yes, Callie."

Callie blinked and reached out, awkwardly wrapping her arm around her mom's shoulders.

Her mom disappeared, then reappeared with a delicate white-gold necklace that looked like icicles. They cascaded down over her cleavage and made her shiver.

Especially when she thought of Jake seeing her.

He didn't want anything to happen between them? Well. Well, now he'd have to resist her.

So there.

"He's going to love it," she said. She squeezed Callie's shoulders. "Thank you. I'm sorry. I'm just... I'm sorry. I know we haven't been close, and I know it's my fault."

That shocked Callie.

"It's *not* all your fault," Callie said. "I... I let some things hurt my feelings a long time ago. And I decided that it all meant something really specific. It's nothing you told me. Nothing Dad told me. It just is. I decided that if I couldn't compete with Sophie's memory I would... Well, that I would just be one of the boys. Because you love them. And..."

"We love you," her mom said. "We love you just the way you are. Anything that seemed different... I'm sorry. I'm not perfect. And I didn't mean to put all of that onto you. But I did grieve your sister. I do. So much."

"Mom..."

"I'm so sorry. I know that I made mistakes with you. I know that I wasn't healed and I know that I had issues that I needed to sort out. I know that. I am so... So sorry that I didn't do it better. That I made you think you had to be some kind of substitute for my loss, because of course you didn't. Of course you didn't, Callie. I'm sorry I didn't do a better job of understanding you."

She wiped at a tear on her cheek before she continued. "Yes, I wanted this. I dreamed about this when I wanted to have a daughter. But I didn't do a good enough job loving the daughter I had. The way that you could understand it. I've always been proud of you. And I've always thought you were wonderful. But it was easier for me to vocalize disappointments that I had about certain things than it was to tell you about that, and that is my fault. That's my fault the way that I did that. It shouldn't have been that way."

"I'm sorry. I... I should've said something sooner. Because it isn't just you—I shut down. You didn't give me what I wanted, and so I just put my head down and never talked to you."

"I'm your mother, Callie. You don't owe me an apology for not being able to figure out how to put up with me. I'm the one that should've realized. Should've realized that something was just not working in our relationship, and rather than wishing that we could go shopping together, I should've sat down with you and talked about horses."

Callie wiped at a tear on her cheek. "I've realized that knowing you and Dad were hurt, were grieving, wasn't the same as understanding. That I really was only seeing this from my own perspective. And I... You know, being with Jake...being with someone like that, I realized how much I don't consider other people. I needed to tell you what I wanted. And I shouldn't have taken a necklace as an insult, when it was a gift. I chose to see everything as an attack and I never chose to see it as a bridge. But I want to...find a bridge. I want to understand, and I want you to understand me."

"I do, too," her mom whispered.

"Next year," Callie said. "Next year, you and I will go shooting. And will make cookies on another day. We'll do both."

"Okay," her mom said.

"I'm not so afraid of trying to do both. I was. I thought doing all those feminine things would just show all the ways that I didn't quite measure up. And I thought it would distract from what I was trying to accomplish in the rodeo."

"What changed things?"

Callie shifted uncomfortably, because the honest truth was an embarrassing one.

"Jake," she whispered. "He makes me realize that I can be more than I thought."

Her mom's eyes glistened with tears. "I'm glad. That's how it should be. That's how being in love should be."

The words hit her like an explosion, and she took a step back. It couldn't be that. It couldn't be.

It was just... Friendship. And sex.

"Yeah."

Her mom reached into the closet one more time and pulled out a white fur wrap, which she placed over her shoulders. "This makes it. Oh, and shoes."

She grabbed a pair of black high heels and handed them to Callie.

"I don't know how to walk in these."

Her mom smiled. "Okay. Compromise."

She brought a pair of black flats this time, and Callie put them on. She wasn't going to try to be that daring. Not all at once. The high heels might've looked nice, but she would've fallen off them in the first couple of minutes.

Her mom led her out of the room, and she walked down the stairs slowly. And as she descended, Jake came into view. He was dressed in all black. Black cowboy hat. Black button-up shirt and black jeans. Black boots. Her heart sped up. She saw that his jaw went tight as he looked at her. And a thrill shot right between her legs. Except there wasn't supposed to be any of this left between them. Except they weren't going to do this again.

She got to the bottom step, and he extended his hand. Reflexively, she put hers out, and he took it. Lifted it to his lips and brushed her knuckles with his lips.

Her heart slammed against her chest. His dark eyes made contact with hers, and she forgot to breathe. With the stubble over his jaw, he looked like an outlaw. And she wanted to get on the back of his horse and ride off into the sunset with him. Disreputable as he looked. Disreputable as he was. Jake her lover, and Jake her friend, didn't seem like the thing she could separate out in that moment. They were all Jake. And he was all beautiful. And she didn't quite know how to breathe around that.

"You look amazing," he said.

"So do you."

If he was lying, maybe he would think she was, too. That she was just playing a part for this. For everything. Maybe he wouldn't know that she was actually, completely, struck dumb by his beauty. Yeah, beauty. Masculine though it was.

"You can follow us out to the restaurant," her dad said. "We'll have to make a convoy. There's too many of us."

Everyone was dressed up, but she couldn't see anyone but Jake. And as they filed out into the pickup trucks, she knew a slight moment of fear when the door closed and left the two of them alone. Because whereas that night when they'd kissed, when they'd decided to make love, and she'd felt free by those endless possibilities, tonight she felt frightened of being alone with him. Because she knew what was possible.

And she knew that he'd said they couldn't do it again. But she didn't know how.

Didn't know how to not do it. To not *want* it. To not *need* it and him.

She didn't know how to keep to the bargain that they'd made to preserve their friendship at all costs. The one that she'd agreed to. Because she'd decided that she was insufficient when it came to sex, and that was why he'd said no, but somehow she was sure now that that wasn't it. That there were other reasons. And other reasons for her, as well, and it was why she let it go so easy. Because they were both running. From what it was, from what it meant.

And here they were again. And the sparks were going off between them like an electric thunderclap, and still, she wasn't supposed to reach out and touch him.

But she didn't jump on him when the doors to the truck closed, and when they started onto the highway after her parents he didn't reach over and touch her, either. She was a little bit disappointed. She had hoped that the thing that was overtaking her might be taking him over, too. That they might be in this together. And it wasn't just her. That was the really scary thing. Not the need to show restraint when she wasn't sure she could, but that she might be in this alone. That maybe he wasn't all that tempted by her, after all. Except she'd seen something in his eyes when she'd come down the stairs that made her feel like he had to be. Like it couldn't just be her. It had to be the two of them.

"Jake," she said softly as the town came into view.

The hotel was at the end of Main Street, all lit up. Two stories high with wooden balconies and a rustic dining area. But she didn't care much about that now.

"Don't," he said, his voice rough. "Don't make this difficult."

She made a huffing sound. "I'm not making anything difficult."

"You wore that dress," he rasped. "You were going for difficult."

"No," she said. "I was trying to patch things up with my mother actually. It didn't have anything to do with you. Though nice to know that your ego is so healthy you figured I couldn't put on a dress if it wasn't to make things hard for you."

"That's not what I meant."

She sniffed. "I think it is."

"Well, think what you want," he said. "I'm not in charge of that."

"You're not in charge of me at all," she said.

But the conversation ended, because her parents parked in front of the building, and Jake parked in the space alongside them. And then they had no choice but to get out, and not linger awkwardly in the truck and create speculation.

So he put his hand on her lower back, and she squirmed

against the heat of his touch as they walked inside the old building.

"My dad reserves the private dining room every year," she said.

"Nice tradition," he said, but he wasn't looking at her. He was still touching her, though, and she couldn't stop fixating on that point of contact against her back.

The fabric of the dress was just so thin. And the nature of the dress was really quite revealing. If he wanted to, he could take her back to the truck. Push the dress up past her hips. And the things that he would be able to do to her...

This was why people were crazy. She hadn't realized it before. Sex made you nuts.

It really took all of your good intentions and reasonable instincts and twisted them. Because for a long time, she'd had very simple thoughts. She'd wanted very simple things. And now she felt like everything had been splintered. Like she had seen her future clearly through a glass windowpane, and someone had taken a hammer and splintered it so that there were fractals of glass, confusing and complex. They fit together—she could see through them. But there were so many different angles, so many different ways something could be.

Wanting him was like that. Filled with absurd angles.

Because she didn't know what she wanted it to become. Didn't have any guess as to where it might take them, but she wanted him all the same. It wasn't like wanting to ride saddle bronc. Wasn't like wanting to get her trust fund. Those things had a clear, straight path. An easy end point. And she could see why she'd kept her focus on things like that for as long as she had. Men and sex and dresses were something she'd written off as stupid, because the reality was men and sex and dresses were complicated. Painful and just a hell of a lot more confusing than she'd ever given them credit for being.

The hostess was dressed in a dark green vest and white shirt with black slacks. An old-fashioned, Wild West look that went with the rest of the place. It hearkened back to another era. When this had been a gold rush town, and the people in it pioneers.

A hotel like this had only been reserved for the wealthiest, most successful members of the town, and those passing through. The lights were still primarily red lanterns, the seats covered in velvet, the tables polished.

And she knew that dinner would be just as elegant as the rest of the place, and for some reason right now she resented it.

Not for some reason. She knew why.

The reason was seated at her right hand. The reason was this man who was making it all feel high stakes when it should just feel like a regular family dinner. And instead, it felt like a date or something. With her friend that she was married to, and her entire family sitting there watching. Her dad had placed the order ahead of time, and when they sat, food began coming out. Braised short ribs and potatoes. Roasted carrots and fresh rolls. And her dad got good whiskey, and poured a measure of it for everyone.

"A toast," he said. "To Callie, and to Jake. May they be happy. And may they go the distance, because I would hate to kill Jake."

Her brothers laughed and knocked back their shots, and Jake did it, too. Callie went quickly, to avoid looking like she was hesitating.

Her mother did not take a shot. But that didn't have anything to do with not joining in the toast, and everything to do with the fact that her mother didn't like whiskey.

They dug into dinner, and chatter was happening easily all around her, but she couldn't stop focusing on the way that it felt to be this close to Jake. Everything seemed to shrink down to that. To him.

But the food was amazing, and she did her best to keep her mind on that. Dinner was followed by a big marionberry strudel and homemade ice cream, along with port, though Callie opted for coffee, because after the whiskey she didn't need to go layering more alcohol over top of it. She was already feeling shaky and vulnerable, and she didn't need anything contributing to that feeling.

Then music started to come from the other room. The sound of live fiddles and stomping feet.

"It's a line dance," her dad said. "We should go join in."

"I can't move," Jace said. "I ate too much. Go on, you ought to get my sister to dance with you."

That was when she realized Jace was talking to Jake.

"I don't dance," she said.

"It's just a line dance," Boone said.

And then Jake was standing beside her, reaching his hand out, just as he'd done at the bottom of the stairs. And she found herself reaching toward him. Like she was being drawn to him by a magnet. Like she couldn't do anything to resist.

She didn't dance. But she didn't wear dresses. And she didn't kiss men. And she certainly didn't go to bed with them. But she had done all that in the past few days. So really, refusing to dance was a little bit absurd.

He drew her from the room, and her mother and father followed, along with a couple of her brothers. The rest of her brothers were already digging out another bottle of whiskey.

They went into the room where there was a lively line dance taking place, and she was somehow hurried over to the side that the women were on, with Jake standing across from her. She did her best to follow along, and she was grateful yet again that she wasn't wearing high heels, because she was already tripping over her feet, and if she'd had to add that to the whole pursuit it would've been a disaster.

She clapped and spun and twirled. And at one point linked arms with Jake, then got handed off to Kit, followed by her father.

When she went back to Jake, her stomach swooped.

She felt dizzy, and it was fun. And she just felt... Free. Out laughing with her family, not trying to play a part. Wearing a dress, but somehow still being herself.

Then the fiddles changed, and a mournful song began. Couples paired off. Kit spotted a pretty girl across the room and went toward her. Boone went back to the dining room. Her parents grabbed hold of each other, and she knew that was her cue to take hold of Jake. But she was frozen.

Jake reached out, took her hand in his and drew her toward him. He laced his fingers through hers, his other hand low on her back.

"I don't dance," she repeated.

"I don't, either. But here we are."

"Why don't you dance? You go out and things like that."

"Sure. But dancing always seemed to me like a poor substitute for the thing you actually wanted to be doing."

She knew what he meant. Before this, she might not have. But she did now. And it brought back visions of their night together. Intense and hot and raw. The sense that she had really seen him for the first time. Not just the facade of a person that he put on display.

She swallowed hard.

"Right."

Except he was dancing with her. Of course, her parents were right there. And if they weren't, he wouldn't be. Oh, that hurt. It hurt so much worse than she wished it did. Hurt so much worse than she wanted it to. She wanted to pretend that all this was fine.

"Well, I don't dance because I've never seen the need to. And I certainly never wanted to do it enough to make a fool of myself."

"You're not making a fool of yourself."

"Am I not? I feel a little bit foolish. Wearing this dress. This dress that you just think of as kind of difficult."

His hand moved over her back, and she felt the heat of it seep through the fabric. It made her want to cry.

"Did I say difficult?"

"You did," she said, her heart fluttering.

"Maybe I meant dangerous."

"How could my dress be dangerous?"

"I think you know the answer to that."

Her stomach clenched tight. "You know what, I haven't worn a dress since I was a child. So I really don't know. That's the problem, Jake, I don't know." She felt like she was begging, felt like she was going crazy. And maybe she was. She had never felt this way before. It had never been like this. She had never been like this. And she had never felt so simultaneously close to her friend and far from him all at once. She wanted to open up the shirt he was wearing and curl up against his skin. She wanted to be closer. She needed to be closer. This man.

He did things to her. He made her feel things. He made her want to do things.

She wasn't squeamish. Not at all. Her lack of experience with sex had everything to do with the fact that she hadn't actually met someone she wanted to do anything with. It didn't have anything to do with it disgusting her. She hadn't spent a lot of time thinking about it, but once she had gotten down to it, with him, she found that there were very few things that she was averse to. But it was beyond that. She wanted to do things with him. Anything. Anything to chase that high that he'd made her feel. Anything to feel closer. To be closer.

"You know," he said. "That's the problem. You know it all too well. You know that you got me over a barrel, darlin', I really think you do."

"What does it mean, though? Because you said that we couldn't. Not anymore."

"We shouldn't."

"I love it when your hands are on me," she said.

And his face turned to granite. No one could hear them. They were close to each other, their mouths a whisper away. And the music was wrapping them up in a sensual rhythm. Carrying them, carrying her, to a place that she didn't think she was going to be able to come back from. Except maybe it wasn't the music. Maybe it was just them. Maybe it was her. She'd put her foot on this path some time ago. Either when she kissed him out at his place, or even when she'd gone to ask him to be her husband. And it was carrying them here. Inevitable as it was anything else. Like the passage of time, or the air they breathed. The way that their hearts beat. Maybe there had never been any getting away from this. Maybe this was always where it was going to go.

And she couldn't see farther down the road. Couldn't see where it would carry them. Couldn't see if it was a terrible, dangerous idea or not. But she had to be here. At this point in the road. There was no other option.

"Callie," he growled, "that is dangerous."

"So now what I wear is dangerous. What I say is dangerous. Seems to me like things have changed. Because we used to just talk, didn't we?"

"You know that changed."

"You keep trying to pretend it didn't. So if it's already changed, then what are we going to do? What could we possibly break?"

"You know the answer to that, too. And you don't want to do it. I know you don't. Any more than I do."

"I don't know what I want. But I think I know what I might need." She was very aware that her parents were standing right there. Very aware that she was attempting to seduce a man for the first time in her life. And really, the worst audience ever was around. But he was her husband.

She was trying to seduce her husband.

It's not real.

It felt real. It felt more real than anything. More real than Christmas.

More real than the food they'd just eaten. More real than the whiskey that still lingered on her lips.

Was there anything more real in her life than Jake?

That's how it's supposed to be. When you're in love.

She didn't want to let her mom's words dwell in her mind like that. She didn't want anything other than this moment. She didn't want to worry about tomorrow. For the first time in her life she wasn't looking way up ahead. This really was like riding. It was the only thing that came close. That moment before the chute opened. When everything was clear.

Right now, looking into his eyes, everything was clear.

"I want your hands on me," she whispered. She wrapped her arms around his neck, put her lips up close to his ear. "I want your mouth on me. I want to be naked with you. Do you remember... Do you remember when I tasted you? I want to do that again. I've never thought much about how sexy men were. But I think about you all the time. About your body. About the way it felt when you were inside of me."

He went rock hard. Every muscle in his body. And she could feel him getting hard in the front of his jeans.

"You want me," she said.

"It doesn't matter what I want," he said, his voice scraped raw.

"Why? Because you don't think life comes with guarantees? Don't you think that maybe that should be your excuse to live? Not just throwing yourself around like you might be disposable, or indestructible, or whatever game you're playing to try and deal with the feelings left behind by the pain that caused you. I don't know. I'm your friend. But I don't have any magic insight into that. What I do know is that I think you want to do something for yourself."

"All I do are things for myself." His face was half an inch away from hers, his eyes intense. She wanted to breathe him in. She wanted to taste him.

It was all she wanted to do.

"Yeah, right. You're here, doing this for me."

"And when I want a woman, I fuck her. I don't call her. And I certainly don't stay with her. Or go to her family ranch. Or try to figure out how the hell I'm supposed to see her again as often as possible for the rest of my life because she's the only friend I have. I ride bulls because it's dangerous. Because it makes me feel something. Because I look at the life my parents made and realize it was all bullshit, that nothing my dad pretended to feel was real. And you can promise someone the world and in the end, it can be a lie."

"All right, Jake. We have right now. Right now... We want each other. Right now, I want you. And who knows where we'll go. Nobody does. We die tonight or we don't. But we can have what we want. Is that what you're on about? You do things for yourself. You don't really. That's all a lie."

And without a care for her parents at all, without a care for anything, he wrapped his hand around the back of her head and brought her up on her toes, crushed her mouth to his. This kiss was different than anything they shared before. It wasn't angry, but it wasn't sweet. There was an intensity to it that took her breath away. That made her knees go weak. She clung to him. Her arms wrapped tightly around him, her hands grasping at the fabric on his shirt. He was perfect. This was perfect. And she didn't care if anyone saw. Because this was real. And she was real. And she was... All the everything that she'd ever been and more. And she felt like she was wearing it. Like this dress. Proud and feminine and strong.

"I think that's our cue to leave," he said.

"Yes, please," she responded.

They slipped off the dance floor, and she turned and saw her mother watching them go. She smiled, and waved. And Callie knew that she had her Christmas blessing.

They went out the front and he kept his hand on her lower back all the way to the truck. Kept contact with her even as he loaded her inside. They didn't speak when they got back on the road. Her heart was pounding hard, the pulse at the apex of her thighs throbbing.

She laid her head back on the truck seat, and a laugh escaped her lips.

"What's funny?" His voice sounded like it was shot through with gravel.

"This. This is crazy. And I really like it."

"Yeah, glad you like it. It's sort of killing me over here."

"Why?"

"I tried to be a gentleman."

She rolled her head to the side and looked at him. "Why start now, Daniels?"

"Low blow, Carson."

"I didn't ask you to be a gentleman," she said. "I asked you to be a good time."

"Well, we all know I can do that." Headlights from an on-coming car cast his face into sharp relief. And she could see the tension etched there. Only for a moment before he was thrust into darkness again. "I tried to protect you from me, Cal, I really did. From the first time I started to want you."

"Tell me about that," she said. "Because I want to go back. In my mind. And pretend maybe it played out differently."

"Well, you were... Maybe twenty-one. And I was watching you ride, and I just thought... Damn, there aren't very many people on this earth filled with that much joy and spirit on the back of a horse. And then it kinda made me wonder what else filled you with that much joy. I noticed the way the sunlight caught your hair. And that it wasn't just brown. It was a little bit of red, a little bit blond. Kind of everything."

"That's how hair works," she said. But she smiled.

"No. Yours is different."

"You're just used to women who have their hair colored by a bottle."

"I'm telling you. I know different."

"Okay. So my hair is different. What else?"

"You don't want to hear this part."

"I do."

"I noticed the way your tank tops fit. You've got a nice rack."

"I've always hated it. I've never seen the point of it." She frowned. "I tried so hard to be this whole other thing. I thought it was my mom trying to make me into something I wasn't. But it was me. Fighting against what I thought they wanted for me. And she told me today... She did want those things. And she has some regrets. But I thought that going ahead and doing the opposite was being freer. It wasn't. I resented the way I was made. The very way that I was put together. And there's nothing wrong with working hard to get what you want, but I didn't let myself enjoy what I could have had. You wanted me. You liked my boobs. I just wanted to strap them down in a sports bra. And yeah, you wanting them doesn't change the fact that they get in my way sometimes. It's just... There's good with the bad. And that goes for my boobs, too."

"That is hands-down the strangest thing I have ever heard anyone say."

"That's just because you don't talk to the women that you sleep with. You would've heard some great strangeness if you did."

"It wouldn't have been the same," he said.

She smiled. "No."

Too quickly and not soon enough the drive back to the cabin was over. He parked, and she waited. Letting him come over to her side of the car and open the door for her. Then she let him undo her seat belt and lift her right out of the car. Because why not? She didn't have anything to prove. He lifted her down from the cab of the truck, and she looked at his face. Shaded as it was by the night. But there was something in his expression…

They had set up a relationship where he was the one who taught her. Where he was the one who knew. He was the one helping her. And she could see right then and there that he didn't know any more than she did what was going on. That he didn't have any more answers. And that didn't make her feel afraid. If anything, it made her feel powerful. She often felt like he had the upper hand. That he was standing on higher ground. Older, more experienced as he was. But not when it came to them.

Because they weren't like anything else.

And she didn't need to have a whole host of experiences to know that. To feel that. He had said multiple times that their relationship was important to him. That he didn't have another person in his life that he prized quite the way he prized her. And that meant something. She knew that it did. It was an expression of vulnerability from this mountain of granite masquerading as a man.

And that made her feel strong. Made her feel powerful.

So she took the lead. She grabbed hold of his hand, and led him away from the house.

"What are we doing?"

"We're walking," she said.

The moon was full, casting a pale glow all around them, enough that they could see the terrain. It was so cold they could see their breath. The pine trees all around them a velvety blue in the night. It was breathtakingly still.

Quiet.

The only sound was their footsteps. Their breath. It was like they were the only two people on earth. Like this was the only moment. It was a strange sort of clarity. To exist like this. With just Jake. Because it was all fine to tell herself that he was her best friend—he was—but if that was all it was, she wouldn't be desperate to linger in this moment with him.

This was the bridge. The bridge between those two very separate things that he talked about. Friendship. Sex.

This walk in the woods was taking them across that gap. This moment that existed right here.

Because if it was sex, then they would be naked. And if it was friendship, then they would be talking. She wouldn't simply be content to just walk, joining hands with his.

But she was. She stopped walking when they got to a clearing, wrapped her arms around his and leaned her head against his shoulder. And just stood. The sky was brilliant and perfectly clear, tiny little stars visible, diamond dust against the black.

"I don't look at the stars enough," she whispered.

She didn't live in moments enough.

She only ever allowed herself that one moment of quiet. That one moment of clarity. When she was riding. A reward for the work she'd put in, that she could enjoy it only then. Only ever then.

And it was like the night sky rained diamonds down on her, glittering realizations that shimmered through her soul.

Suddenly she felt like the whole world might be full of these moments and she'd been missing them. Suddenly she felt like she was realizing for the first time that moments of peace and quiet and brilliance could be found any which where. If only she stopped long enough to look. If only she could be comfortable in who she was long enough to be in them.

The greatest and strangest gift that had come from making love with Jake was that kind of comfort in her own skin. That understanding of why she was put together the way that she was.

Jake hadn't made her a woman.

But he'd made her appreciate the complicated angles of what it meant to be one. Made her want to explore all the dimensions of her feelings, her body, her world.

He had given her the gift of the stars. Of these diamond dust moments of quiet. Where standing with the person was just as gratifying as talking to them. Where leaning her head against his shoulder was just as intimate as lying with him naked.

She turned to face him, and he stayed looking away.

She stretched up on her toes and pressed a kiss to his cheek. Migrated to the corner of his mouth, then reached across and turned his head so that she could have access to his lips.

She kissed him. Slowly at first, then taking it deeper, and deeper still.

His restraint began to fray, and he turned his body toward hers, wrapping himself around her, but she wanted this. To simply kiss. She knew that it would challenge him. She just knew. Suddenly she knew a whole lot of things that she had never learned. It just seemed to come from somewhere inside of her. Brought up to the surface by the way his hand skimmed over her curves. By the growling sound he made low and deep in his throat as they continued to kiss. She wrapped her arms around his neck, pressed her body against his. And she could feel the exact moment when he lost his composure.

"House," he said, his lips still pressed against hers.

"Sure," she responded.

He grabbed her hand, and they began to walk back toward the cabin. His hold on her was firm, his pace much quicker than when they had first walked into the grove of trees. It was so similar to that first night they'd been together, going into the house, consumed with hunger as she was. But it was different, too. Because this time she knew. She knew where this was going to go. She understood what he would make her feel. And even more importantly, she understood what she had the power to make him feel in return. She didn't feel nervous. Didn't feel embarrassed about the desire that was pulsing through her like a heavy rain.

As soon as he closed the door, she shrugged the fur wrap

from her shoulders and slipped her shoes off. Then she tipped his cowboy hat off his head, letting it fall to the floor.

"I had a thought earlier," she whispered, grabbing him by the collar of his shirt and dragging him toward the couch.

"What was that?" he asked, coming down onto the couch with her.

"I've never really worn a dress. I mean, not since I was a kid. And I was thinking, the really neat thing about a dress is how you could reach up underneath and touch me without even taking my clothes off."

"You're killing me," he groaned, braced halfway over the top of her, his eyes glittering with need.

She lifted a shoulder. "I just thought it might be fun."

And then that last word was cut off by his kiss. She parted her thighs, as much as she could in the dress, and the fabric pushed its way up as he settled between them, his denim-clad arousal hard against the thin fabric of her panties.

He rocked against her, and she moaned, rolling her hips so that she could feel him better. So that she could feel this.

All of it.

It was so powerful. That was what surprised her the most. Because the way the conversation had swirled around her when she was with the cowgirls, there had been this idea that the women who gave it up so easily to the cowboys were weak in some way.

But she could imagine they felt like...like they were shifting the earth and the stars, making those big men shake like this.

Those powerful, masculine men who tamed bucking broncos and bulls. Maybe one of those women couldn't ever do that, but they held the men themselves in thrall, in the palms of their hands.

And it was a different kind of power.

Different than the one she'd been trying to claim for herself. Different than the one she aimed for by competing in men's sports. Honing her body into something stronger and more fit.

That was strength. A strength that she enjoyed and admired. But this was a different kind altogether. This sort of softness that seemed to curve itself around all that hardness, and make it bend.

Make it weak.

She had the power to do that. Just as she was.

Just as she was.

They kissed. Endlessly. Like it was the only destination. Like it was the only game. His hips bucked against hers, and she felt herself getting wetter and wetter, more and more ready for the insistent throb of his arousal. But she also wanted to stay in this moment, in this torture, for as long as possible. Because it was a gift. An undeniable, magical gift, just as much as it was a torture.

Then he grabbed hold of her hips, pushing the fabric of her dress up her thighs. "Was this your fantasy?" he asked, his voice rough. He moved his hand between her legs then, hooking his finger around the elastic band of her underwear, right where it covered the most intimate part of her, and swept it to the side. The sound he made, the way the air rushed through his teeth, sent a bolt of lightning straight through her.

"You are so pretty," he said. "You make my mouth water."

She wasn't nervous. He'd done this before.

But now she knew, and that made it different. Made her antsy. Desperately so. Hungry for his touch. For his mouth. Hungry for everything that he had in store for her.

His eyes intent on hers, he pushed two fingers through her slick folds, stroking her. And he never looked away.

"Jake," she whispered. Saying his name like that, looking at his face… It ramped up her desire.

Jake.

Her Jake. Her best friend.

He was the one touching her. He was the one stroking her. Drawing the wetness out from inside her body and slicking it over that sensitized bundle of nerves right there.

She moaned, grabbing hold of his arm, looking for something, anything, to brace herself as her hips worked in a restless rhythm. He pushed two fingers inside of her again, relentless in his torture of her.

"Jake," she said again.

"What's wrong, Cal? Too much for you?"

It was absurd. His use of her nickname right now. That familiarity, combined with the huskiness of desire. Combined with the way that he was touching her.

She thought she was going to burst with it. Combust.

"You wanted me to push your dress up and take you like a dirty girl," he said. "That's what you really want, isn't it? You don't have to be strong all the time," he growled, leaning forward and biting her neck. "You can just be mine."

She shivered, shuddered, coming around his fingers with embarrassing ease.

She threw her head back, a cry of desire reverberating through her.

"You like that, don't you? Being mine. My wife."

"Jake," she said again.

She wanted desperately to tell him not to tease her. Because all of this hurt, and she didn't know what game he was playing. Why he'd gotten so intense, why he was saying these things when they both knew that wasn't real. This was real. The way that he touched her. His body buried inside of her... That was real. Everything else... It would end. It had to end. She knew that as well as he did. So why say that? Why bring up that she was his wife and he was her husband when it was going to end in just over a month?

But then he was pushing her dress higher, exposing her stomach, pressing his hot lips to the skin there, and it didn't matter. Nothing mattered but the moment. Like that isolated piece of time they'd shared looking at the stars. There was nothing before this and nothing after. And in this moment, she was his wife. In this moment, he was her husband. And his mouth was creating havoc on her body.

Keeping her underwear pulled firmly to the side, and his fingers deep inside of her, he moved his mouth to the center of her pleasure, sucking on her mercilessly, pushing her further, faster, than she had imagined possible. And just like that, she climaxed again. And then again. Until she was begging him to stop.

"It's what you wanted," he growled against her slick flesh, lapping at her with the flat of his tongue. "You wanted to play games with this dress. With this fantasy. So let's play games. But we'll play by my rules."

"Don't torture me," she sobbed. "I need you."

"You have me." He looked up from his position between her legs and she was certain that she couldn't take anymore. Certain that she was going to expire on the spot. Then he pinched her. Right there. And set her flying one more time.

She was limp and boneless when she realized that he had moved up her body, that he was sitting her up and unzipping her dress, stripping her naked. He took her bra off, his eyes glittering as he looked down at her breasts.

"You're beautiful."

"Tell me again."

"You," he said, leaning in and taking one nipple between his lips, sucking hard, then blowing on her wet skin. "Are beautiful."

He created a symphony of desire in her that she hadn't known was possible. Made her feel things, want things, she hadn't been aware existed until recently.

"The most beautiful woman I've ever seen. The strongest. You're incredible."

And she felt it. Right then. All the way to her soul.

But there was something bleak in his expression that made her wonder if he knew how amazing he was. Because he had poured it all out onto her. All of his praise, all of his admiration, and what had she given in return?

Orgasms.

He knew that she wanted him, because she could hardly hide it. But it wasn't everything that she felt. How could she begin to put that into words. So she sat up, launching herself onto his lap, straddling him, completely naked as she did so, the rough denim scraping against her thighs and that soft, melting place between them.

The buttons of his shirt rubbing against her breasts. "You're beautiful," she said, kissing his chin, then opening her mouth and biting it. "You make me want to do… Crazy things. Dirty things. I don't even know if they're real things. I just know you make me want them. I want to climb your body. Like a tree."

"Damn," he said, his voice like gravel.

"You know how wet you make me."

"Cal…"

She started to unbutton his shirt. "Your chest is amazing." And more words tumbled out of her mouth. Without thought. Without planning. She didn't know if they were elegant or sexy or anything other than ridiculous.

But she talked about all the things that she wanted to do to him. The way that she wanted to taste him. How badly she wanted him inside of her.

And by the time he was naked, his hands were shaking as he flipped her onto her back on the couch and settled between her legs.

He had paused only to put on a condom, and she had to stop herself from begging him to do it without one. A moment of insanity that she could hardly believe had risen up inside of her. Because condoms were important. She didn't want any consequences from their time together. For a host of reasons. But there was something primal about her desire to be with him. Skin to skin, nothing between them. To experience being filled by him.

He made her something entirely new. Or maybe it was just something whole. Complicated and difficult to reconcile, and there was a host of realizations that went with that but she wasn't entirely certain she was ready to deal with that. He pressed the head of his hardness to her slick entrance, and pushed into her slowly. She groaned as he filled her. As stars burst behind her eyes. And when he was fully seated inside of her, his eyes met hers, and she was overwhelmed yet again by the sensation of Jake.

He was…

He was in her. And it was perfect. He was her best friend. And he was her husband. He was her teacher, her lover. And she felt overwhelmed by the need to be just as many things to him as he was to her. To find a way to fill the need that she sensed inside of him. The endless well of darkness that she could see behind those eyes in his unguarded moments.

She wanted to make promises to him. Wanted to tell him things. Things she hadn't even let go fully formed in her own mind.

But she was afraid. So she kissed him. So she kissed him and rocked her hips, and took his every thrust. His every growl of pleasure. Swallowed every groan of desire that escaped him. He pounded into her until the couch proved too narrow for the intensity of their need, and he braced himself against it, lowering them both to the floor, without breaking off where they joined. The floor was hard against her tailbone, and he was merciless with it. But she didn't care. Because it was perfect. It was everything. And they were on fire.

Words rained down in her mind like a thunderstorm. Promises. Declarations of need. And when he shattered, so did she. His pleasure like a thunderclap that radiated through her body and pushed her over the edge.

They lay there, tangled in each other, breathing impossibly hard. It was the only sound in the room.

"If that's what dressing like a lady gets me," she said. "I'm going to do it more often."

She was exhausted, too exhausted to move. But he chuckled,

and lifted her up off the ground, pulling her against his body. She kissed him. Willing him not to leave her. And he didn't. He gathered her up against him, and carried her down the hall. Carried her into her bedroom, where he set her on the bed, and put the blankets over her.

"Jake..."

"Get some sleep."

"Tomorrow's Christmas," she said.

"Yeah," he said. "It is." And she couldn't puzzle out quite what he meant by that. She knew what she'd meant.

She'd meant stay with her. Sleep with her. But he was leaving, and she wasn't brave enough to ask.

And when the door closed behind him, all she could think was that sex was some kind of insane witchcraft. Because she wasn't afraid of a bucking bronco, but she was afraid to ask a man to stay in bed with her. To sleep with her. And what kind of stupid thing was that? She had felt so powerful only a few moments earlier, and now she felt... Now she felt weak and sad.

And she refused to let those words in her mind take shape. She refused. Because this hurt. But she acknowledged the full depth of what she felt—that she might break entirely.

CHAPTER EIGHTEEN

It was Christmas fucking morning. He woke up feeling like he had a bad hangover. He had fallen asleep on top of his blankets, bare-ass naked, and he was freezing cold. But he supposed it was what he deserved, and no less. And he knew that they had to go over to the main house for their Christmas morning, knew that he had to face her.

He also knew that she hadn't been happy that he'd left her in the bed, and he pretended that he hadn't realized. He felt like a dick for that. But he got dressed in blue jeans and a thermal shirt, and went out into the kitchen, where she wasn't.

She'd made herself scarce, clearly.

There was no coffee in the pot. He wondered if she'd gone ahead for Christmas. Then he looked at the clock. It was eight-thirty in the morning. He never slept that late. He was always up with the sun. And here he'd gone and slept that late on Christmas.

Dammit, this woman was messing him around.

This woman.

Your friend. Your friend, *you damn asshole.*

Yeah, he was an asshole. He had…

He hadn't been able to get enough of her last night. He'd

stroked her and tasted her and let her come all over him for a good hour before he thrust home. It had been the hottest, most erotic experience of his life.

And everything in him had wanted to crawl into bed with her. But he hadn't done it. He hadn't been able to bring himself to do it.

Yeah, you're perilously close to a whole lot of things you know you're not allowed to have.

He looked out the window and saw that the space in front of the house was empty.

She had taken the truck.

He got dressed, made himself some coffee and started to walk over to the main ranch house.

The truck was outside the great spread, so he figured she was inside. He walked up the front steps, and knocked on the door.

It was Callie who opened it.

"It's about time," she said, appraising him with a cool expression.

"Good morning."

"Merry Christmas," she shot back.

Then she took a step out the front door, wrapped her arm around his neck and kissed him. Not a light good-morning kiss. A deep, passionate kiss that made him want to slam that door and take her right back to their cabin, where he could have his way with her again.

"Merry Christmas," she said even more firmly when they parted.

"What's gotten into you?"

"Last night?" Her lips twitched. "You did."

"Cute," he responded.

"You just looked so peaceful this morning sleeping naked on your bed that I couldn't bring myself to wake you. Had we been together, it might've been a different story. But we weren't. So, anyway." Her voice shifted to a singsong he'd never heard from her before. "I hope you don't mind, the cinnamon rolls have gotten cold."

"It's fine," he said, successfully shamed as he knew she had intended him to be.

She took his hand and dragged him inside. Then led him to the grand living room. The massive Christmas tree was all lit up, the presents underneath it mostly open.

"Merry Christmas," he said.

"Merry Christmas," her family said back with varying degrees of humor in their faces.

He was the fool who'd slept through Christmas morning, and he didn't know how to process all this togetherness and cheer, and he hadn't had any time to warm up to it.

The deep sleep he'd fallen into had definitely been comatose, and it had most definitely been because the woman had nearly blown his head off.

And he didn't know how to interact with her brothers and dad now. Hell, he barely knew how to interact with his own family half the time and here he was, feeling like his skin had been peeled back a layer, dealing with family that wasn't even his.

"We got you a gift," her mom said, and that stopped him short.

"Oh," he said. "I'm sorry, I didn't bring—"

"It's all right," her mom said. "We understand that all this came on really suddenly for you. But still."

They handed him a bottle of whiskey with a red ribbon tied around the neck of it.

"Thanks," he said.

"We all got the same thing," Boone said, lifting his bottle up, and he really didn't quite know how to process that. He didn't want to. Didn't want to go over the full implications. Anyway, they didn't matter. Because he wasn't actually their son-in-law. Not like they thought.

This wasn't permanent. And it was a damn good thing he

hadn't fallen asleep with Callie, no matter that it had hurt her feelings at the time. He was playing with fire and he knew it. Last night had been his breaking point, and there had been no resisting her.

She wanted him, so why not give her what she wanted? Wasn't that why he was here? It hadn't made any sense to put her off. Hadn't made any sense to deny her.

Laughing and gift opening continued around him. And for half of it he felt like he was having an out-of-body experience. Because this was a family. A regular old family with a mother and a father and children. Even if they were all grown.

And it wasn't at all like his life. But he just kind of had to sit there and be part of it without actually being part of it.

"Hey, Jake," Callie's father said, clapping his hand on his back. "Why don't you come have a drink of that whiskey with me. Since I so generously bought the bottle for you."

"Sure," Jake said, knowing he couldn't deny the older man, but also feeling a little bit afraid.

"Let's go to the den," he said, leading him out of the formal living room and into a place with a big TV and high-backed leather chairs.

There were two tumblers sitting on the table, and Jake felt very much like he had been railroaded into the moment.

He took the bottle of whiskey from Jake's hand, sat in the chair and pulled off the top. "Set a spell." He poured a measure of the amber liquid into the glasses, and gestured to the seat across from him.

Jake complied.

"You know, I don't think I've ever told you how much I appreciate the way you've been there for Callie over the years. You've been a real good friend to her."

Jake gritted his teeth and sat back in the chair. "I try."

"She admires you. Looks up to you. She always has. It's been clear to me from the beginning just how crazy she was about you. And I can tell that's even more true now."

Jake had the distinct feeling that someone might have if he was being held under a microscope.

"So thank you for that," he said. "Because you know, that's what a man wants in life. To know that his daughter is taken care of. That she's protected. And that she's happy."

"Her happiness is important to me, too," Jake said. "Nothing is more important than that."

"Glad to hear it. You know, Jake," he said. "I remember years ago, I got a stallion. Big one. Supposed to be a great stud. I put him in the field with this filly. And you would think for all the world that the stallion and the filly were going to make something of it. But I knew for a fact that the stallion wasn't doing his job. Everybody else that worked for me kept saying there was no way that stallion wasn't covering that filly. But I just had a feeling. I had a feeling things weren't what they seemed."

Jake shifted uncomfortably in his chair. He had no idea if he was actually hearing a story about a stallion and a filly or if this was a metaphor, and he couldn't decide what made him more uncomfortable.

Mostly because he had absolutely, completely, covered Callie, so to speak. And he really didn't want to be in this discussion with her dad.

"When you work with as many animals as I do, you have a sense for it. Well, it turned out that I was right about the stallion. Now, then the question was, was something wrong with him. Turns out he'd injured himself. But it wasn't obvious. What happened was he got spooked in the trailer on the way over to my ranch. He jumped up, and a piece of metal had come down into his abdomen. Had sunk all the way in. But it wasn't immediately clear that was what had happened. So he had this piece of metal that he was carrying around inside of him. Prevented him from functioning in all kinds of ways. Made him averse to the filly, even though we all know that a stallion wants a filly, Jake. We all know it. But because of that wound he couldn't take her. He had to pull that shrapnel around he was carrying inside of him. And then… Everything worked just right. I got me a champion little colt out of the deal. But you know, the point is, I had to see what was in front of me first. I'm good at seeing what's in front of me."

The old man's eyes met his, and again, Jake couldn't quite puzzle out exactly what he was claiming to know. Because if it was that he wasn't… With Callie, then he was wrong. But if it had to do with the marriage not being real…

"You can't let the shrapnel stay there forever," he said. "Keep you from doing what needs doing."

"Yeah, I'm not quite sure what you're getting at."

"I think you do."

"I think you're giving me more credit than you maybe should."

Abe shifted. "Well, I don't think so. But if that's the case… I think it will become clear when it needs to. But just to let you know. I'm a man who sees things."

"Well, I don't have any trouble believing that."

"One more thing to go with that. When the dust settles, if my daughter is hurt in any way, I'll be hunched down. So will Boone and Kit and Jace and Flint and Chance. Just because you're not in the rodeo don't mean I don't know where you live."

Jake believed it. But threats against his person were not his primary motivation for making sure Callie came out of this unscathed. "I would never hurt Callie."

But as soon as he spoke the words he had to wonder if they were alive. And that bothered him. Down into his soul it bothered him, because he would never want to hurt her. Not for anything. But he was afraid he'd maneuvered himself into a position where it would be all too easy.

"See that you don't."

Then the older man leaned back in his chair and knocked back his glass of whiskey before setting the empty tumbler back down on the table. Jake did the same.

"Cheers to you," he said.

"And to you."

He put his hand on Jake's shoulder. "I have faith in you, son."

The word blindsided Jake. Made him feel like he'd been punched in the face.

Or in the shrapnel wound. Whatever the case may be.

His memory of his own father was damaged. There was no way it couldn't be.

His father hadn't been the man Jake had believed him to be.

There were so many unanswered questions.

And he didn't have it in him to be an optimist, not with the way his life had gone.

But he still missed his father.

He still missed being a son.

And for the whole rest of the day he felt bruised.

They said goodbye to the family, and it was a real goodbye, because they were about to head back to Gold Valley, and to his ranch the next morning.

"We gotta get an early start," he said to Callie when they got inside.

"Okay," she said, her gaze veiled.

And she knew that he had hurt her feelings. Which pissed him off. Because he hadn't wanted to do that. But he also needed… Just a bit of distance.

The next morning, they were up bright and early, loaded into his truck and headed back toward Gold Valley.

This time, they didn't stop by the Painted Hills, but when they drove by the sign, he had the strangest sensation that he'd been living a whole different life on his way over to her parents' house than he was leaving it.

And her dad's words echoed in his head.

You can't let the shrapnel stay there forever.

Showed what he knew. You damn well *could* let the shrapnel stay there forever.

Because some mistakes were forever. You didn't get to heal from them. Just because you felt like it.

His mother was dead.

End of story. That was all. There was no bringing her back. There was no amount of penance that could be paid. He wasn't trying to atone for anything, because there was no atonement for certain things. But by that same token, there were just some wounds that didn't go away. No matter what. And you couldn't make them.

Don't hurt her.

He didn't want to. He really didn't want to.

"I practically could've stayed at my parents'," she said, holding on to her seat belt shoulder strap as they continued to drive. Like she was trying to brace herself against whatever he might say.

"We had a deal, remember," he said. "You're supposed to help at my ranch. I have horses coming soon."

"Yeah," she said. "I know."

She didn't say much else for the rest of the drive.

When they got back to the house, she went and put her stuff in the separate bedroom.

"I guess we have chores to do," she said.

"Guess so," he responded.

He set her on an assignment, away from him, and he felt a little bit like an ass, but he wanted the distance. They'd been trapped together for an awfully long time, and it didn't seem like a bad idea for them to spend a bit of time apart. And by the time he got back in cell phone range, he had a voice mail from his cousin reminding him to come to dinner on Sunday night.

CHAPTER NINETEEN

It felt different going to Hope Springs Ranch this time. She hadn't been sleeping with Jake the first time she'd been, and their marriage not being real had been a funny joke—well, it had never been all that funny to her. It had been embarrassing. But now it all felt fragile and sacred, and she didn't like what she was walking into. But she also didn't want to spend the evening away from him. Didn't want him to go to their house without bringing her along. She hadn't slept with him the last couple of nights.

Well, slept with was only a euphemism.

They'd had sex twice.

He'd *never* slept with her.

But since leaving Evergreen Ranch he hadn't touched her, hadn't kissed her, hadn't anything.

She had thought about starting a fight, seeing if a little bit of anger could ignite a spark between them again. She thought about throwing herself off the back of a horse, to see if he would get mad again and if she could get a kiss that way.

But it just felt... All that felt cowardly.

That night that they'd walked together under the trees had

been real. It had been deep and intimate, and it had felt like something. She had to figure out a way to get back there again.

To what end?

Well, she didn't want to think about it. She just wanted to focus on the next thing. The next step.

Though she didn't know what it was.

She had never minded her inexperience, but about now she was getting pretty annoyed with it. She had figured out the inner workings of a man's pants. But she had not figured out the inner workings of a man's mind. And you would think that she would have some insight into that growing up with the many brothers that she had. But it was a far cry to be a man's lover than it was to be a man's sister. Or his friend.

When the front door to the ranch house opened, the two dogs came running outside, tangling between her legs. She laughed, bending down to pat the Australian shepherd on the head.

"They're so cute."

"Menaces," a voice shouted after them.

Callie remembered Iris, Jake's cousin, who was standing in the doorway, looking more amused than angry.

"You don't even live here anymore," Jake said. "What do you care if the dogs run wild?"

"I care for common decency," Iris said.

"Yeah, well, they don't," Jake said.

He put his hand on Callie's lower back, and she flinched away. Mostly because she felt a little bit too raw for him to be giving her casual contact in front of his family. And anyway, it was just a reflex, because they weren't even putting on a show for them.

She looked at him, and he lifted a brow in question.

"Don't forget where you are," she said.

Great job, Callie. Be petulant, and ruin your chances of figuring out how to get close to him again.

She didn't mean to be petulant. It was just... He was being thoughtless. And nothing about her right now was thoughtless.

She was brimming with thoughts.

Here was an unforeseen downside to this embracing all aspects of womanhood thing.

The thing about her life being all about saddle bronc was that it was simple. She either got to do it or she didn't. One was acceptable, one wasn't.

Wanting Jake…

Well, she wanted him, but it hurt. She wanted to get her way but she was also afraid of it.

It was so complicated, and so internal, and so…

Nothing she was used to at all.

Jake dropped his hand, and she was immediately upset. Well, she'd gone and cut her nose off to spite her face.

The Christmas decorations were gone from the ranch house, but it was still brimming with color and activity. She found herself fascinated by each and every one of his family members. Where her brothers were all sort of cut from the same cloth, this family was something else entirely.

His cousin Ryder was a Captain America type. Good, heroic. And adorable with his baby daughter. Ryder's wife, Sammy, was a flurry of motion, hair and diaphanous fabrics. Police chief Pansy was the female counterpart to Ryder, with Rose the youngest, most stubborn and outspoken. Iris, the oldest of that sibling group, was maternal, but with a dry, quiet wit that snuck up out of nowhere. Then there was Jake and Colt. The cousins. She noticed that they talked and laughed easily enough with each other, but that they didn't seem to ever talk about anything beyond the weather.

After dinner, she found herself in the kitchen with the women, and a few weeks ago that might've bothered her. But now… Now it didn't. She liked these women. She had from the first time she'd ever been here. And she'd been fascinated by all the different ways that they were women. And now she felt like she fit. A part of them. Her own kind of woman, and just as much of a woman as anyone.

"Jake used to be an absolute hell-raiser," Sammy said. "I thought he was going to give Ryder gray hair even back when we were kids."

"I don't understand how that worked," Callie said. "Ryder taking care of everybody when they were so close to the same age."

"The only reason we even got away with it was that this is a small town with limited resources, and it was easier for people to come check in on us than farm a bunch of unwilling, angry teenagers out to foster homes," Pansy said. "At least that's what I figure. Not that Ryder didn't do a great job—it's just...you know, that was a lot to put on him."

"But he was the best," Rose said, unfailingly loyal.

"And did you all listen to him?" Callie asked.

"Oh, they resisted it," Sammy said. "The boys especially. It was only Iris and me cooking good food that kept them coming back at night. Colt and Jake were assholes."

"It's true," Pansy said, nodding.

"I don't remember," Rose said, shrugging.

"Yeah, because you're the baby," Sammy said, patting her on the head.

"What was Jake like... Before?" She felt slightly like a turncoat asking that question. Like she shouldn't try to get information about her friend that wasn't directly from him. But things had changed. She wanted to talk to him in a different way. She wanted to talk to him more deeply, and she didn't know how to access him. She didn't know how to get down to that level. There were a whole lot of things that she just didn't quite know about him right now, and she couldn't pretend that their friendship was going to power them through it. Not when things had changed.

You know why they've changed.

"Oh," Iris said, frowning. "I don't know. I mean, he was always a smart-ass. But he... He liked to be at home. I figured he would be a rancher like his dad."

"But he never really worked on the ranch, did he? I know he went into the rodeo. I remember that."

"Yeah," Iris said. "He just lost his interest in the place after our parents died. It's strange, because it didn't have that effect on Ryder, but Ryder ended up taking care of everybody, and I feel like in a lot of ways his future was decided for him. Ryder always planned to leave. He was going to play football. Jake... I never got the impression he did plan on going anywhere else, and then he ended up leaving right when he turned eighteen."

"I never got to know him all that well," Sammy said. "Not like the others. I mean, we know each other. But I didn't know them before. He's fun. But... There's more to it than that."

"Yeah," Callie agreed. "I got to know him about eight years ago. I was sixteen. And I just thought... He was the best man I'd ever met. And he is. I..." She stumbled over the next few words. "I cared about him almost right away. He became my best friend. But I didn't notice until recently that all that is just covering... He's sad." She looked up, meeting Iris's gaze. "He's really sad."

She felt guilty, revealing him like that. She had never felt the urge to talk about her friend to anybody. And here she was, talking about him. Not because he was less of her friend, but because there was something she needed to work out, and he couldn't help her do it. He wouldn't help her do it. The space that they were standing in. That bridge that she'd realized they were on that night under the trees... That space between friendship and sex. This uncharted territory that she didn't know how to map. That's where they were.

"He just doesn't like to talk about anything serious," Sammy said. "He's hard to know."

Would she ever know him?

That ate at her.

Because she always felt like she had, but she didn't in the process of realizing just how one-sided their friendship was in that way. He knew all her hopes and dreams. He'd up and left the rodeo without so much as talking to her. He'd started a ranch, when she hadn't even realized he'd wanted that. So how good of friends were they really? He held her at a distance, and she hadn't even noticed it.

"I want to do something for him," she said. "But I don't know what. I don't know how to…"

She realized that they were all looking at her sympathetically. "What?"

"It's like that, is it?" Sammy asked.

"Like what?"

"He's… Important to you," Pansy said slowly. "And maybe this isn't as fake as it was in the beginning?"

She scowled. "I don't know. Maybe. But he's difficult."

"Oh, that's the Daniels family trait," Sammy said.

The other women looked at her. "Hey," Rose said.

"Sorry, but it is. You are all singularly pains in the ass."

"If I recall right," Iris said, "you broke Ryder's heart."

"He got better," Sammy said, waving a hand.

"Still," Pansy said. "Just be careful who you're calling a pain in the ass."

"I didn't say I wasn't. But I'm just saying, it is hard to get to them when they decide to be problematic."

"Problematic," Rose muttered.

"He's taking care of you," Iris said. "Maybe it's time for you to take care of him."

"That's the thing," Callie said. "I want to. I want to take care of him. I just don't know what he needs."

"I do remember," Pansy said, "that his mom used to make sugar cookies."

"Oh, right," she said. "He mentioned that."

Rose looked edgy. "A word to the wise about attempting to reproduce cookie recipes without warning. Sometimes it doesn't go over well."

"Oh, right," Pansy said, looking at her sister. "Logan got a little bit weird about that."

Rose shrugged her shoulders. "It did work out in the end. So, I'm pro-cookie. I'm just saying... It's gonna get a reaction."

"That's what I need," Callie said. "I need a reaction. I feel like things happen with him, and then... He pulls away, and there's nothing I can do to reach him. I considered throwing myself off a horse."

"Baking cookies seems less extreme."

"I'm actually more comfortable getting thrown off a horse than I am baking a cookie."

"It's simple," Iris said, waving a hand. "I run a bakery. And actually, I know how to make those cookies. I make them in the shop."

"You do?"

"I absolutely do," Iris said. "I have the recipe. If you follow that, it's not dramatic. I promise you."

"Well, I haven't got any other ideas," she said. "So maybe I'll bake some cookies."

"You were warned," Rose said.

She nodded. But she was ready. For whatever. Because she couldn't keep going back and forth with him. She couldn't continue on in this pattern. And their marriage was ending at the end of next month. Another few weeks, and the marriage would be over. All of the trust fund money would be transferred to her... And they wouldn't need to be together anymore. So yeah, she would see what happened with this. She would just see.

Because she needed time. More than a few weeks.

And she didn't know how else to get it.

"I've never really had a whole lot of girlfriends," she said. "So this was really nice."

"Well, if everything works out…" Sammy grinned. "We'll be seeing a lot more of you."

Callie held that close, but tried not to think it through too deeply.

If she let herself think about this too much, she would pull away. She would get afraid, and she would stop.

And she wasn't going to let herself do that.

CHAPTER TWENTY

He hadn't run into Callie at all when he was out working that morning. It was strange, but not entirely unusual. They hadn't seen each other at all that first day, either. But this time, he had looked for her a few times, and hadn't found her in any of the places where there were tasks to do, so he wasn't really sure what she had found to busy herself with.

He had gone and checked the corral, and she wasn't there. But it was late, and he was hungry, and he was about to go inside and open up a beer and get a TV dinner out of the freezer.

She could join him if she wanted to. Maybe she was off at a bar finding a man to pick up.

He gritted his teeth against the anger that thought produced inside of him.

She'd better not be doing that.

And then what? If she were? What would he do?

Yeah, he didn't really know. Because he had waived his right to be in her face about that, he expected. When he had acted like nothing had happened between them while they were at her parents' ranch.

But it was for the best.

Yeah, maybe they had talked about it, but things had gotten too heated, too real, back there and they needed time to cool down.

Soon enough, this whole marriage thing would be over. And he wouldn't have to worry about it anymore. He walked up the steps into the house, and was immediately surprised by the smell coming from the kitchen.

It was food.

He frowned, making his way toward the smell, and the sounds that went along with it. Clattering and banging. When he walked in, there was a pot sitting on the stove with steam billowing out of the top of it, and Callie was standing in front of a skillet, red-faced.

"Cal?"

"Oh," she said. "You're back."

She looked at something on the counter, and then grabbed the pot, taking it over to the sink and dumping the water out, and some pasta along with it. He presumed there was a colander down there to catch it, otherwise she was throwing out a whole lot of food.

"I cooked," she said.

She picked up the colander in the sink—as expected—and dumped the noodles back into the pot. Then she picked the skillet up off the stove and dumped something looking like red sauce into the pan after the noodles.

"I had to do a little bit of research." She wrinkled her nose. "But I figured out how to make spaghetti."

He held back a smile. Even he could make spaghetti.

"Well, that's an achievement."

"Thanks," she said. She looked genuinely proud, and it warmed him.

Why exactly are you letting it warm you, asshole?

The moment splintered. He didn't know what he was doing,

standing there, with this woman cooking him dinner. He didn't know what she was doing.

"Well, we both have to eat."

And that simple declaration saw him pushing aside his concerns. She was right. They both had to eat. And this was infinitely better than a freezer dinner.

"True," he said.

"Grab some plates," she said. "I'll bring the pot into the dining room."

He did as instructed, getting a beer, some plates and forks, and following her into the dining area. There was a bowl of salad sitting on the table, with two forks shoved into it. And there was a bottle of ranch dressing sitting beside it.

"Thanks," he said. "This is way better than what I had planned."

She twisted her hands together. "You're welcome."

And then he sat. And it was just nice. To have this done for him after such a long day. She sat across from him, holding her own beer. And she watched as he served himself, taking a heaping helping of spaghetti and putting it on the plate. He'd eaten meals with Callie countless times, but there was something different about this. Something different about her having prepared the food for him. Warmth spread in his chest, but at the same time, so did the discomfort.

They ate in silence, and he enjoyed it, and then she popped up and went back into the kitchen. "I have something else."

She came back, and returned with a plate of sugar cookies.

Sugar cookies. The crunchy kind.

Just like they'd talked about at the ranch when she had discussed making cookies with her mom.

"What's that?"

"I hope you don't mind, but I got the recipe from Iris. She said that she had it. The one that your mom used to make. I know that I'm stepping all over emotional stuff," she said. "But

I wanted to do something for you. I wanted to do this for you. I… You take care of me, Jake. You've done so much for me, and I just really wanted to do something for you, too."

All he could do was stare at her. And then down at the cookies. And he couldn't… He couldn't for the life of him understand why she was doing this for him. Why anyone would do anything for him. And he was so damn stymied by the cookies that he couldn't really focus on much of anything else. Because he just couldn't make sense of it. Not heads nor tails.

"You didn't have to do that," he said.

"I wanted to," she said. "Jake… You have been there for me for the last eight years. You are the most important person in my life. You've taught me so much. And then you… You married me. Cookies really aren't a fraction of that. Not even the beginning of some kind of repayment."

"You don't have to repay me."

"It's not that. Sorry. I just said it wrong. It's just…" She made her way from her seat, and took the chair right beside him. "I care about you." She put her hand over his. "I would… I would do anything for you. I would."

The earnestness shining from her eyes, the plate of cookies… He felt like she had reached into his chest and grabbed hold of his heart. Felt like she had… Done something to him. And he was reminded of that night when they had stood out under the trees. Before they'd made love the second time.

That night when he felt like the only way to get the pressure off his chest was to kiss her.

Hold her.

Make her scream his name.

Because at least if they shifted the feelings inside of his chest into something physical it might make some kind of sense.

And he couldn't even bring himself to pick up a cookie.

He just couldn't. He was frozen. Absolutely and completely

frozen. And he didn't know what in hell his next move was supposed to be.

So he kissed her. He kissed her because he wanted to. He kissed her because if he didn't, the siren that was going off in his head was only going to get louder, that feeling that was expanding in his chest was only going to get more powerful. Except kissing her didn't do anything to get rid of it. Kissing her only amped it up. Joined the physical in with the emotional, and it hadn't been like that last time. He had been able to find a way to get caught up in her body and forget.

That was what he needed to do. Forget. Because it was the friendship that was being too intense right now. Her looking at him. As if she expected something.

And he had no idea what in hell to do with expectation.

With hope.

Because his own had been burned clean out of his soul. Because the feeling that was swelling in his chest was something he wasn't equal to.

He couldn't be. Not ever.

This was feeling. Pure feeling.

And he wanted to wipe it out. Eradicate it.

Sex.

Not anything else. He was a master at that. Sex without feelings. He knew it so well. And he could capture it now if he wanted to. He knew that he could. So he kissed her. He kissed her and he tried to block out who she was.

What this was.

He kissed her, and he tried to make himself feel nothing. Because hadn't he spent years doing exactly that? Jumping on the backs of bulls, and feeling nothing. Picking up a new woman every night and feeling nothing.

Nothing but the blessed hollowness that was there to comfort him. So much better than an evening spent alone in silence where he remembered. What it was like to have a family. What it was like to be loved. What it was like to be happy.

And feel all those things in return.

Yeah, he tried to find that space. Tried to focus on her lips, on the softness of her mouth, the flavor of her. But there was nothing in this kiss that didn't scream her name.

And her name could never be divorced of emotion. Ever. Her name always rang inside of him like a bell.

And adding a kiss didn't do anything to fix it.

And he was at a loss to explain why that was.

Why he couldn't just take charge of it.

"Jake..."

"No talking," he said. "I don't want to talk." He grabbed the front of her shirt and pulled her toward him, and he heard the collar of it rip, but he didn't care. Didn't give a damn.

"I'm filthy. I've been out working all damn day. And I need a shower."

He grabbed the hem of her top and pulled it up over her head. Did his best to stop himself from looking at her face. He looked at her tits, because that was easy. They were beautiful, and they could be anybody's breasts. It didn't have to be Callie. He unhooked her bra, and threw it down, but it landed on the table.

"Shouldn't we...?"

He picked her up, wrapped her legs around his waist, lowered his head to her breasts and sucked her nipple between his teeth. And he bit her. She cried out.

Yes, this he could do. He could act like she was just another buckle bunny. A plaything. And she could pleasure him. She liked to. So why not. It didn't need to mean anything. Didn't need to be anything special. That was the problem. He had stopped sleeping with her and turned it into some kind of holy grail of pleasure.

It was just sex.

He'd had lots of sex.

For Callie it was all new, and he let that get in his head. He let it mean something that it was brand-new to her, but it didn't have to.

It didn't have to be anything. Holding her in his arms, his hands under her ass, he walked them up the stairs, to the master bathroom. And then he set her down on the floor.

"Strip for me," he said.

Hell, if she wanted to do something for him, she could do this. She swallowed hard, visibly, and began to take her jeans off.

"That's not really stripping," he said. And then he pulled her toward him and did away with her jeans and panties himself.

It was methodical, almost mechanical, but that's what he was on a mission to make it. This thing that he knew all the moves to. A practiced dance, not unlike the line dance that they'd done at the restaurant.

That was fine. It was more than fine. It was the dance they'd had after he didn't want to think about it. It was that dance that he couldn't risk again.

But this…this was just sex.

He turned the shower on and finished stripping them bare. Then he pulled her in after him, sliding the water over her bare skin. Drawing her close to him and kissing her, deep and long.

He knew the steps to this dance. Well practiced. Well rehearsed.

But then she wrapped her arms around him, fierce and tight, and not the way a woman caressed a lover she simply had for the night. It was like a hug, her breasts pressed flat against his body, one hand on the back of his neck, the other pressed between his shoulder blades. And she whimpered when they kissed, opening her mouth wide and invading him. She wasn't shy or teasing. She wasn't coy in any way. She wasn't practiced or expert, either. She was just enthusiastic.

And just like he'd been on the couch with her, he suddenly got lost in it. There was nothing that he could refer back to, no map that he could follow. Nothing in his extensive personal backlog of experience could give him a blueprint for the way that she clung to him. For the eager boldness that seemed to guide her as her water-slicked body rubbed all up against his. He couldn't pretend that she was someone else.

And he couldn't pretend that this was anything like what he'd done before.

Except with her.

But even then, it was different than that first time. Different than that second time. Like he was being drawn deeper and deeper down an endless well that he had tried to avoid his entire adult life.

Because everything she did screamed *Cal*.

It couldn't have been anyone else.

Her body was slim and firm, shaped by the hard work that she did. Soft, as well, her skin like silk against his.

He *knew* that body.

From years of being near her, around her. Trying not to look at her. He knew her voice. And every sound of pleasure only reminded him who she was.

He lifted her up off the ground, pressing her against the back wall, burying his face in her neck and kissing her. She was open to him, and he slid his slick cock through her folds, groaning at how good it felt. How good she felt. He looked up at her, and her grin was impish, and so decidedly her.

Callie.

His Callie.

And it was all he could see. All he could feel.

Like a horrible bright joy, which was a terror he had tried to stay away from for so long.

He couldn't make her a stranger. He couldn't do that to her, couldn't do that to them. Because of all the dark, terrible things that he had in this world, she'd never been one of them.

She had been the sunny spot. His hope, when he'd felt none of his own at all.

That's what had brought him to her in the first place.

This woman who was all fire and optimism and everything he couldn't find inside of himself.

She had given him purpose. He could remember meeting her, and seeing that drive in her. That passion. And it had been almost an obsession to pour what he couldn't give himself into her. He treated bull riding like a gamble. Like some kind of a game to tempt fate. But that wasn't how he saw her dreams. On her behalf, he could want something bigger. Could want something better.

Things that he couldn't want for himself. Things that he wasn't allowed to.

But how had he ever tricked himself into thinking that it wouldn't all lead here?

Yeah, they were friends, and it wasn't that men and women couldn't be friends. So he told himself. Over and over again.

It wasn't that.

It was that Callie had always been somewhere underneath his skin, from the moment they first met. It was that she had hooks in him, that one particularly deep, and he never had an explanation as to why.

It didn't matter now.

It didn't.

They were here.

The future didn't matter.

The future was… The future was maybe nothing. There were no guarantees in life. There was no amount of happiness that could insulate you. No amount of good deeds you could fling yourself into that couldn't end up as a pile of shit. There was nothing.

And the only thing that felt real was her. Everything else felt bleak and terrible or wrong. Everything else felt hopeless, and she was like a beam of light that he could hold in his arms. That he could test himself against, more dangerous and harder than any bull could ever be.

He thrust against her and she shuddered, and he knew that she'd come, just from that slick friction against her delicate body.

She moved her legs, unwinding herself from him, putting her feet back on the shower floor. Then she slid down his body, pressing a kiss to his erection, before taking him into her mouth.

He braced himself against the shower wall, water and pleasure washing over him in a wave.

"Callie," he said, his voice rough.

"Hush," she said.

And he was lost. There was nothing to say, nothing that he could do. He wanted to tell her to stop. He wanted to tell her that it didn't need to end this way. He wanted to tell her not to give so much to him. Because she'd made him dinner. And she'd made him those cookies. And now she was giving him mind-blowing pleasure with her mouth on his body, and he didn't deserve any of it.

He had been her mentor, her helper, her husband when she demanded it. He had been happy to stand in the gap between herself and her family. Had been happy to give her all those things, but when she turned around and tried to give anything back to him he wanted to push her away.

That had been the point of this, but now she was on her knees in front of him, and he couldn't push her away.

It wasn't that he thought a blow job was innately deep or service-oriented, and she'd put her mouth on him before. But there was something about this. About the way she looked up at him…

He had to close his eyes. Had to turn his head away. Had to try and keep his grip on that dark, rocky version of reality that he had spent so many years clinging to. But it was slipping. He was slipping. All because of that slick slide of her lips over his skin.

All because of her.

Callie.

He said her name. He said it out loud, and it reverberated off the tile walls.

And he shoved his hips forward, not meaning to, but not able to restrain himself. She braced her hands on his thighs, taking everything that he gave. And he was lost. Past restraint. Past control.

It was never supposed to be like this. Not with her, not with anyone.

Especially not with her.

She made a sound in the back of her throat, and his eyes opened. His gaze met hers.

And his orgasm ripped through him like a freight train. He lost it. Completely. Didn't have a chance to warn her, nothing.

He opened his mouth to apologize, but she moved away from him, a satisfied smile on her lips.

And he felt... Unmanned in a way he hadn't, not even when they'd made love those first two times. He felt exposed. Robbed. Like she could see the innermost parts of him, and he didn't like it. Because he didn't like those things. How could he ever expose her to them? How?

He shut the water off, and all he could hear was the sound of his own jagged breathing, and he liked that even less.

He hauled her up off the floor, and kissed her. Kissed her deep and hard, because at least it blotted out that raggedness in his breath. At least it swallowed up the sound of his beating heart.

Covered up those jagged pieces in him that were starting to show no matter how hard he tried.

Was this it in the end?

Did you break?

No matter how hard you worked to keep yourself together?

Could you only go through so much of life being made of fragments so loosely pressed together?

And he had lost.

Lost the reason why he'd started any of this. Lost his defenses. And what he wanted to do was surrender, because he didn't feel like he had the strength to keep on pushing her away.

He took them both out of the shower, and wrapped her in a towel, drying her off.

By the time they were in his bedroom, by the time they were back to the bed, he was hard again. He opened up his bedside drawer and got out a box of condoms. And she took one out, her face filled with near-comical concentration as she tore the packet open and rolled the protection over him. And then, with the same look of fixed determination, she put her hand against the center of his chest and shoved him back on the bed.

"It's about you tonight," she said.

And she mounted him like he was a bucking bronco, that same fixed expression there, all stubborn and uniquely her, as she lowered herself down onto his erection.

Then her mouth fell open, soft and feminine, her head dropping back, her hair a wet cascade down her back, over her breasts. "Jake," she whispered.

Like a prayer.

His name.

Because she wasn't just any woman, and he wasn't just any man.

She was Callie.

Strong and fierce and the person he cared about most in the world.

Giving him the greatest pleasure he'd ever experienced.

She flexed her hips, all those well-developed muscles in her thighs taking them both on a race to the finish that took his breath away.

His heart was thundering fast, his every muscle tense. And when he exploded, he dug his fingers into her hips, hard, his orgasm like a raging fire that seemed to ignite hers. He pulsed inside her, and her slick body squeezed around him like a fist.

And for a moment, everything was blank. Black. Void of anything and everything except for feeling. He was bleeding with it.

Hemorrhaging.

This bright white sensation of heat and fire and flame. This overwhelming blanket of need.

It was suffocating. Then somehow... Also the first real breath of air he'd taken in more years than he could count.

And when it was over, she collapsed against him, curled herself firmly around him. And everything in her body language told him something he didn't even need to ask.

She wasn't going to leave him. If he wanted her out of his room, he was out of luck. He would have to leave.

But he felt exhausted. Undone.

And it was easier... So much easier to just lie there with her. To let her curve her soft, warm body around his. To feel that warm weight of her against his chest.

And for the first time in his life, Jake Daniels shared a bed with a woman all night.

CHAPTER TWENTY-ONE

The next morning, Callie woke up sore but happy.

What had happened between her and Jake last night had been a revelation. A new step, just like she'd hoped.

He had stayed with her. In bed. All night.

She grinned when she woke up, looked across his broad chest at his profile. And then she kissed him. On the cheek.

He stirred slightly, looking at her out of the corner of his eye. "Good morning," she said.

"Morning," he mumbled.

"See how much more convenient it is when we share a bed?"

She proceeded to show him all the perks involved with the arrangement.

And that was how it went for the next few days.

She did her best to ignore the fact that the time was ticking on their marriage. Tried to tell herself that it didn't matter. They busied themselves with chores around the ranch, and he kept to his end of the bargain. Instructing her on the minutia of riding saddle bronc, and not overprotecting her. Instead, he gave her solid advice, and good training. And when it was done, they would eat dinner together. Sometimes she would cook, sometimes they would get food at a restaurant. And they always ended up back in bed together. They didn't talk about it, though, and that bothered her a little bit. Because they were friends, and it was a strange thing that the deeper they got into this physical relationship, the harder it was for the two of them to talk.

He had also not eaten the cookies that she had made him five days earlier, and they hadn't discussed it all.

The Christmas cheer of December faded into a gray January, but it was all just fine as far as Callie was concerned, because she was with Jake.

And it was beginning to become obvious that the words she was avoiding thinking in her mind were there whether she gave them voice or not. But they filled her, invaded her limbs, soaked down to her bones, flowed through her blood.

That it just was. In everything she did. And in the shifting tide of what she thought about. What she wanted.

It was an odd thing, because a few months ago she would've seen it as a failure. To want something—anything—more than success in the rodeo would be heresy. But now, she felt like she could see it clearly for what it all was. She had used the rodeo to avoid dealing with certain issues that she had. Certain things in her family. And once she had begun to break those things apart, once she had stopped erecting barriers inside of herself, limiting herself when it came to certain things, telling herself stories about what she could be, who she was and what she was allowed to be good at, the scope of what she wanted began to get broader.

The scope of who she was was widening, and her dreams along with it.

It was easier to love a sport than to love a person. Easier to pin all of your goals on something like that. Because it was just the luck of the draw with horses. A rodeo ride just went the way that it did. Caring about a human... Well, you weren't going to be able to strap on a saddle and try to subdue another person.

They had to be willing to meet you where you were. And the risk in that was... The risk in that felt terrifying.

Still, it was becoming more and more difficult to deny it.

They had just finished another ride out in the arena when she'd let herself think it for the first time. When she'd looked at his profile and realized that she loved him in ways that went so deep it was terrifying.

She loved him.

She loved him so much she was nearly sick with it.

Not just friendship love, no, she had known that she loved him for a long time. But she had tried to tell herself it was like a friend. Like a brother. Like anything other than what it was. Which wasn't just one thing, but everything.

A lover, a man, a friend. A piece of her.

Woven into the fabric of all that she was. That was Jake. Jake Daniels was a part of her. She would never be able to lift him away. He was part of why she loved the rodeo. Part of why she learned. He had introduced her to passion, and given her his physical presence when she needed it. Had legally married her when she had asked.

He was... There wasn't a single person on this earth that understood her the way that he did. Not a single person who supported her quite so unconditionally.

What she'd asked of him was insane. And he had gone along with it. And when he let her care back... Oh, it was hard for him. But when he let her cook for him. When he shared his bed with her. When he let her lavish his body with attention, she could feel it coming from him, too. That rightness. The sense of completion.

She loved it more than anything. Just like she loved him. All of him, even the difficult pieces.

She also knew, down to her soul, that it wasn't something he would want to hear. Wasn't something he would want to deal with. He would consider it a betrayal. A change.

She didn't know how she knew it, only that she did.

The man was utterly and completely walled off to admissions of feelings, but he felt them. He went to his family's house for dinner every Sunday night. The way that he showed up in their friendship was yet more evidence of it. He was just...

There was a brokenness to him that she couldn't quite get a grasp on. That she couldn't quite nail down. The last little fragments of what he wouldn't share with her. The things that made him who he was. The things that would give her that full picture of Jake, everything he was in, everything he resisted.

They were in the barn, putting the horses away, when she let it come right out.

"Jake," she said. "I don't think I want to get divorced."

He turned sharply. "What?"

"I don't want to get divorced. I want to stay with you. I want to stay like this."

He was frozen for a moment. "I don't think that's such a good idea."

She had known that it would go like this. So she just had to be strong and push through. He was like a stubborn horse. And no, she couldn't quite rest on that old confidence that she'd felt before starting a relationship with him—because that's what this was, whether he wanted to admit it or not—couldn't pretend that just because she understood how to bait a dog with snacks she understood men.

But she *did* know Jake.

And everything in her knew this wasn't going to be anything other than a fight.

Because for all that she'd been broken, and hurting and pro-tecting herself...she'd been slowly growing and changing, ex-panding the definition of what she could be as she cried out with pleasure in his arms. And Jake? Jake might just be as much of a rock face as he'd been at the beginning.

Just because she'd been on an emotional journey, while lying in his bed, didn't mean he'd been walking the same path with her, not with his heart or his soul.

"You're going to have to do better than that," she said. "You're going to have to explain yourself. Why exactly don't you think it's a good idea, Jake?"

"Because…" His face went blank and she knew he was about to lie. "I'm not built for this. It's… It's been good. I like you a lot. We're good friends. It's convenient for me to have sex right here on my ranch, but I'm not the marrying kind. And you're going to go back to the rodeo, as you should."

She felt like she was standing on the edge of a cliff. About to offer something insane. Something that she realized she was now willing to sacrifice.

"I don't need to go back."

"What?"

"I don't need to go back. I could stay here." Her chest went tight, her throat constricting. This laying herself open like this… it was new to her. But it was right. It was what she needed. It was what they needed if they were going to not just survive but truly live. "I could work the ranch with you. Be a ranch hand and your wife. We could be together. And we could work on making this life. If that's what you want, if that's what would make things better for you, if that's what would make them more, then I'm all about it. I'm all about the two of us making something out of this."

"Callie, you can't be serious. We literally got married so that you could get your trust fund, so that you could ride saddle bronc. It's the most important thing in the world to you."

The words washed over her like rain.

The most important thing in the world.

Being seen. Being the best at something. Not the second daughter who was a poor replacement for the first, but one who was singular. Unique. The first of her kind.

A girl who rode like a man and took no prisoners.

She didn't know her anymore. That shield. That certainty.

Oh, sure, there was a safety to it. To being one thing. Honing herself into a sharpened blade that could only cut, rather than making herself into something who could cut, be cut. Hurt, be hurt. Want so many things deeply, desperately, that she might never have.

That was terrifying.

But she was on the edge of something beautiful. Like seeing a gilded ray beginning to crest a mountaintop. This time with him, that hope of winning against her family and getting a chance to ride in the rodeo was nothing more than a fraction of what could be.

That whisper of light wasn't the entire story.

They were the whole sunrise.

One that could light up the whole world, and she couldn't live on a sliver of gold anymore. Not when she knew just how much more they could have.

A whole life.

Not pieces of things. Friendship and trophies and applause. But all of it wrapped in love. Commitment, children, a home. Sickness, health and everything else.

"It *was*," she whispered. "It was the most important thing in the world to me, Jake. And I thought it was what made me... me. I thought it was what was going to make my parents respect me. See me as my own person, a valuable person because of what I was doing, what I was achieving, and that if they did it would make me feel...fixed. But the problem is, I was wrong about myself. I'm not saying they were right—it's just that I was immature. I probably still am. I've been growing and changing over these last couple of months, and it's not a simple thing to admit or realize. But I went into all this like a rebellious teenager. Willing to defy anyone and everyone, willing to stamp my foot and say that no one understood me. That they all wanted these things for me that weren't me. But... I didn't know me. I didn't know enough about life. Yes, I would still like to compete in the rodeo. But I can put it on hold. It's not what defines me. And it's not the most important thing to me. It isn't what's going to make or break my life and my happiness. Look at you, you're done with the rodeo. You're thirty-two, and you're done."

"What does that have to do with anything?"

"It's not going to be my life. Not my whole life." Certainty flooded her. Freedom flooded her. "I have to want more things. I have to be more things. I was afraid of that. I think because I was afraid of being rejected... Really rejected. You know, it's easy to pick a straw man and throw him up there for people to light on fire. Because that was a goal, a dream, even, but it wasn't me. A rejection of me riding saddle bronc in the rodeo isn't the same as being rejected. What I was afraid of was putting on a dress and not being the daughter my mother wanted. Trying to bake cookies with her and not being the person that she wanted standing beside her. What I was afraid of was not being loved as much as the sister that died, and as much as my brothers who are here. I was afraid that I didn't matter. That I didn't have a place and I had to make myself one with grit and exceptionalism. And I just... I'm not afraid of that anymore. I'm not afraid at all. It was never about loving the rodeo so much. It was about being afraid of losing what made me special."

She wasn't afraid. She wasn't afraid she'd lose the rodeo and lose her chance to be loved.

She wasn't afraid she could only matter if she did certain things.

Moments were more than holding your breath in the chute.

More than eight-second blocks of time.

There were moments all around. In every piece of life.

And she was more than success.

She was diamond dust.

As unique as the stars and just as fast.

And she felt it. Deep.

"My parents do love me," she said. "I just had to quit being a coward. I had to tell them what I wanted, not just…stubbornly do things without ever explaining myself. I had to stop being so shut down and small and focused only on what I wanted. It doesn't mean they weren't wrong, too, but those things aren't insurmountable. If you don't deal with the molehills they become mountains you'll never be able to climb. But I climbed them, and they met me there. And now I'm more at home in my own skin than I've ever been, and don't you see your part in that?"

"What? So I'm your new saddle bronc? The thing that's going to make you feel complete? It's not any different, then, is it?"

He was trying to push her away. She could feel it. Desperately scrabbling to try to put distance between them as she continued to talk, but she wasn't going to let him. It could hurt her if she let it. Because it was scratching at that very worst fear of hers. That rejection of who she really was. Of what she really wanted.

Of her deepest heart.

But he was wounded, the same as she'd been. And she knew that wounds didn't heal overnight, and they didn't heal easily. You had to fight, and you had to be honest with yourself. You had to be willing to change. To look at yourself and understand where you might be wrong. And she knew that it wasn't easy, but it was what had to happen.

She'd had difficult conversations with her mom, and she'd had to have difficult conversations with herself. About why she needed the rodeo so much, and why she clung to those ideas of who she had to be.

And then she had to let herself change. And metamorphosis wasn't painless. A shift in who you were wasn't painless.

"No," she said, shaking her head. "I matter because I'm me, and I get that now. Along with…understanding that *me* doesn't begin and end with a rodeo event. It's just that when you open yourself up, and when you quit trying to make yourself into something and just let yourself be, things change. I don't need you to make me feel any kind of way about myself. I feel a whole lot more than I ever have. And I'm not hiding." She looked him full in the face, there in the brightly lit barn, standing underneath fluorescent lights. The smell of the hay, and the sound of the horses in their stalls providing a backdrop to the moment. Perfect, really. Because this was what they were grounded in. Even if it wasn't who they were.

"I'm willing to give up something I care a whole lot about to stay here and be with you, because while I care about the rodeo, Jake, I… I love you, Jake."

The words left her mouth and she felt like she had grabbed hold of her heart, pulled it out of her chest and showed it to him. That she was naked and vulnerable and on the verge of death, standing there with the most integral part of what she was on display. For him to accept or crush. For him to embrace or push away.

And while she had never felt more terrified in all her life, she had also never felt stronger. Not on the back of a bucking bronco, not asking him to marry her, not at any point in time. Not ever.

In her terror, in her vulnerability, there was a strength that she had never imagined existed in her.

This whole journey had led her here. Peeling off her protective layers, one by one. Dealing with her family relationships. It had brought her here. Changed her, broke her open. So she could feel it all.

So she could risk it all.

"I love you," she repeated. "With everything that I have. You are the future that I want, Jake Daniels. And if I can ride in the rodeo right along with that, then I will. But if it doesn't fit in, then I know which one of those things I can leave behind. And it's not you."

She felt free. Weightless. This deep, unending revelation that washed over her was like light. Like the key to chains she'd put on herself.

It wasn't about what she could do to prove herself.

It was just about love.

About loving what she did. Loving those around her.

Believing they loved her.

It was about loving Jake.

"Please don't say that," he said. "I can't... I can't do anything with that."

"Why not?"

"Dammit," he said, his word echoing in the barn. "You know why. I've explained why to you. I told you. I'm not going to do marriage or family or anything like that. I don't do it."

"You're a liar," she said. "Because this isn't friendship on one side and sex on the other. It's both together, and I am pretty damn sure that's just love."

"Callie Carson," he said. "You are without a doubt the best woman that I have ever known. The most talented, the brightest, the best, and you can't love me."

"Why not?"

"Because this is... Domesticity might as well be dying. My parents were miserable and then they died. What is the point of that? That's what I learned. You can do all these things and make a life that looks a certain way and just have it all fall apart. You can die, anyway. Your husband can be ready to leave, anyway. Your wife can hate you, anyway. And if there's a higher power out there, then it's bullshit. I don't believe in anything. And you... Look at you. You are strong, and you have dreams, and you believe in the beauty of things that I can't. That's not a love that you can survive, Cal. Believe me."

She faced him head-on, and she made him look her in the eye as she put voice to her next question. "So you don't love me?"

He turned away. And he didn't say no. He didn't say no.

"Jake," she shouted his name. "Don't be a coward."

He turned around, grabbed hold of her face and looked at her, his eyes blazing. "It doesn't matter. None of it matters, because this isn't going to happen. It's not something that I can... I can't give this to you."

"Then why don't you let me give it to you," she said. "Why don't you let me...carry this for a little while, because I figured some things out about myself, and I can wait. We can just do this while you figure out what's going on. While you figure out how to fix yourself."

"I can't be fixed," he said, his voice low. "I can't even have a... I can't even have a conversation with my damn brother. You're the only person on this planet that knows what happened with my parents. That knows the truth about that situation. About me. And you can't fix that. Because my father is dead and I can't ask him. I can't ask him if it was going to be okay."

"We don't know," she whispered. "You don't. I know that bothers you, I get it. But you can't... Things happen. I can't know how things would have been if Sophie would have lived. She didn't. And we had to go on. You have to go on."

"It lives in my head. That moment when my mom left to go on that trip, to go after my dad. And I felt like it was all right. Because I believed in a fairy tale, Callie. Love wins. They lived happily ever after. But they didn't live, happily or ever after, at all."

"But you are alive, Jake Daniels. *You*. Are. Alive. And whether it's happy or not is up to you. But you have to be brave enough."

He started to walk away then, and she felt her grip slipping on this thing between them. On what they had. "What about me? Maybe I need you. Without you I wouldn't be here. I wouldn't have learned how to ride bucking broncos. I wouldn't have learned how to stand up for myself. I wouldn't have figured out what I wanted."

"You would have," he said. "I know you would have."

"Maybe," she said, a tear falling down her cheek. A tear that didn't make her feel weak or embarrassed. "Maybe so, Jake Daniels, but I wouldn't have been able to love you. And it matters. It does. It made me something different, and it changed me. And I like it. I am so tired of my life being shaped around people who are gone. People I didn't know. I'm sorry about your parents. I know they matter to you. But why do I have to always take leftovers because there are people gone from this world that I never even met?"

"I'm leftovers," he rasped. "I'm too damaged by all this. That's it. That's what you get. I'm sorry if that bothers you."

"I'm fine with it actually. It's the not getting you that I'm not fine with. You love me, you damn coward, admit it."

"I love you," he said, the words scraped raw against his throat. "And it doesn't make any difference. Did that help? Did that help you? Because if we move into this house together, and we do this, if we… It's like dying. I can't handle it. I can't take it."

"You're *scared*," she said. "You don't trust the world, and you are afraid that one wrong move is going to take something you care about from you, and that's not the same as having no hope, or not believing. It's just cutting all the hard parts out so you don't have to deal with them. You keep telling me you don't know how life will end up, that no one knows, but you just decided it's all bad so you can do your best to not get hurt and then you get to be this monument to death. To being alone. You get to love me, but not have everything, and tell yourself you're being noble with it. Not just afraid."

"It amounts to the same thing."

And then he turned and walked away, leaving Callie standing there, shattered. And she knew there was no arguing with him, because…

He loved her.

He loved her, and he wasn't going to let it be enough. There was no arguing against that. If he'd said that he didn't love her, she might've had some hope. That he was lying to himself. But he was just choosing the wrong thing. He was just choosing to be alone.

She went into the bedroom on numb legs and sat down on the bed. And she saw her duffel bag there on the floor, saw a peek of yellow down there.

She leaned over and opened it, and saw her wedding bouquet.

She picked up, and crushed it to her chest, a sob rising in her chest.

Oh, these weeds. These silly weeds.

She'd been sad that day because even she'd dreamed of a real wedding day. But that wedding had been real. These weeds meant more than a dozen roses ever could.

And she tried in that moment to imagine her life without him. She tried to imagine the future that she'd wanted when she'd first come here and asked him to marry her. She tried to imagine when the rodeo had been the most important thing. When her trust fund had been the only thing that mattered.

Along the way, it had changed. Along the way, it had become something bigger and deeper.

Along the way, it had become Jake.

There had been other changes, too. And there were two things that were true. She couldn't stay here, couldn't stay with him.

And she had to go tell her father the truth.

CHAPTER TWENTY-TWO

He shouldn't have been, but he was shocked when he discovered that Callie was gone. There were still two weeks left of their marriage to fulfill. Not that her being in residence was a requirement. But he had no idea where she had gone.

But her duffel bag was gone. Along with everything else. Her presence. He could feel it. The difference in the air. The difference in everything. He sat down on the couch, numb.

He had avoided this feeling since that terrible week when his parents had died.

That awful hollow feeling. Where there was nothing. No future, no past. Just nothing. Nothing but the endless lack of a person that you wanted desperately to be with and couldn't.

Knowing it was his fault.

Knowing it was him.

He thought maybe he was having a heart attack. Right then. Because he couldn't catch his breath. Couldn't breathe past this god-awful realization that it was just him again.

He let her down. But he told her, and it still didn't matter. He should have done different. He should have done better. He should have protected her from himself, and he did.

You're afraid.

You're afraid.

Did it matter? Did any of it matter?

His life had changed that day fifteen years ago, and his world had shattered. And it had broken again when he'd learned the truth about his father. Every room in that house had felt packed full of lies and unanswered questions.

The wedding pictures on the wall had felt like photographs from a play, and when he'd started to get older and his face had begun to take the shape of his dad's, he'd wondered what that meant. Who that man had actually been.

A man who'd bought a plane ticket in a moment of insanity?

A man who had a secret life.

Secret plans to leave.

A man who had changed his mind when his wife had decided to go on that trip with him, after all.

Everything had felt wrong and uncertain. And hope had felt like something with teeth.

Contentment had felt like the calm before a plane crash.

Loving a person felt like the edge of disaster.

He'd cared about nothing. For a long time. And then there was her. And she had always been an exception. And he let her get too close. He'd let this all go too far. But no more. It had to end.

He'd ended it. And she was gone.

It was why he left the rodeo in the first place, and he should've just left it as it was. He never should've let her come for Thanksgiving.

Holidays were a bitch.

This whole holiday season had ruined years of rules. Years of them.

It had to be done. It had to end. And thankfully, it was.

Because she was gone.

And he had a feeling it was for good this time.

And he knew that it was for the best.

Callie slung her duffel bag off her shoulder and set it down on the porch, looking up at the front door, feeling... She didn't know. Not like a failure. She hadn't failed at anything. It was just that it was time now, to have a real conversation with her father. Be ready for the answer to not be what she wanted. But she was going to have to put herself out there. And she was going to have to tell the truth.

All of it.

She breathed in deep, then knocked on the door. It was her father who answered.

"Hey there," he said, taking a step back and letting her in. "Didn't expect to see you."

"Yeah. I know. Are... Boone and Kit and...everyone still here?"

"No. They all went home. Right after Christmas."

"Of course. I... Yeah. I'll come in, then."

She followed her dad into the kitchen. He pulled out a stool at the island. "Have a seat."

"Is Mom here?"

"No," he said, moving to the fridge. "Off getting her nails done."

"Oh. Right."

"Well, spit it out," he said, getting a cheesecake out of the fridge and setting it on the counter in front of her.

"What's this?"

"Your feelings," he said. "If necessary."

And then she just started to cry. Absolutely burst into tears. And she couldn't remember the last time she'd done that. Ever. She didn't do tears. Other than the times that Jake had kissed her, and they just kind of escaped. But even then they'd both been too wrapped up in what they were doing to really talk about it. And she didn't even know if he'd noticed.

"Do I need to get my shotgun?" he asked.

"No," she said, reaching out and putting her hand on her dad's wrist. "But I do have to tell you some things. Jake and I didn't get married because we were in love."

Her dad sighed, and sat in the stool next to her. "I see. Well, I suppose this is about the time I tell you I knew that."

"You... You knew?"

"Yes, I knew. I knew you didn't just decide to get married after never showing any interest in it. And I knew it wasn't like he was that old-fashioned of a guy. Though it was a nice story that you told."

"Oh."

"I think he's the kind of old-fashioned guy who would've done what he wanted, sneaked around, then asked my permission to marry you when he was good and ready. Not that I have any experience with that."

She winced. "I don't need to know about your and Mom's personal life."

"Well, I don't need to know about yours, either, but I think I got the hint of a bit more than I cared to while you were here. I know it's not that you're just friends with him."

She slumped down on the stool, picked up a fork and dug into the cheesecake. "No. We were supposed to be. But no, it didn't end up that way. But that's not the point. When everything went to hell yesterday, I realized something. I realized that I had to let that cover go. And I had to tell you why I did it. Because I needed the trust fund money because I wanted to enter the rodeo. And we had some honesty between us, Dad. And you told me you were going to try to be brave. So it's my turn. I have to be brave. And I have to tell you that I spent a lot of years trying to be one of the boys because I thought then I could be approved of."

"I never disapproved of you."

"I get that now. But I shut down and I tried to protect myself, and I tried to make my life as simple a thing as possible. I did all that to keep from getting hurt. Because I've always been afraid that I wasn't really the daughter that you wanted. So I just didn't try to be one."

Her father looked broken then, his face contorting. "Callie. You are a blessing. You always have been. What your mother and I went through was a terrible thing. And I know it must be hard for you, because you don't remember that time. You weren't even here for it. It affected each and every one of us, because we were there. Because we remember Sophie. But you don't. And I'm sorry for all the ways that loss has hurt you, too. But in a way... I don't want Sophie to ever be forgotten. I want her impression on the world to last. So of course I always wanted you to know about her."

"I understand that," she said. "I do. But so much of it was me just being afraid. I thought I needed to be tough and perfect, and then when I had my accident and you didn't want me to compete anymore...it confirmed it. And I understand now. I don't need to just be one thing. I have to be myself. I care an awful lot about saddle bronc, I really do. I want to do it. But I care about other things, too. And more important than the rodeo is my relationship with you and Mom. It's coming to some kind of understanding. More important than the rodeo is that we tell the truth. That we get to know each other."

"I want you to ride," he said. "Because it's important to you. And I'm going to work on letting go enough to let you be who you need to be. Even if it scares me. Callie, when you fell I realized if something happened to you it would have been because of how I raised you. What I encouraged you to do, and that would have killed me."

"Dad, I'm myself. And while I appreciate your worry, and you know I want your support... I don't do anything I don't want to do. It could never be your fault."

He chuckled. "Well, that is true. I'll tell you, when I thought you married Jake Daniels, I was pretty terrified."

"I mean, I did marry him," she said. *"Legally."*

"No, I know. But I just... All I could see was you getting hurt. And not only that, I had to face the fact that you were a woman, and I didn't much like that, either. Because a lot of that overprotective stuff... It only works when I can convince myself that you're a child. And that's the way that I feel I can protect you."

"I'm not a kid. But... It's okay that you want to protect me. I have to remember that it's not you thinking I can't do things. It's... It's just loving someone. I get that now. I want to protect Jake, from his own pain, and I can't do it. I feel inadequate, and I feel I can't reach him. And I don't like it."

Her dad nodded, and picked up his own fork, going into the other side of the cheesecake. "Yeah, I could see that he had some issues. And I could also see that you two were falling in love."

"Yeah. He does love me. He just says it doesn't change anything."

"The wound has to be addressed," her dad said. "You can't just cover it up and let it fester. That's the hardest thing to do." He sighed heavily. "Listen to me. I say that, and I've never done it in my own self. I told myself that grief over losing a child is something you're not supposed to heal from. And I'm afraid I've made you suffer because of it."

"No. I'm an adult. And I should've talked to you, and I didn't. If you treated me like a child it was because I kept on acting like one. A rebellious child who didn't want any kind of honesty, because I was too busy protecting myself." She sighed. "For just a little bit I felt so powerful because I was brave enough to show him my whole heart. But I didn't feel so brave when it was finished and he told me we couldn't be together."

"But sometimes that's just the step," her dad said. "Failing before you figure out how to make a life. We do it over and over again. I did it with you. We could've had this conversation and you might not have married Jake to get what you wanted. But then you wouldn't have fallen in love with him. And maybe this is an important step, too. You just can't see to the end of it yet."

"I didn't take you for an optimist," she said, taking another bite of the cheesecake.

"I don't know that I'm an optimist. I've seen some pretty terrible things in life. I lost a child, and that's about as bad as it gets. But I've got six more. And they're as wonderful as that was terrible. So what I know is that life is good along with the bad. I have your mother, and she loves me, even when I'm a bullheaded ass. I love her even when she's badgering you about making cookies. Everything is good and bad, darlin'. Every damn thing. And it doesn't end on one spot or another. It just keeps going. So it's bad right now, but it'll be good later. And maybe... Maybe this will never be okay. Losing your sister was never okay. But other things have been. Other things have been damn great. Like having you."

Emotion rose up in her throat, and she swallowed it, along with another bite of cake. "Thank you. I guess I just have to hope that... Hope that in the end I find something that I want just as badly as I want him."

"Don't count yourself out just yet. Let time do the work. Let him think about it. Let him taste what it's like to live without you. It was easy for him to make a decision not to be with you when you were standing right there. But he's been through... Grief. And I understand grief. When you lose someone the way that he did, the way that I did, you want that person and there's no way you can have them back. Well, he could have you. So any hopelessness... That's all his choice. Let it marinate for a while. See where it gets you."

"I will," she said, not feeling much better, but knowing that someday she might be able to reflect on her father's words and find some comfort.

"Come on," he said, hitting the top of the counter.

"What?"

"I want to watch you ride again. I want to be involved. Even if it scares me."

And while Callie wasn't sure how this would all untangle, and she wasn't sure how she would ever not have a broken heart, she had gotten something. She had become a more whole version of herself. And she had this moment.

Maybe in the end, that would be enough.

Maybe.

CHAPTER TWENTY-THREE

Jake was damned miserable but he knew that if he didn't go to Sunday dinner it would only bring more questions than not, and Colt was still in town. And he... He found himself wanting to talk to his brother. Because he'd been alone all by his damn self for days, and the echoing inside of his chest wasn't going away. Wasn't getting any better.

And maybe it was time. Maybe it was time to talk to Colt, even if it wouldn't fix anything. He felt like there was poison inside of his chest and he had to drain it out.

He managed to eat lasagna, even though it tasted like cardboard to him, and had two more beers than he normally did.

And then, when all was said and done, he found himself out on the front porch with his brother.

"Where's your wife?" Colt asked.

"You're the first person who asked that," he said, looking out on the backyard miserably, and wishing he still smoked cigarettes, that it wasn't a habit he'd left behind along with his teen years. Because he could sure use something. Something to help distract him. Something to numb the pain. "Nobody else asked."

"Everybody else is afraid of you."

"She left me."

"I didn't think it was a real marriage."

"Yeah, funny thing about that."

"Shocking," Colt said dryly. "You married your best friend, who you have so clearly had a thing for for a number of years, and it blew up in your face."

He stared out into the darkness for a long time. "She's in love with me."

Colt looked at him. Long and hard. "I don't have to ask you if that's a bad thing or not."

"No," Jake said, his voice rough. "You don't. You don't have to ask me because you damn well know."

"Look, we've all got our own issues from this. And I know it's not a thing we do. Prying. But…"

Jake felt resigned. Like he was going to the damn gallows. But he knew it was time. It was time. "Dad was going to leave. When they got back from the trip."

"What?"

"I found a plane ticket in his things when we were cleaning the house up. He was going to LA. He wasn't coming back."

Colt's face went hard like stone. "But he asked Mom to come."

"Yeah, he did."

"She wasn't going to."

"Yeah."

"It doesn't make sense," Colt said, his tone hard.

"Maybe it was goodbye, I don't know. We'll never know. They died. That's it."

Colt nodded slowly. "Son of a bitch."

"You can never know. You can't trust instincts or anything because it could all be a lie."

"Or it could be the truth," Colt said. "I mean, really. One's as likely as the other. I understand feeling like you can't fix things. I get that. Under my soul. I don't know what to tell you about relationships. I really don't. Because… I don't want one, either.

It's all fine for them." He gestured back toward the house. "I'm happy for them. It's not for me. Maybe because for our parents it wasn't domestic bliss in the same way it was for theirs."

"Maybe."

"I get the feeling like fate is jerking you around, believe me." His tone suddenly went hard. "Maybe it's random. Maybe someone's in charge. I don't know what concerns me more. That anything could happen. Or that there's a plan and it might mean I have to go through more shit."

"Cheering."

"It's not supposed to be, it's just what I think. Maybe it'll be good. Maybe it won't. That's a risk. Every damn thing is a risk. And you're right, we can't even go back and ask Dad…we can't ask what he was thinking. We can't ever know. Anything. If you don't want this, then don't. But I suspect that you do. I think you want her. I thought that for a long time. And if you want her, then you want to have her. Don't… Don't keep yourself from having her because you're protecting yourself. Because you're living your whole life with the expectation the cops could come to the door again and tell you that you lost everything when a few minutes ago everything was great. Protecting yourself because you thought… Hell, at least they died together and loved each other and then you found a plane ticket that meant Dad might leave and now you think every good thing out there might just be a lie. Because it had all seemed like it was getting better. Until it went to hell."

Jake felt like the room was spinning. Because that was exactly it. The damn truth. Everything had seemed better until it went to hell. And maybe that was the real reason he trusted nothing. Believed nothing. Maybe the real reason was that… He couldn't stand the idea of wanting to be happy again and losing it.

Maybe that was the real reason he didn't want her doing anything for him. Because he just didn't want to feel good only to have it taken from him. Not again. Never again.

"I really love her." He shook his head. "I don't know how to… I don't know how to be brave enough to live in it. Cannot just be sitting there waiting to be blindsided."

He looked at his brother, and he realized. He realized that was why he held Colt at a distance, too. He was a master at lying to himself. That was for damn sure.

"Damn," he said, his chest sore. He lowered his head and pushed his hands through his hair, his elbows resting on the porch rail. "This is hell."

"I don't know how to do the feelings thing," Colt said.

"Neither do I," Jake said, feeling mad about it. "I don't know how to do this. I don't know to feel this. But I am. Damn her."

"I guess the way I see it is you could go on like you have been, and then you're certain of what you've got. Not her. Right? Or you have to step out not knowing, and learn to live with that. But then you have her."

"I really want her. But people think it's brave or stupid to bull ride—it's nothing compared to this. If I love her, that I'm going to stay with her. And I'm going to want to keep her. Have kids with her. Somehow cope with the idea that everything I care about is running around *out there*. With any number of dangers all around. And I can't just keep them safe. I can't guarantee what's going to happen from one moment to the next. And if something did I… I wouldn't see it coming. It could all be great and then…"

You have to take the shrapnel out.

Her father's words echoed inside of him.

He was walking around with a wound inside of him. And it wasn't based on nothing. Life had been a damn bitch to him. That was the truth of it. Life had screwed him about seven different ways. And right now, it wasn't life or faith or God that was his enemy. It was him. Life wasn't fair, but here they were, living it.

And he'd walked through a world where he'd tried his best

to care about nothing, and in the end, he kept coming back to Gold Valley.

Why?

Because of his family. Because it was home. Because the things that he loved were what made it worth being on this goddamn planet. That was the thing. When you cared enough to take the risk, that was when it mattered.

And he couldn't let a wound decide anymore how much his life meant. Because the value was in those people. The value was in that love.

In Cal.

Callie. The love of his life. The woman literally owned his heart. Seeing her fall off that horse and break her arm… Entering into a tailspin that he hadn't been able to get himself out of, and rather than walking toward her, he'd run away from her.

"I'm a damn coward," he said.

"Well, I have always thought you were vastly less impressive than I was."

"I love her."

"Clearly."

"I love her so much. I'd die for her. But the scary thing… The scary thing is living for her."

"There's a whole lot of people in there who would tell you that it was worth it."

He looked at his brother, the hollow look in his eye, and he knew that whatever was going on with Colt, he wasn't ready to take the next step forward. And all he could do was hope that someday the right woman came along and pushed him there. Because that was what it had taken for Jake.

Being more afraid of living life without her than trying to live one with her.

"I've got to go get her."

"Good luck. And I hope you're good at dodging bullets."

"Why is that exactly?"

"Come on. You know her dad as well as I do."

"True," he said. "But it's worth the risk."

CHAPTER TWENTY-FOUR

Callie was dirty, sweaty and cold along with it. She was just coming in from riding, and running laps around the arena with Boone, who had just taken off to go grab a drink, when she saw a familiar truck coming up the long drive to Evergreen Ranch.

"What in tarnation... Jake Daniels?"

She stood there. Just stood. And waited for his truck to get to where she was.

"I'll shoot you," she muttered when he pulled up, killed the engine and got out.

They just stared at each other. Just stood there. She was rooted to the spot, and he was... As beautiful as he'd ever been. It enraged her. That she wanted him still, even with how he hurt her. That he was still... Jake.

"What exactly are you doing here?"

"I came to tell you that I love you. And it does make a difference."

She could have been tipped over with a feather. "You did?"

"I kept thinking about something your dad said to me. He was talking about a stallion and a filly. I couldn't tell if it was a metaphor or not."

"Well, he knew about us. So I expect it was a metaphor."

Jake chuckled. "Well, it was a damn good metaphor. I love you. But I needed to get the shrapnel out. I needed to heal that wound. And the thing is, when something is just... Unfair, it's tough to do that. You can't fix losing someone. It just is. So it's a wound you have to decide to let heal. Because you can't reconcile it, and you can't make it fair. You can't get a guarantee that you'll never lose anyone or anything ever again. You just have to decide that love is worth a hell of a lot more than fear. And it is, Callie. It is. Loving you is worth it. It's worth the cost. It's worth the risk. I want you. I want you even knowing I can't control everything. That I can't see into the future. I want you. I want you even knowing I don't deserve you."

"I don't know, Jake. You hurt me. I laid my heart and soul out there for you and you hurt me."

"Do you need me to get down on my knees?"

She laughed. "That might be a start."

"I'll do it."

And he did, just that. Dropped onto his knees in the dirt right in front of her. "Stay married to me. Marry me again, please. Love me, because I have loved you for a very long time. Do you want to know the real reason I left the rodeo?"

"Yes," she said. "I do."

"It was because of you. Because you fell off that horse and you broke your arm, and that was when I realized. That whatever I felt for you, it was too strong. That I was on dangerous ground, and I couldn't pretend that... That I wasn't falling for you. I have been in love with you for years. And I was just in denial this whole damn time, and when you hit the ground and I realized that I could lose everything if I lost you, that was when I knew I needed to leave. When I had to confront the fact that you were breakable. I had to admit that you made me vulnerable. So I left. And you came after me. And you asked me to marry you, and I couldn't tell you no. Because... I didn't want to. I didn't want you to ask some other man. I just wanted you. With me. That's what I want, Callie Carson. I want you with me. But I also want you to be you. I don't want to stop you, so I want you to be you. Even if it scares me. Because what I feel for you scares me, and that's a good thing. That's how I know it's big. That's how I know it's love. Because I didn't care for anything for a long time. Not until you. Not until you."

"Jake, I love you," she said, flinging her arms around his neck and kissing him. "And of course I'll stay married to you. And marry you all over again for the spectacle of it. Of course I will. We'll have a big wedding, and I will wear a ridiculous dress. And my mom will be so happy. And we'll be… Ridiculous. Forever. I would have your babies and screw you silly for the rest of your life."

He laughed. "That is the most ridiculous thing I've ever heard anyone say."

"Well, I pledge to be ridiculous. Were not going to get married and turn into other people. We're Jake and Callie."

"We sure as hell are."

He picked her up off the ground and kissed her. Deep and long and hard and with everything he had in him. And she kissed him back. Like she would die if she didn't.

"Thank you," she said. "For not only being all my missing pieces, but for showing me everything that I could be. For believing in me when no one else did. And for being the first real-life naked man I ever saw."

"Him to be the last naked man you ever see."

She smiled. "And I'll be the last naked woman you ever see."

"That's the best news I've ever heard."

"Well, that does it. You must be crazy."

"Or just in love."

Callie Carson had never been accused of being a shrinking violet, or shy and retiring, or anything of the sort. She'd always been up-front and honest. At least, she thought so. It turned out, she hadn't even known herself all that well. But she did now. Thanks to her best friend. Who was also the man that she loved, more than anything in this world.

"Thank you for being mine."

Because that's what he was. Hers. In all the deepest, most profound ways imaginable.

"Thank you for being mine," he agreed.

And when they kissed, she was excited. Because she couldn't remember how many times they'd kissed. And she knew that there wouldn't be a way to count. Because they would be kissing like this. Always and forever. Whether she went to saddle bronc events or didn't, whether she ended up staying at the ranch or not.

It didn't define her. And it never would.

It was love that defined her.

And she was glad about that.

EPILOGUE

The real wedding was on Christmas, at Evergreen Ranch, the following year.

Well, Callie didn't think it was any more real than their courthouse wedding, with weeds and jeans, but her family was here for this one. And so was Jake's.

They lived in Gold Valley now, on Jake's thriving horse ranch, near the other Danielses. A clan that was ever expanding with Colt's recent marriage, Iris and Griffin's upcoming baby and Rose and Logan's new one.

This was the wedding for everyone.

Callie was riding high after her first season riding saddle bronc, and finishing with some decent standing. No, she hadn't gone in and won everything. But she'd done well, and that felt like enough. For now.

So much of that was down to the unfailing support of her family.

And of course Jake's.

She felt secure. Secure enough that she was wearing one of the girliest wedding gowns in all of creation. It reminded her of a meringue that Iris might make for the bakery. So fluffy and airy and bright.

Delicate lace covered every inch of it, with long sheer sleeves and an off-the-shoulder neckline. Complete with a necklace, presented to her by her mother, one she'd worn at her own wedding. Her something old.

And a pocketknife from her dad.

It was in her garter. Her something new.

Her wedding bouquet was roses, mixed with scrubby yellow weeds, and she didn't care if anyone else understood.

It was her.

It was them.

The wedding was outdoors, in the frosty air, with evergreens and Christmas lights all around. And even though she'd been Jake's wife for over a year, her father still gave her away. Because it was his one and only chance to be father of the bride, he'd told her.

And this time, with witnesses, she and Jake made traditional vows.

Before God and everybody.

And she knew this time they meant them.

But they'd decided traditional vows weren't enough, not for them.

"If you ever need me," he finished. "I'll be there for you. Whatever, whenever. I'm your go-to."

She smiled. "I'm yours. Whatever. Whenever."

And then it was time for her to kiss her husband.

Her best friend.

Her everything.

And she felt whole.

★ ★ ★ ★ ★